The Rest of Your Life Soundtrack

Benjamin Roesch

Winnipeg, Canada

Developmental editor: Margaret Larson
Proofreader: Sanford Larson

Published September 2024 by Deep Hearts YA, an imprint of Story Perfect Inc.

Deep Hearts YA
PO Box 51053 Tyndall Park
Winnipeg, Manitoba R2X 3B0
Canada

Visit deepheartsya.com for more great reads.

For my grandparents (I miss you)
For Elliott Smith
And for anyone and everyone impacted by cancer

The Rest of
Your Life Soundtrack

Side One
Jesus Wears a Blonde Wig
August, 1997–September, 1997

Track Zero
Let There Be Decision

I yank on my winter coat and step out into the bitter December cold, trudging through calf-deep snow toward the treehouse. The rope ladder sways and creaks as I climb. I haven't been up here since the leaves turned to scarlet, then to brown, then to so much fallen dust.

Sitting down on the love seat, I click on the camp lantern, hoping the batteries still work. *Let there be light.*

With my breath blooming in the frozen air, I slip my headphones over the thick wool blanket of my beanie, then click on Elliott Smith's *Either/Or*. *Let there be sound.*

Finally, I pull the two envelopes out of my coat pocket and set them on the table. Bright white and blandly official, their blank faces are utterly indistinguishable, like creepy robotic twins from a Philip K. Dick story. *Let there be decision.*

Eeny, meeny, miny—

Thump. The treehouse trembles with sudden sound. A heavy, dull *thud.* I rip my headphones off and stop the tape. Is it midnight already?

But there's no sister sound to follow the first, which means it can't be the fireworks yet.

"Hello?" I ask stupidly, trying to make sense of the noise. I try to re-settle on the task at hand—no biggie, just figuring out what I'm going to do with the rest of my life—but I can't focus now because, seriously, what the hell was that? Curiosity has me first down the rope ladder, then back into the heavy snow. I catch a whiff of woodsmoke from the fire Dad was still stoking when I came outside, even though he looked terrible and way past tired, and Mom was already snoring on the couch.

I look up at the side of the treehouse, not sure what I'm expecting to see. Then I see it, not up but down. An inky black swell.

It's a small raven, still and silent, atop the crystal white blanket. Holding up the lantern to get a better look, I can see that one of its wings is twisted unnaturally down like someone whose pen drifted off the page. The bird's neck is similarly off its axis.

I look up at the treehouse again, then back down at the smashed raven.

Taking off my mitten, I hover my hand over the raven's body, which emits a barely perceptible, but already diminishing warmth. I watch the bird until my ribs rattle with the cold, but the raven's chest reveals no movement. Not even a final tremble.

Now feeling really good and freaked out, and even further away from figuring out my life, I go back up to the treehouse and wait for my heart to slow down. The envelopes are still there on the coffee table, staring at me, daring me to open one and choose already.

What do YOU want?

Thump.

Not again, I think, picturing a flock of ravens storming out of the woods and going full kamikaze against the treehouse, then dropping to the frozen Earth.

But this sound is different. Concussive and reverberating. Followed by another, and another, an unsteady drum beat out there somewhere, the sound giving no hint of the dazzling sprays of light that I can't see, but can imagine so clearly.

"Happy fucking New Year," I say to nobody, then give the envelopes a final look before I lay back on the loveseat and listen to the fireworks, wondering what I'm going to do.

Press the rewind button. Right there. Stop.

Track One
A Sea of Smirking, Squinting Raineys

"She's here again," Walden says, ducking back into the dressing room.

"She is?" I ask, sitting up (cue the clammy hands, cue the tense belly). "Are you sure?"

"She's the only person here over twenty-five. Except for Poser."

I steal a look at my makeup. Double-thick black mascara, smoky gray eyeshadow, deep purple lipstick. I give my hair a quick tousle until it's *fuck-you* messy.

"Who are you talking about?" asks River, my best friend and guitar player. Sunk deep into a purple La-Z-Boy that must hold a thousand layers of stinky punk rock sweat, he's lazily plucking strings on his white Gibson semi-hollow body.

"Rainey's weirdo geezer groupie," Walden says, examining the set list, which he's re-written five times already. He scratches the willowy fuzz on his cheeks he calls a beard.

"Whatever," I say, thinking *she's hardly a geezer*. "Besides," I add, nodding at River, "pretty boy is the one with the groupies."

"Hey, yeah," Walden says, turning to River. "That reminds me. Tonight, during 'Ordinary Girl,' do more of that thing you did in the video. The chicks love it." Walden dramatically flips his hair from right to left, then smushes his lips out into a faux-sexy pout.

"I didn't even mean to do that!" River grins.

"*Please*," I say. "You totally meant to do that."

"Wait, what groupie?" River asks. "I've lost count."

"She's *not* a groupie," I say, picturing the woman with the right cheek beauty mark and the pixie cut that's been to our last three—now four—shows. "I think she's another journalist."

Except I don't really think that. I think she's the answer to the question. The one everyone keeps asking me: *Rainey, when are you going to get signed?*

"God, I wish they'd just leave me alone," River says, pitching his voice up. "Don't they know I'm going through a silent, emo phase right now!"

I give River a big sarcastic air kiss, which he gives right back. He sets down his guitar, then comes over and sits down next to me, opens an imaginary notebook, and clicks an imaginary pen.

"Tell me, Miss Cobb," he says, slipping into a syrupy British accent, "where *do* you get your song ideas. Our readers are dying to know."

I twirl my hair and chew a wad of fake gum. "I don't know, they just sort of come to me."

"Freak," River says, putting his face inches from mine, then tousling my perfectly-mussed hair. He knows how hard I work at making it look like I don't care.

"Stop it!"

"But the *chicks* love it," River whispers and I push him away.

"Will you two please get your heads in the game," says Walden.

Paul Posen, the owner of Club 182, who we call Poser, pokes his head in.

"You guys planning on starting anytime this century? Generation X is getting restless out there. Oh, and Evan said to tell you the nest is already empty, whatever the hell that means."

"It means we're out of CDs," River says. "Again."

"I told you," Walden says, looking over at me.

"I know, I know."

We're now through our fifth order of *The Treehouse Tapes,* my debut album that Walden and I recorded and released last summer. At the time, I thought we'd be lucky to get through the first five hundred, but they just keep selling. And selling. So do the stickers and T-shirts that Evan, my other best friend, and manager, sits out there and sells every show. He convinced me it was a good idea to put my face on the shirt, but now that I'm assaulted by a sea of smirking, squinting Raineys at every show, I can see that it was a mistake of galactic proportions.

Note to self: If you have mixed feelings about your face, maybe don't put it on a T-shirt.

After Poser leaves, I reach into my makeup bag and palm my black film canister.

"Be right back."

"Where are you going?" Walden asks.

"Bathroom," I say.

"You went ten minutes ago. Are you nervous or something?"

"I don't get nervous. It's girl stuff. You want to come and make sure?"

"Gross," he says.

In the hallway, I'm slapped by a wave of thick and steamy late August heat. Anticipatory, pre-show chatter hums from the sell-out crowd, kids giddy and wired, ready to rage away the last days of summer break. Skirting past a couple of girls at the sinks, keeping my head down, I slip into the middle bathroom stall, the one with *my heart is a thousand years old, I am not like other people* carved into the inside of the door. It's the only one I ever use. My lucky stall. Yes, I have a lucky stall. Sue me, I spend a lot of time at Club 182.

I sit down and put my head in my hands. My heart is racing.

It's true what I said to my brother. I don't get nervous. Not when it comes to music.

Not until she started showing up.

I wait until I hear the two girls leave, then pry the gray cap off the film canister and shoot down the vodka inside, hot against my throat and then warm in my belly.

Show time.

In my memory, I'm four. Maybe five. Legs dangling off the piano bench, air thick with cigarette and pot smoke and the smell of grilled hot dogs and spilled beer, surrounded by my parents' musician friends, this tiny little me at the center of their grown-up universe.

Even at that age, my freaky musical memory already had over a hundred songs locked inside of it, and my famous parents loved to keep me up late and show me off to please the masses. They'd call out requests—showtunes, blues, Motown—or put random songs on the turntable for me to play back perfectly, down to the last note, after a single hearing.

It was their eyes I remember the most. That strange surrender, as if I'd cast some kind of spell. When people ask me how I got so comfortable on stage, I'm always four or five sitting at that piano bench, legs dangling, learning how to let all those eyes look.

But in a lifetime of being looked at, no one has ever looked at me quite like her before. And it's messing with me. Causing a tectonic rearrangement, a minor earthquake deep in the ocean of my nervous system.

Out there in the darkness, she's leaned against the bar in her usual spot. Ripped jeans. Ramones T-shirt. Massive hoop earrings. Jet black pixie cut. She looks like an older version of most of the kids in here. Except that she's always alone. No drink. No pretzels. No plus one. Just those dark eyes doing their slow-motion, back-and-forth dissection of the girl standing center stage.

As I play, everyone in the crowd pushes slowly forward, but not her. She seems to soak up all of it without needing to be a part of it. Like how the Terminator is there but not there, if the Terminator was a cool-seeming woman in her late twenties. And kind of hot.

After our hour-long, fourteen-song set, I slink to the merch table and autograph CD sleeves and T-shirts with a Sharpie. I pose for pictures with kids who never say hi to me at school. I sign my name on some girl's bare abdomen. I let a college guy cut a small lock of my red hair.

I look around, wondering if she'll be the next in line. But by the time the crowd has thinned to Evan, Walden's girlfriend Bethany, and a handful of stragglers, by the time the house lights are up and I'm loading amps and drum parts out the back door of Club 182 and into the Cobb Family's rusty, trusty RV, which I lovingly call Howard the Duck, She Terminator is gone.

Walden, nodding at my ripped fishnets and the fingernail streaks and grip bruises on my arms, says, "You don't have to keep doing that, you know. One of these days you're going to get really hurt."

Bethany, draped off Walden like an appendage, says, "Don't listen to him. He's just being a good big brother. I think it's badass. I've never seen a girl crowd surf like you do."

"Don't encourage her," Walden says, but he says it sweet and then they're kissing. And, well, gross. I'm still not used to seeing my brother with his lips smashed against somebody else's, let alone those of Bethany, this chatty community college girl who works with me at Cuppa Josephine, where I've been slinging lattes and cappuccinos three days a week all summer to earn some extra money, which I mostly blow on CDs and clothes.

When I introduced the two of them, I didn't think much of it. Even when Walden started hanging out at the shop more, pretending to read Rimbaud while he nursed a bottomless cuppa but actually studied Bethany's dark bangs and hazel eyes, I still didn't think anything would happen. Walden's never had a real girlfriend. Then, six weeks ago, he took her to the movies to see *Contact* and they've been pretty much joined at the lips since then.

"Rainey, you got a second?" Poser asks, perched in the back door. I follow him down the dark hallway to his office, which is splatter painted with band posters and empty two-liters of Diet Coke. Poser, who has the sobriety symbol tattooed on his left forearm, sucks the stuff down like water.

Back in his early twenties, Poser was in this band called Willow Lake Road that was briefly signed to Columbia before getting dropped after their charismatic lead singer drowned in Lake Champlain on the Fourth of July. Their debut album was only a month from release, but the label found a contract loophole and the album never saw the light of day. After he emerged from a five-year alcohol bender and went to therapy, Poser opened Club 182, the all-ages night club in downtown Burlington, Vermont where I've been playing for the past two years.

Poser regularly pulls me into his office after shows to dispense his brand of take-it-from-someone-who's-been-there wisdom, which is why I'm ready for another lecture about the dangers of crowd surfing. Or how it's time to find a manager who's not my best friend.

Instead, though, Poser takes a business card out of his pocket and hands it to me.

Cassie Plimpton, Talent Scout
Shore Records
212-878-9821 (w) / 212-655-2543 (h)

My whole body buzzes. Shore is one of biggest record labels in the country.

"From our mystery woman," he says.

On the back, in tidy script, she's written:

Everybody wants you. But what do YOU want? PS, you totally rock. -Cass

A warmth floods my chest. My cheeks flush. "Is this real? Because if you're just messing with me."

"It's as real as it comes. This is how it starts."

I read the cryptic message again.

"You should tell Walden," he says.

"Yeah right. He'll freak. You know how he is about labels."

"Have you thought about it?" he asks, swigging from a two-liter. "What you want?"

I shrug, feeling embarrassed at how much I have thought about it. About how sometimes I can't sleep because I want my musical dreams so badly. About how every time someone asks me the question I've been getting at least once a week for the past year—*Rainey, when are you going to get signed?*—I've dreamed of saying: *Any day now.*

But barely any of the people who ask me that know what I did to my family two years ago. How I blew up my family's band so I could stop being homeschooled and try to be a normal kid for the first time in my strange, meandering existence. Something I seem to be failing at miserably. They don't know how it's more than a little bit crazy that I want to get right back on a train I fought so hard, and broke my mother's heart, just to get off in the first place.

"Look, I know I've been telling you this pretty much since the day I met you, but be careful, Rainey. I mean it. Watch your back. They only care about one thing."

"Artistic integrity?" I ask.

"Yeah, that's it."

"Did she say anything about me?"

Poser chuckles. "There's that gigantic ego you're so good at hiding," he says.

"Shut up."

Track Two
Welcome to My Minimalist Phase

I don't want to wake Mom, but her head is tipped back so far against the sofa cushions, I know she's in for a serious case of Tin-Man neck if I don't get her to bed.

Since we left the club, I've been buzzing with the weight of what Poser told me: that Cassie Plimpton—that Shore Records—is interested in me. That they want to talk to me about my music, my future. About signing me. I felt so light and giddy on the way home that Walden asked me what I was smiling at. *Nothing*, I told him, having already decided to keep the business card, and Cassie Plimpton, to myself. For now. Thanks to the way my parents got screwed over by Elektra Records earlier in their career, Walden is cynical about any and all things to do with major record labels, and I'm not ready to fend off his needles around my new balloon.

I click off the TV where Humphrey Bogart is wearing a trench coat and has a smart looking dame on his arm. Django, our geriatric mutt, eases himself off the couch and hobbles over to his dog bed on the far side of the room, plopping down like he's been dropped.

I re-cork the half-empty bottle of red wine on the coffee table, then gently squeeze Mom's shoulder until her bloodshot eyes flutter open. Her breath is an acrid musk of sleep and cheap merlot.

"How was it?" she asks.

For a second, I almost tell her about the business card, almost say *I'm going to get signed and we can pay the hospital bills and we'll never have to worry about money ever again.*

But I already made a promise. College. Then music. And signing a record deal is pretty much the opposite of going to college.

"It was good," I say.

"Jesus, Rainey," she says, sliding her fingertips over the scrapes on my forearms.

"It's because they don't want to drop me," I say, my voice muffled and froggy from the show. "Nobody's trying to hurt me."

"Maybe you should tell them that." She lets me help her to standing. "I've done my fair share of stupid things to get attention, but—"

"It's *not* about attention," I say, my voice, and my blood, rising slightly. But I don't want to fight, and I'm definitely not in the mood to explain to her, again, the admittedly confusing ethics of mosh pits and crowd surfing. So, I just mumble, "Forget it."

Mom waits a beat, then says, "Walden?"

"Driving Bethany home. He said he's going to stay over there. Dad?"

"Guess. Peek in on him before you go to bed, will you?"

"Sure."

"Oh, and can you take him up tomorrow morning for treatment?" she asks.

"Again?"

"Melissa's baby is still sick and I have to open the store," she says matter-of-factly.

"I have to work too."

"What time?"

"Noon."

"I'll be there by then."

"Okay," I say, already dreading another trip to the hospital. I hate the way it smells.

She kisses me on the cheek, then walks right past her suitcase and guitar, both still packed from when she got back from tour almost a week ago, and vanishes into the darkness of her bedroom. The toilet flushes; the bed creaks.

I still haven't gotten used to seeing Mom leave and come back from tour by herself. Every time I see gear and bags piling up by the door, my lizard brain tells me to pack my duffel bag, pick out the longest books I can find, and get ready for restless overnight rides in Howard the Duck's creaky bunks as the highway hums beneath me.

But the Cobb Family Band doesn't exist anymore and things are different now.

Mom's debut solo record, simply titled *Tracy Cobb*, came out six months ago. I think it's some of her best music ever. But the sales haven't been great, and from what I've overheard listening to Mom and Dad bicker about money, this tour, like the last one, and the one before that, was pretty much a wash financially. Which is why Mom is back part time at TJ Maxx and the mortgage notices and overdue medical bills are still piled up on the kitchen counter.

If I sign with Shore, I can get enough money to help. But I made a promise. College. Then music.

While I suck on a Ricola, I microwave some water and drop in a chamomile tea bag and stare into the back yard. The studio lights are still on, a trio of yellow rectangles that draw a misshapen face in the darkness. While the tea steeps and cools, I munch a stale chocolate chip cookie, dipping it in the tea to soften it up. My throat is scraped raw from singing, and a low hum of post-show adrenaline still buzzes in my bones. But it's nice to be alone.

I step barefoot into the backyard. The temperature has come down, but the air is still thick with late summer humidity and insomniac mosquitoes. The dewy grass tickles my toes. When I walk into Paradise Avenue, the recording studio my dad slowly built out of what used to be our two-car garage, I find him passed out on the couch with his arm draped across his face as if trying to block out the sun. On the coffee table there's a hunk of wood my dad has started carving into something, its eventual form not yet clear, though it will likely find life as a bird. For the past couple years, since Dad's stage fright got so bad he had to stop touring, he's sold his woodwork for a few bucks here and there. Birds. Bookcases. Beaming suns and crescent moons. Pretty much whatever you can dream up he can conjure from a slab of wood. The table is littered with sawdust and curly wood shavings. I sit down and put my arm on his shoulder.

"Trace," Dad says, his eyes opening to slits. His face is

all cliffs and sharp edges. His thick auburn hair is reduced to chemo peach fuzz. Before he can say another word, his breath catches on a violent wave of coughs, which bend and rattle his wiry frame. "I'm okay. I'm...sleep...here."

"Dad," I say. "It's me."

His eyes open a little wider.

"Rain Man," he says with a sweet little half smile.

"C'mon. Let's get you inside."

But he's already asleep again.

Using a pair of scissors from the control desk drawer, I snip last week's plastic hospital bracelet off his wrist. He always forgets to cut them off. There's a faded green and white blanket balled up beneath Dad's feet, and I gently slide it out and drape it over him, then stuff the bracelet into my skirt pocket.

Against the studio wall sits a messy cluster of boxes. The neck of my first ukulele, recognizable by its lacquered red finish, draws me over. I pick it up and laugh at my name clumsily painted on the back in white nail polish. I tune it up and quietly pluck a few notes.

Another of the boxes is packed with Luce and Tracy Cobb show posters dating back to 1973. Carnegie Hall. The Ryman Auditorium. The Flynn Theater. Red Rocks. The Fillmore West. There are piles of newspaper clippings and set lists. An envelope bursting with yellowing receipts. Old AAA road maps offering to decode entire swaths of the country between their silky covers: The Midwest. The Pacific Northwest. New England.

Last time I saw these boxes, they were dying a slow, dusty death in our basement so it's strange to see them all piled here in the studio. I look over at Dad, still snoring softly on the couch. *What are you up to?*

Another of the boxes is stuffed with a million Polaroids. Dad and Mom backstage. Slurping champagne. Goofing on somebody's tour bus. Walden and I asleep in our bunks in Howard the Duck. There's pictures of Eric Clapton and Neil Young. Toots Hibbert. Mavis Staples. There's one of me and Willie Nelson that always makes me smile. I can't be any more than three and I'm balanced on Willie's knee in an oversized T-shirt, one of Willie's braids gripped firmly in my right fist. Willie is mid-laugh, a fat joint tucked between his lips.

I find another picture I've never seen before. I'm probably six or seven, wearing cut-off jean shorts, a ringer tee, and a pair of red cowboy boots. The picture captures me in motion, mid-air, knees bent, arms flexed, hovering above the rain puddle I'm about to stomp in. My teeth are gritted with the effort. I get this weird, sort of electric feeling looking at it, in awe of the fierce, flying girl in the picture, who I recognize but somehow doesn't feel like me at all.

Taking the picture with me, I turn off the control room lights, then cross to the far side of our backyard and climb the rope ladder up to the treehouse. After clicking on the twin camp lanterns, I stick the puddle jumping picture to the wall with a thumb tack, then plop down on the loveseat and stare at Cassie Plimpton's business card.

What do YOU want?

I put Dad's hospital bracelet on the coffee table, then pull open the table's only drawer and take out the other bracelets. First, I use the blade of my Swiss army knife to dig a small hole into one end of the new bracelet, then, using a small length of fishing line, tie it to the six other bracelets I've already collected, each one with my dad's name and arrival date written in various colors of ink. I loop the threaded bracelets around my waist, stopping when I run out of real estate, probably three bracelets short of a belt. When the belt is finished, or when the doctors pronounce him cancer-free, I'm giving it to Dad as a present.

Exchanging the bracelet belt for my journal, I flip to a fresh page, then crank the stainless-steel body of my grandfather's pen until the tip slides out. I haven't been making as many lists lately as I used to, but Cassie's question has me thinking, and old habits die hard. At the top of the page, I scrawl:

Things I Want
1. For my dad's cancer to go away.
2. To sign a huge record deal with Shore so I can pay off all my family's hospital bills. And so I can be a famous musician.

My pen hovers, but I can't think of anything else. Welcome to my minimalist phase.

The crickets chirp while I examine my arms some more, my pale limbs like art pieces. There's one particularly long scrape running up the back of my left forearm. I could never say aloud why I go into the crowd. That I like that it hurts. That the pain helps me forget about how afraid I am that my dad is going to die. And about the promise I made.

"I've done my share of stupid things to get attention," I

sing softly, a melody drifting out of my brain like steam from a sewer grate, then hum the line on a loop, sending it up, down, and across the range of my voice.

"I've done my share of things to try and disappear," I echo over the same melody.

My cherry red Telecaster is in a stand next to the loveseat and I pick it up and strum until I find the chords. A minor to C major, hammering on the F in the C shape with my pinky.

I scrawl the two lines down in my journal where the rest of my list should be.

Track Three
World Domination, I Assume

I know the routine well by now. Check in at the front desk. Bracelet for Dad. Visitor's pass for me. Quick stop at the café. Regular for me, decaf for Dad. Then down the long hallway and through the high-ceilinged atrium with the massive fake maple trees to the bank of elevators with the polished steel doors and then up to the third floor. Quick stop at the bathroom, quick sip from the water fountain, and then into the treatment center.

No matter where you go in the hospital, it always smells the same. Antiseptic and a little bitter with a hint of lemon cleaner. A hospital is full of people, but it doesn't smell like people.

Claire, one of the nurses who always seems to be here, greets us warmly, comments on the nice weather and the disappointing score of last night's Red Sox game, and within a few minutes, has gotten my dad settled into a padded beige recliner and plugged a chemo pump into the medical port in his chest. The drugs always make him cold, so without asking she lays a thin white blanket over his lap. Brings him a ginger ale with no ice.

He's nearly bald so even though it's still summer he wears a thin skull cap.

"You mind if I close my eyes?" he asks because the drugs make him tired.

Sometimes the drugs make him sick and he wheels the cart into the bathroom looking like a man making the slowest getaway ever staged. Sometimes I hear him throwing up and I feel powerless because I don't know how to help him.

They measure cancer in stages, one through four. Basically, the higher the number, the closer you are to death. When Dad first found out he had lung cancer, it was already Stage II. It's now progressed to Stage III, which means that the cancer has spread. Recent scans show that the chemo and radiation are helping slow the spread, but they haven't stopped it yet. Or shrunk the size of the tumors, one of which is the size of a small lime. A black lime lives in my dad's chest.

"A week from now we'll be in Boston," Dad says.

"I know."

"Boston University. Even the name sounds exciting, doesn't it?"

"Yeah." Thinking about how we were sitting right here when I made my promise. College first. Then music. Dad says his biggest regret in life is that he didn't think about planning for his future until it was too late. He doesn't want me to make the same mistake.

I desperately want to tell him about Cassie Plimpton and the business card. About what I really want. About how I might be able to help with the hospital bills. About how the promise wasn't really a promise. It was just something I said to make him happy. But how do you tell the truth to a man who might be dying?

"After we tour the campus, I'll take you guys down to the Noname restaurant and we'll eat the best fish chowder you've ever had. It's this old place right on the docks. Makes you feel like you're about to go out to sea."

I smile. "That sounds amazing."

I'm reading *Bluebird* by Kurt Vonnegut and I read aloud to him until he falls asleep, at which point I tell Claire that my mom will be there by noon, then kiss Dad's forehead as softly as a whisper and barely make it back to the car before I start crying.

When Cassie Plimpton walks in the front door of Cuppa Josephine that afternoon, my body, at the sight of her, literally screams: *Hide!* I take a couple of nervous steps backward before realizing that, with Bethany in the stockroom, I'm the only other human standing there.

As Cassie walks toward me, heat rises and swarms my body. I feel slow-motion aware of everything: my beige Cuppa Josephine hat with the smiling coffee cup logo, my black apron stained by milk froth and cream cheese smears. The way the ceiling fan wafts loose strands of my hair into my periphery. It feels like I'm watching a nature documentary about myself.

Cassie Plimpton studies the menu, as if she's just another customer.

"What's good here?" she asks, slipping off her aviators

and stuffing one of the arms down the middle of her white V-neck.

"Um, well," I say, surveying the menu, as if I don't have it memorized. "The maple lattes are made with real maple syrup." Then, like a robot who can't stop talking, I add that "A lot of people like the popovers, which are made by this lady Jan who calls herself the Popover Princess. That's the name of her popover business."

Oh my God, stop talking, Rainey.

"Sold," she says, pulling out a Vans checkerboard wallet attached to her jeans by a silver chain. I make change from her twenty. She drops two bucks in the tip jar.

"I'm Cass, by the way."

"Oh, hi. I'm Rainey."

"Nice to meet you. I've been to a few of your shows, but it's nice to actually meet you."

I'm still holding up her cinnamon sugar popover with a piece of pastry paper.

"Do you want your popover heated? We can heat them up. Sometimes people like them heated up. But sometimes not. Some people eat them like this."

Cassie's eyes do a thing I'm used to seeing because it happens all the time. People see the version of me that performs, and to them that's *me*, but then they meet the version of me that has to talk to other people in real life, which is somehow me too, only half as confident and twice as awkward. There's genuine doubt in their eyes, as if I might actually be the twin of that other person.

"Surprise me," she says, then takes a table by the window.

By the time the popover is heated and I've made the latte, Bethany is back, so I walk over to Cassie's table with her things. She says I didn't have to do that, but then jokes that since I came all this way, I might as well sit down for a minute. If I can. Which I can. So I do.

Cassie says she loved my show last night. I tell her thank you. She asks how I think it went, and something in my face must betray the fact that I didn't think it was perfect.

"What?" she asks.

"Nothing. We have this new song," I say. "I don't think the arrangement is quite right."

"Third from the end, right?"

I look up from my fingers, which I've been nervously rubbing against each other while I study patterns in the floor's wood grain. She's right. "Yeah," I say, feeling impressed.

"I could tell. You were all holding back a little."

She breaks off a piece of her popover.

"How long have you been crowd-surfing?" She gestures at the bruises and scrapes on my arms. Her eyes pivot to my choker, then to my nose ring. I can tell she's sizing me up— my look, my choices—and that she's a little bit skeptical.

I shrug as if I'm not sure, but that's not true because I remember with searing detail the exact moment five months ago when I dropped my guitar during "Anger, Part III," walked to the front of the stage, turned around, and let myself fall backward. How amazing it felt to have all those hands catch me, then hold me aloft and pass me around like I was floating. How my mind was blissfully empty.

I keep waiting for Cassie to live up to the slithery stereotype of record company people my brother and parents have always painted in my mind. But Cassie seems nice. She asks me what I do for fun.

"Books, movies," I say. "Sometimes I go fishing with my dad."

Talking to Cassie reminds me of talking to my aunt Becky, my mom's younger sister, who's always upbeat and cool and curious about my life. Because of who my parents are, I've been around music industry people my whole life. You get used to it. But knowing that Cassie Plimpton is here for me and me alone makes it different. It makes her different.

"I grew up in a small town too," she says. "In Ohio. Except I worked at the local pharmacy instead of the local coffee shop. God, I couldn't wait to get the hell out of there. Now I kind of miss it."

She asks me whether or not I have a boyfriend. I tell her no. I find myself curious about Cassie's age and decide to take a chance.

"A lady never tells," she says.

I open my mouth to apologize, but Cassie smiles.

"I've never been much of a lady. How old do you think I am?"

"Twenty...something."

She smiles. "Good answer. I actually turned thirty-four last week."

We talk about how my senior year is about to start. I tell her about being home schooled. What I miss about it and what I like better about going to public school.

"And after high school? World domination, I assume."

I shrug. "My parents want me to go to college."

"Really?" She sounds genuinely surprised.

I shrug again. One of my New Year's resolutions when 1996 became 1997 was to shrug less, and I have failed utterly. I hereby resolve never to make another resolution again.

"Can you keep a secret?" she asks, motioning me forward, then whispers, "my parents wanted me to go to college too."

I laugh.

"Then again, my parents aren't Luce and Tracy Cobb. Is that what you want? College?"

"No. My parents say having a degree will be useful, later. A safety net, or whatever. But I love music."

I ask her what she thinks. She looks out the window for a few seconds, then turns back and stares a hole right through me.

"I think anyone can go to college," she says. "But that pretty much no one else in the entire world can do what you can do on that stage. That no one else will ever make a first album quite like *The Treehouse Tapes*. Or the second album we're going to make together." She sits back and smiles. "That's what I think."

Cassie's words feel like a language that only I can understand, and I can't help but smile. "What?" she asks, eating another tiny nugget off her popover.

"Nothing. Just. You're different than I expected."

"Good different? Bad different?"

"No, good. You're, I don't know, cooler?"

"I'll take cooler," she says. "Look, I won't beat around the bush. I think you're incredible and I want the next Rainey Cobb album to be on Shore Records. And to show you how serious we are about your future, I want to fly you to New York so we can hang out some more. Would you like that?"

"Yeah," I say. "I'd love it."

"Good. Talk to your parents and let me know. I think for the moment, it's probably easier if you talk to them about this instead of me."

"And what about my band? My brother? And River? He's the guitar player. Should I tell them so they can make plans, too, and stuff?"

Cassie turns and looks out the window. "Rainey, your band is amazing. You guys are so great together. The chemistry you have is fantastic. And I'm sure you feel really loyal to them." She turns back to me and I know what she's going to say before she says it. "But you're the one we're excited about. Do you know what I mean?"

"Yeah," I say. "I think so." I think she means that if I want to sign with Shore, I'll have to ditch my best friend and my brother to do it. I hate the thought of losing River, but he also has college plans and has never been that serious about a musical future. But the thought of leaving Walden behind after everything we've been through makes me want to puke.

Cassie waves at the air. "But let's worry about that later. In the meantime, if you ever need anything, or just need a fake big sister to talk to, hit me up. You've got my number."

Track Four
Sad Bastards and Constant Tragedy

The Pena Twins have made me their project.

"You're a freaking rock star," says Rachel Pena at lunch on Monday, the first day of our senior year.

"A freaking rock star," echoes her twin sister, Clara.

I met the twins at the very beginning of sophomore year. They were new to town. I was new to public school. Though I sometimes wonder if we'd have become friends without our newcomer status to bond us, they've been my daily lunchtime companions for two years now. And they always make me laugh.

"And it's time to finally act like it in the dating department because senior rock stars can go out with whoever they damn well feel like," Rachel says, jerking her head to the right as Clive Brewer, quarterback and king jock in residence at Green Valley High School, walks by. We watch as Clive occupies the last seat left at a table packed with buff guys and buffer girls. With bulging calves and glimmering white teeth, they all might as well have been manufactured in a lab.

"Not my type, you guys," I say, revealing only the tiniest

tip of the iceberg that is my complicated relationship to high school dating. Hidden well beneath the surface, way down there with the shipwrecks and the anglerfish—and all my letters to Juliet—is the rest of the story.

"Um, that ass is *everyone's* type," Clara whispers, and we all start giggling because, truly, as a specimen, the quarterback's ass is fairly undeniable in its quality.

"Gross," says Evan, sitting beside me, and as usual, a little closer than I'd like as he squeezes a mayo packet onto his chicken patty, the smell of it mixing with his normal bouquet of Old Spice and Clearasil. "I'm trying to savor my first mouthwatering deep fried chicken product of the year. Can we not talk about Clive Brewer's butt?"

"You don't have to sit here, bro," Clara says.

"Yeah, bro, you don't have to sit here."

But there's not much sting behind the twins' words. When Evan first started eating lunch with us, there was a period of time where the Pena twins didn't like Evan, and he didn't much like them back. But for some reason, even though they've evolved into a begrudging level of mutual affection, they've never let the animosity routine drop. Honestly, it's a little tiring, as if they're sitcom characters who the show's writers won't let evolve.

"What's with the winter clothes?" Clara asks, tugging at the full-length waffle shirt I'm wearing to cover the scrapes and bruises on my arms.

"You know I'm always cold," I say. As the only girl in school who wears a nose ring and a choker, I already get enough weird looks and whispers without passing out free ammunition.

As usual, the Pena twins are scarfing French fries dipped in way too much salted ketchup, and though Clive Brewer's butt isn't my idea of quality conversation, it's at least better than soccer, which is the only fall topic the twins seem to talk about.

As if they can read my mind, the conversation naturally segues into the soccer team's home opener this coming Saturday against Green Valley's biggest rival, Lincoln High. Apparently, last season, Clara almost got into a fight with one of Lincoln's defenders after a no-call on a dirty play that sent Clara face planting into the grass. She wants revenge.

"You coming?" Rachel asks. "Get ready to watch us slay."

"Slay," Clara says. "I'm gonna destroy that chick. Like, dead. Plan the funeral. Write the eulogy. I'm very sorry for your loss Mr. and Mrs. so and so."

"Oh, I can't. Sorry. Family stuff," I say, being deliberately vague.

But then Evan pipes in with "What family stuff?"

"You know," I say, then gently knock my leg against his.

"Do I?"

"Yeah, I told you." I knock his leg again.

"Don't think so," Evan says.

"It's no big deal. I just. I have to go to Boston with my dad," I reluctantly admit.

"Boston? What for?"

"I don't know. There's this thing at BU. He wants me to go with him."

"Boston University?" Evan asks. Now he has the Pena twins' attention, which is exactly what I didn't want.

"Yeah," I say, then bash his leg hard enough to knock him off balance and send his chicken patty flying, leaving a mayo smear across the tabletop.

"Oh right, right," he says, gathering up his sandwich. "Boston. Family. Right. Got it. Sorry. Forgot."

The twins both burst out laughing at his awkwardness.

"Oh my God, you are so weird," Rachel says.

"Weird, squared," Clara says.

Rachel leans forward conspiratorially. "I'm friends with Clive. Just say the word when you're ready and I'll make the intro."

"Pass."

"Eyes on the prize, Rainey," she says, drawing an ass shape with her hands, sneaking another giggle out of me. "Eyes. On. The. Prize."

"Sorry about that," Evan says as we navigate the packed hallway on my way to AP English, just a couple of salmon swimming upstream. "But now my leg really hurts."

"Well, then pick up the cues quicker."

A couple of nervous freshman girls appear beside us and tell me how much they loved my show the other night. One of them is shouting. I keep walking. That's the key. If you stop, you're screwed. The girls proclaim they're coming to every single one of my shows from now on. One of them, the quieter one, says, "Last year, my sister got super depressed. Like bad. She just kept listening to *The Treehouse Tapes* and she started to feel better."

I shrug my awkward thanks, feeling humbled by this notion, but also, not sure what to say. Seriously, what can you say in response to the possibility that your music helped pull somebody out of depression? Finally, they vanish into the melee.

"When are you guys leaving for Boston?" Evan asks.

"Saturday morning," I say. "My dad wants to get a BU sweatshirt so he can wear it as a badge of honor."

"You didn't swear a blood oath, you know. You were just talking with your dad when you said it."

"I know, but all of the sudden me going to college has become the central preoccupation of his entire life. He's trying to re-write history and make up for all his mistakes."

Lockers slam left and right, syncopating the conversational rhythm.

"I have to tell you something," I say, feeling a sudden impulse to tell him about Cassie, for somebody else to know. "But you have to *swear* you won't tell anyone."

"Oh my God, you're not...gay, are you?" Evan whispers, dissolving me into annoyed laughter. I punch him in the shoulder as hard as I can. Evan is one of the only people in the world who knows the truth about me. He accepts me completely—and I love him for that—but he can't stop with that joke. Probably because it always gets me.

"Ouch," Evan says, rubbing his shoulder. "Okay. I swear."

But before I can tell him, the bell rings, meaning we're both now officially late to our next class.

"Forget it. I'll tell you later."

"Fine. Wait. Do you still want to check out those new poster designs after school?" He's looking at me the way he sometimes does, like my face is the answer to a riddle he just solved. Even though Evan knows that I'm not into boys, deep down, I don't think he ever quite got over his crush on me. Little pieces of his heart are always slipping out without him realizing.

"Sure," I say, then hustle down the hallway and slip into AP English where I spot River in the third row, halfway back. He doesn't know it, but the two girls behind him are whispering about him. He slides his backpack off the desk he's been saving for me.

"On behalf of a grateful nation," he says, "I'd like to thank you in advance for letting me copy all your homework this year."

Our teacher, Ms. Ofalko, who's far and away my favorite teacher at Green Valley High, assumes a place at the front of the room and stares us all down with her fierce hazel eyes until all the side chatter slowly dries up. She's chewing one of the arms of her glasses and pondering something imponderable. Nobody holds a room's attention like this woman.

"The idea first came to Mary Shelly in what she later called a waking dream," Ms. Ofalko begins, and slowly winds her way into her opening day lecture, which I would normally love because Ms. Ofalko always knows these elaborate backstories about the novels we're going to read, but between thoughts about BU, the record label, and my sick dad, I can barely focus. I try to bring my attention back to my teacher's words, but before I can get the thread back, River hands me a piece of paper, which I open in my lap.

Will you please do Mia's radio show Friday night? She won't stop asking me. It's annoying and I don't want to have to kill her. My mom would be majorly pissed.

I laugh way louder than I mean to, distracting Ms. Ofalko, who's holding a copy of Mary Shelly's *Frankenstein*.

"Something to add, Ms. Cobb?" she asks.

"Uh, no."

"I know *I'm* funny. But I didn't realize that Mary Shelly's mother dying shortly after giving birth to her was so comical."

"Sorry," I say. "It's not."

"You're forgiven."

I look at River and nod yes. He mouths *thank you.*

On my way out the door, Ms. Ofalko hands me a copy of *Frankenstein* from a tall stack. On the book's cover, a strange figure kneels over a body of still water, gazing down at its own hideous reflection. We never read anything funny in English class. Why is that? Everything we read is always sad bastards and constant tragedy.

"Read anything good this summer?" Ms. Ofalko asks.

"*The Handmaid's Tale*," I say. "And *Hitchhiker's Guide to the Galaxy*."

"Ooh," she says. "Two of my favorites. Welcome back, Rainey."

"Thanks. You too."

"Thank you. Now go away."

After school, I trail River into the woods behind the high school. Squirrels scatter up into the maple trees. Birds squawk overhead. River winds his way to his regular spot, an abandoned, decaying sugar shack, then sparks a joint he's got hidden in an Altoids tin in his backpack. He takes a hit, then hands it to me. I look around, then accept it.

"Thanks for doing Mia's show," he says, his voice smoke-bent and stilted. "But get ready, she's a little weird."

River's older sister Mia, who dropped out of college last semester, hosts a weekly show on the local college radio station. She plays indie rock and interviews local musicians. Our paths have crossed at River's a handful of times, but we've never really spent any time together.

Exhaling a small cloud of smoke, my shoulders instantly relax. I can't believe how good it feels. How necessary. "Look at us," I say. "How weird can she be?"

"Speak for yourself. I'm just a perfectly average Joe."

"Right."

We pass the joint back and forth a couple more times, not talking. River is one of the only people I know who can shut up and just be.

"Crap," I say, remembering Evan. "I was supposed to meet Evan in the library to look at new poster designs."

"You could show up after dinner and he'd probably still be sitting there."

"Don't be so hard on him," I say. "You want to come?"

"Jeez, I'd really like to, but I got all that stuff to do," River says, smiling. River loves making music, loves arranging and investigating the caverns and valleys inside my songs, but he finds everything else about being in a band pretty boring. For a second, I almost tell him about Cassie and Shore. It's hard to imagine River being anything less than excited for me. We both know our paths are diverging in nine months anyway. We've always known it. But even the possibility of hurting his feelings, of seeing his face filled with the pain of rejection, stops me. I can already tell this is going to be harder than I thought.

We pass the joint back and forth two more times, which is twice more than I need.

"Do you think you can get me some?" I ask.

"What, weed?"

"Yeah. Just a little that I can keep at home."

He cocks his head.

"It's been stressful lately," I say. "I just want it to help me chill out."

River doesn't worry about much. But there's a hint of concerned curiosity in his eyes. Eventually, though, he shrugs.

"Let me see what I can do."

Two days later, I'm scrubbing vanilla syrup off the counter at Cuppa Josephine when the phone rings. It's a little after eight and the shop just closed for the day. Bethany answers.

"Cuppa Josephine, this is Bethany. Yeah, she's here. May I ask who's calling? Okay. Hang on a sec." She cups her palm over the receiver and turns to me. "Somebody named Cassie?"

I knock over the bottle of cleanser, which rolls and plummets to the ground with a splat.

"Crap, yeah, hold on," I say. Cue the clammy hands. Cue the jackrabbit heart.

A few feet away, my brother is perched at a table for two reading *The Fountainhead* and waiting for Bethany so they can go to her apartment and do whatever unspeakable things they do behind closed doors. As I scamper around the counter and pick up the cleanser bottle, his eyes drill a hole in my back. I accept the cordless phone from Bethany and hurry to the office and close the door behind me, realizing how suspicious my behavior must look.

"Hello?" I ask.

"Hey, it's Cass," she says. "Is this a bad time? I took a chance and tried you at work."

"Yes. No. It's fine. This is fine. Sorry. I mean, I can talk."

Cass explains that she's hoping I can come to New York for the weekend in two weeks. She wants to give me a tour of the Shore offices, and then take me to a recording session at Electric Lady Studios in Greenwich Village. Electric Lady is the studio that Jimi Hendrix designed and had built in the late 60s. His dream palace. Everyone has recorded there. Stevie Wonder. Patti Smith. Zeppelin. The Stones. I feel like I've been invited on a trip to the stars.

"Your whole family can come," Cass says. "Or just you and one of your parents. Whatever works. Let me know and I can have our people set it up. Does that sound okay?"

"Yeah," I say, wondering how the hell I can pull any of this off. "That sounds great."

Cass tells me to call her back in the next day or two when I know how many of us are coming and she'll set up everything. Flights. Hotel. All of it.

"You won't need to do a thing but show up," she says. "Cool?"

"Cool."

When I come out of the office, I casually hang up the phone and take off my apron. I'm trying so hard not to look at my brother, but finally give in.

"Who's Cassie?" he asks.

"Just a friend from school."

He nods, mulling this over. I can't tell if he believes me or not.

Track Five
Mushy Pea Green

On our way to a festival gig in California where the Cobb Family Band was playing a million years ago, I ordered fish and chips in an English style pub in Portland, Oregon called The Elephant and Wheelbarrow. Beside the fried fish and chip wedges was a shallow, sloped hill of green mush that looked like chunky baby food. I jabbed at it with my fork before my dad said, "Mushy peas. It's better than it looks."

The taste is still growing on me, but I never forgot that color, somewhere between grass and guacamole.

I mention all this because River's older sister Mia's eyes are mushy pea green. And when she leans way forward on her elbows and asks me questions, her eyes go almost iridescent with her excitement. She wants to know how my new songs compare with the songs on my first album.

"Lyrically," she says. "And sonically." She chuckles a little bit nervously at herself. "If that's even a word. Is sonically a word?" She consults the small stack of 3x5 index cards on which she's written her interview questions in neat block print.

"I think so," I say. "It sounds like a word. Anyway, I know what you mean."

"Okay. Cool. Sorry, sorry."

I'm glad she's nervous because it helps me hide the fact that so am I.

Since I was a little girl, I've been exposed to the delicate art of being asked questions about yourself and answering them in real time, as practiced by the Jedi master Tracy Cobb. Mom always seemed comfortable with the attention, able to articulate her ideas in a way that sounded honest and effortlessly cool. But the second I'm asked a question, my brain-mouth pathway turns into rush hour traffic. Nothing I say feels equal to the question asked, and so I end up in my head and babbling a stream of nonsense.

"I'm a different person now than I was when I wrote the songs for *The Treehouse Tapes*," I say. "I know we're always evolving, but just more so I mean."

"Oh. Like, how?"

"I think I'm a little more myself," I say. "I'm proud of those songs, but sometimes when I play them, I'm like, who wrote that?"

Mia laughs as she flips cards, then asks me about the origin story of "Ordinary Girl," which was the very first song I ever wrote, and is probably my best-known song, in part thanks to the video, the one where River flips his hair in that way the chicks love. I notice that when Mia moves the top card to the bottom of the stack, she aligns the corners so they're nice and crisp and there's no overlap.

I tell her about the fight I had with my mom one day. How I told Mom that after growing up homeschooled on the road and becoming a working, touring musician before I could even drive, I just wanted to be ordinary for once.

"I took that idea of being ordinary and made it look in the mirror," I say, completely overdramatizing the lyric writing process, which happened spontaneously one morning in a hotel room on the shores of Lake Michigan while I was nursing my very first hangover. The lyrics came out so fast that I barely had time to think about them. "I think there's too much pressure on all of us. Especially girls. Everybody's always telling us to be ourselves, but those same people are the ones pressuring us to be like everyone else."

She asks me where songs come from. I sip my water to give myself a second to think. "My dad says that songs are like butterflies. And that a songwriter's job is to safely capture them without breaking their wings. Or something like that. It sounds way better when he explains it. I think he means that songs are already out there somewhere."

"That's really beautiful," she says.

I've heard Mia's show before and whenever she has musicians on, they usually play something, so I brought my acoustic guitar. Just in case she asks me to play, which she does.

"I just wrote this one," I tell her. "It's called 'Stupid Things.' At least for now."

I strum softly with my thumb, A minor to C, getting the pulse into my body, then sing:

I've done my share of stupid things to get attention.
I've done my share of things to try and disappear.
I'm softening, like melted glass.

Forget the sea, forget the mast.
I never win, I'm paper thin,
Cause stupid things are always in my way.

When the song is over, Mia re-centers her microphone and says, "I love that so much. But it sounds so different from your other songs. It's very *Either/Or.*"

"Either or?"

"Elliott Smith's new album?"

"Oh, right," I say. I know the name Elliott Smith, but I've never heard his music before.

"I'll dub you a copy," she says.

River and his sister don't really look alike. So much so that I wonder if one of them is adopted. River is kind of, well, perfect looking. A sort of ageless *Interview with the Vampire* meets elves of Rivendell kind of thing. Beautiful, but detached, like a statue walking around. Mia's face is softer. Less angular. Full lips. Low cheek bones. She has short blonde hair, cut just above her ears, and two earrings in her left ear but only one in her right.

And those mushy pea green eyes.

Her style is different from River's, too. Whereas River favors ripped designer jeans, crisp white T-shirts, flannels, and Chuck Taylors, Mia is wearing a mustard-colored sweater vest over a bulky white T-shirt, brown suede sneakers, and black corduroys. It's an outfit that's quietly defiant. Confident. Grown up.

After the interview, as I'm packing up my guitar, my stomach growls loud enough to wrestle a smile out of Mia and an embarrassed giggle out of me.

"Sorry," I say. "I haven't eaten dinner yet."

"Me neither," Mia says. "I hate eating before I have to talk a lot because then I have to burp the whole time. Sorry, that's really gross."

"No, it's the same for me. It's why I never eat right before I sing either."

"I was going to go to the Neptune. They have good food and free coffee refills."

"Oh," I say.

"If you feel like getting something to eat? But it's fine if not. It's not a big deal if—"

"Yeah, sure."

Mia left her purse at work before she came to the studio, so on the way to the Neptune, we make a quick stop at Sullivan Street Jeans, the thrift store downtown where she works, which is only a few doors down from Cuppa Josephine.

While Mia gets her purse, I flip through the T-shirt rack and try on a couple of flannels. Having been forced to wear a lot of second-hand clothes over the years, I've always had an aversion to thrift stores. They've always been a reminder about how my family never had enough money. How everything Walden and I had—toys, clothes, books— used to be somebody else's. I longed for new things that were mine and mine alone. But there's this vibe in Sullivan Street. It smells rich and layered. It smells like history and experience. And the clothes have a lived-in quality that makes them mysterious and tantalizing.

"This place is cool," I say.

"Wait until I get my hands on it."

When I ask what Mia means, she confesses that Sullivan Street's owner is thinking about selling the store, and that she wants to buy it. "If I can get my mom to co-sign on the loan," she says. "She's still holding out hope that I'll go back to school next year."

Mia pulls a small notebook out of her bag and flips pages until she finds a series of rough drawings of the room we're standing in, only re-arranged and re-imagined.

"The coffee bar will go over there," she says, pointing to where the sweater racks currently live. "And a small stage in that corner." She thinks that Sullivan Street could be more than a store. "Imagine you come in looking for a great pair of jeans, only there's live music playing, so you get a coffee and a sandwich and hang out while you shop. I think this could be a place where people can come together and share their love of clothes and music and whatever." She has that nervous way about her that I'm already getting used to. Her green eyes are lit up and blazing with child-like excitement.

That's the moment I start to fall for her.

All the dishes at the Neptune Diner have these silly names.

The burger is called Thank You Mr. Cow. The cheesesteak is called the Philadelphia Flyer. And so on. Mia, who neatly arranges the coffee caddy and salt and pepper shakers the second we sit down, says she always gets cheese fries with melted Swiss and a side of gravy.

Who orders Swiss cheese on fries?

A waitress appears and fills both our mugs with

steaming coffee. The waitress has just turned when Mia says, "Excuse me," then hands her the silver cream pitcher. "Can we get some fresh cream, please?"

The waitress considers this, then accepts the cream pitcher and walks away.

"Always get fresh cream," Mia tells me, sounding serious.

"Why?"

"Because people spit in it," she whispers.

"They do not," I say, and sip my water while I study the menu. I try not to think about all the times I've put cream in my coffee and how many of those times people may have spit in it first. The waitress comes back with a fresh pitcher of cream and we doctor our coffee.

"Can I ask you a weird question?" Mia asks.

"Okay?"

"Is it true you have a photographic memory?"

"Is that what River said?"

I hate it when River tells people that because, inevitably, they want me to prove it.

"How does it work?"

"It's not a big deal. I just remember stuff."

"Can you turn the menu over right now and remember all the appetizers?"

I shrug, knowing I probably can.

"Sorry," she says. "I would hate it if someone put me on the spot like that."

I wait a few seconds, then, unable to resist the urge, rattle off the appetizers, in order, complete with prices. Mia's mouth opens wider and wider the further I get down the list, which ends with a dish called I'm Stuffed (stuffed mushrooms) for $5.99.

"Oh my God, that was insane!" Her eyes narrow and focus into a look I recognize. It's the same look that Evan often gives me, like my face is the answer to a riddle. Except Mia's version makes me wonder how her lips would taste.

Last year, when I came out to River, he helped me know he was okay with it by telling me that his older sister Mia was gay too. I'll never forget how comfortable he was with that tiny, stupid, everything word. Gay. How he was the first person I'd ever heard say it like it wasn't wired to explode. I've been wondering if River told Mia that I'm like her, and though I might be projecting, the way she looked at me just now feels like a big yes.

I get the You Cheddar Believe It (grilled cheese on sourdough). Mia gets her usual. While we eat, Mia talks about being back home, sleeping in her childhood bed after two years away at college in Rochester, NY. She and her mom argue sometimes, she says. But she likes being close to River, and their little sister.

"Why did you?" I ask. "Leave school?"

"It's a long and boring story," Mia says, dragging one of her cheese fries through gravy, but the way she says it reveals that while it may be a long story, it's probably not a boring one. I wonder about Mia's life. What being gay has been like for her. I want to ask her, but can you just ask someone that?

Mia drives me home at a speed that can only be described as geriatric. With her hands firmly locked at 10 and 2, she studies the road intently, rarely cracking the 25 mile per hour speed limit. I flip through her massive CD book, realizing halfway through that the CDs are in alphabetical order. Radiohead comes before Red Hot Chili Peppers, which come before The Rolling Stones, which come before The Smiths and Talking Heads and Tortoise. When I ask her what CD she's currently playing, I'm not surprised when she tells me it's Guided by Voices' *Alien Lanes,* since there's a CD missing between Green Day and Guns N' Roses.

It's yet another interesting oddity about this most interesting girl.

As we sit in my driveway, Mia turns down the music and thanks me again for doing the interview. I want to hang out with her again. In truth, I don't really want the night to end. But I don't know how to ask her without it sounding weird. I'm no good at this. Then it comes to me.

"Pick a color," I say.

"A color?"

"Yeah, pick a color. Any color."

"Why?"

"Just do it."

Last spring, while I was studying SAT vocab words, I bumped into this word, *synesthesia,* which means one of your senses automatically stimulates another one of your senses. The sound of a person's name makes you see a shape. Or you see colors when you hear music. That idea started this kick of making "color" mixes. I made a dark and brooding "black" mix for when I want to burn the world down and a light and sunny "yellow" mix for my dad to listen to during his chemo sessions. It gave me an excuse to look at music in a different way.

"I don't know. How about marigold?" she asks.

"Marigold?"

"What's wrong with marigold? It's like yellowish orange."

"Nothing," I say. "Marigold it is."

Track Six
I'm Not Like That

It's nine o'clock on Saturday morning and I-89 is mercifully quiet as I strangle the wheel and put all my concentration into keeping our car between the lines.

"I'm happy to take over anytime," Walden says from the backseat, looking up from his book. He hates the way I drive, but Dad says I need the highway practice.

"Stop it, I'm trying to concentrate," I say.

Dad's eyes droop with fatigue from yesterday's chemo, and his Egg McMuffin is getting cold in the paper bag at his feet, but as we head south, he's in a good mood, telling stories from yesteryear Boston gigs, trying to remember the name of the diner near the Paradise he and Mom used to love and quoting Thoreau when we pass the exit for Concord, Massachusetts.

"I still can't believe you named me after a pond," my brother says.

"A book," Dad corrects.

"The book is named after the pond," Walden says.

"That's true," Dad says. "But you're missing the point."

"Which is?"

"The book isn't named after the pond so much as the idea the pond represents. It wasn't just about getting off the grid and living simply. Thoreau was after something even deeper."

"Marrow of life?" Walden says, drawing an impressed turn of the head from Dad.

"I thought you never read it."

"I skimmed," Walden says. Dad chuckles.

I fight not to roll my eyes. I've read *Walden*. Parts of it I've re-read. I love a lot of what Thoreau says and feels. But it's infuriating that my dad doesn't even see the fact that, like Thoreau, he went out and lived the artist's life he dreamed of without worrying about what it would mean for the rest of his life—not to mention his family, including yours truly—but still expects me to be practical about my future.

We park at a garage near the BU campus and walk to the student center, where we're met by my dad's old friend, Cleo Brown, a bearded guy with horn rims and a bald head that gleams in the afternoon sunlight. Cleo is a killer bass man who played on some of my parents' early albums, but he left music a long time ago to get a PhD. in biology, which he now teaches here. He looks ten years younger than my dad, and it's hard to believe they were born within a month of each other.

"Shit man," Cleo says after they hug hello, lightly gripping my dad's arms, "does Tracy have you on a diet or something? You're about ready to blow away."

Dad just laughs and doesn't address the comment.

Cleo looks at me and Walden and shakes his head from side to side in disbelief.

"Last time I saw you two," he tells us, holding his hand three feet off the ground, "you were about this big. C'mon, let me show you around."

The college talk started in early spring, shortly after the cancer diagnosis. Dad and I were out fishing on the pond near our house, both bundled up against the cool April morning.

"You ever think about college, Rain Man?" he asked, sipping from a thermos of coffee and eating the last bite of a chocolate frosted donut.

"Once in a while," I said. "But not really. Music is going so great right now."

"I'd like you to give it some more thought."

"Oh," I said, surprised, "okay." I paused, then added, "Why?"

"Because a college education will give you options you can't get any other way. And with a degree, you won't have to make the same stupid mistakes your mom and I made."

Until I went to public high school two years ago, my parents were the only teachers I'd ever had. And they were surprisingly great at it. Insightful and passionate. They challenged me and Walden and helped us learn how to speak and listen. They were also deeply contemptuous of public education, which they believed was mass-produced, fast-food learning that lacked the ability to teach us true critical thinking or reasoning. Instead, the world was our school, the road was our textbook, and our family was our classroom. All this meant that, up until the moment I quit the family band to live a so called "normal" life, it was always a given that Walden and I would take over the family business and follow in our parents' musical footsteps.

But in the past two years, and more recently with my dad getting sick, the sizable cracks in my parents' own life and planning gradually revealed themselves. And with no health insurance or money saved for lean times, let alone retirement, they've found themselves woefully unprepared for the rest of their lives. Dad can't play live anymore, and Mom's solo career hasn't taken off, which means they've been quickly chewing through their savings.

"But how would that even work?" I asked.

"Scholarships," he said. "Loans. And anyway, let me and Mom worry about that."

Even in that moment, I knew I wasn't serious about college. When I first got to public school, I briefly flirted with the idea. But when *The Treehouse Tapes* took off, all I could think about was my music and how to keep playing it.

We fished in silence for a while. I got a couple nibbles, but no bites. Dad's line was as silent as he was, but by the way he kept chewing his lip, I could tell his internal machinery was on overdrive. Three different times he shook a cigarette out of his pack of Camels, only to stop himself and slide the cigarette back in, as if each time he had to remember all over again that he had lung cancer. He looked like a confused little kid.

"Are you okay?" I asked.

"Yeah, but I do have some regrets, Rain Man," he said, then burst into silent, horrible tears. I didn't know what to say, so I watched the water while my dad cried three feet away from me, wondering about what he meant.

Shortly after that day, Dad learned that Cleo was teaching at Boston University, and the college conversations got more and more serious. Walden called the game *Cleo says*.

Cleo says that scholarships are available.

Cleo says that a degree gives you endless options.

Cleo says that Boston is the best college town in the world.

Cleo says that even if you go to college, there's no reason you can't keep writing and recording your own music on the side.

Cleo says that if you try hard enough, you can fix all your own mistakes through your kids.

Cleo says.

Dad kept suggesting we take a ride down to Boston to tour the campus, and I kept putting him off. Saying I had a show. Saying I had to study. Saying we'd do it soon.

Then, one day, during an especially bad chemo session, Dad took my hand. His breathing was short and labored. His eyes were closed against the pain.

"I want you to go to college, Rain Man," he said. "And then you can keep playing if you still want to. There are no guarantees in the music game and you've got so much life in front of you. Promise me. Please."

So, I said it.

I promise.

Two words. Two stupid little words I can never take back.

With Cleo as our guide, we walk the BU campus, its own little city within a city. There are entire clusters of polished stone buildings dedicated to single subjects: business, engineering, law, fine arts, social work, communications, medicine. I keep wondering: *how can all this be one school?* There's a student center, a fitness club, an aquatic center, a food court, a chapel, even a police department dedicated just to the university.

Manicured flower boxes line the red brick sidewalks, lush with colorful, late summer blossoms. Cleo leads us into classrooms and through computer clusters. Everywhere we go the floors are hospital clean. A swarm of college kids bustles around us, coming and going, tucked into corners, scrawling into notebooks, drinking coffee, laughing at nothing.

With Cleo in the lead and my famous father in tow, we make an unusual quartet. I feel like everyone is looking at us. My all-black outfit feels conspicuous, my purple lipstick too bold. My choker over the top. And yet I like this place, so much more than I expected. It's as if I've been invited to a party I'm not supposed to be at. There's secret information on offer, and all I have to do is ask for it. Just walk up to those two girls laughing in the student union and say: *Hi, I'm Rainey.*

But I'm not like that.

The dining hall's massive floor-to-ceiling windows

flood the space with daylight and peer out onto a busy street, cars and pedestrians blurring by like a scene from a silent movie. We get sandwiches and cups of soup and sit at a table by the window. Dad has a few swallows of chicken noodle before nudging his tray away. I notice Cleo noticing how little he eats. Walden is doing his best to seem unimpressed by the whole thing, which is no big surprise, but I can tell his mind is swirling, that he's wondering the same thing I am: what would it be like to go here? To be swallowed up by this place and spat out a completely different person.

"It's easy to get anywhere in the city on the T," Cleo says, dipping his turkey sandwich into his clam chowder, "and there are student discounts everywhere you go. Museums, even Red Sox games. You also can't go ten feet without bumping into some famous spot where John Adams did this or George Washington did that." He looks out the window, then back at us. "But to me, the coolest thing about this place is all the doors its opens. I don't just mean opportunities out in the world. There's that. But I more mean doors in yourself."

At one point, Dad, looking pale and sweating, excuses himself and is gone a long time.

"Is he okay?" Cleo asks. Walden and I don't say anything, but our silence speaks for itself. "Sorry," he adds, holding up his hands, "none of my business."

When Dad gets back, he grills Cleo on scholarships and financial aid. About all the different majors there are at BU, a list which seems bottomless.

"Do you know what you might want to study?" Cleo asks.

I shrug. "I'm not really sure."

"The music school here is one of the best in the country," Cleo says.

Dad shakes his head. "The whole point of all this is to get into anything *but* music."

Cleo's eyes watch me as I look at my dad.

"Hey, that's cool," Cleo says. "One of the best parts about college is that you don't have to know at first. Part of the fun is figuring it out along the way."

Dad asks him how hard BU is to get into.

"What's your GPA?" he asks.

"3.75."

"SAT scores?"

"1275."

"Extracurriculars?"

"I do stuff with the drama department," I say. "Stage crew and stuff."

"Volunteering?"

"I played for free at our school's spring fest last year," I say and Cleo chuckles.

"Admission is highly competitive. But with your grades and SAT scores, you should be good. And it doesn't hurt that a few people still know who your old man is."

Cleo directs us to the business office where we get a pile of forms from a woman with large round glasses and a frilly white blouse. Application. Financial aid. Scholarship. They all have tiny writing and are printed on expensive stock.

After BU, we eat steaming bowls of fish chowder at the Noname Restaurant down on the docks, then buy cannoli from Mike's Pastry and share them while we look out over the harbor where fed-up patriots threw in all those crates of tea to protest a distant king. The dark water rolls in on the breeze, waves whispering as they break against the harbor walls. Dad brought along a camera and makes Walden and me pose for a picture, then asks a passing pedestrian to take a picture of the three of us.

As the picture taker, a fifty-ish guy with male-pattern baldness and stone washed jeans, is handing back the camera, he says, "Sorry to be a pest, but aren't you Luce Cobb?"

Dad confesses that he is, or at least what's left of him, and the guy shakes his hand and says that he and his wife got married to "Just Like the Day We Met," one of the early Luce and Tracy hits.

"We're divorced now," the guy says, chuckling, "but I'm sure it's not your fault."

By six o'clock we're on 93 North, Boston in the rearview, Walden at the wheel.

Dad, wearing a brand-new Boston University sweatshirt, asks what I think. I can hear the hope in his voice.

"It was pretty cool," I confess from the back seat.

"Cooler than you thought, right?" Dad asks.

"I guess."

"Cleo said to say the word when you want to go back. You can shadow some students to their classes, even stay overnight in the dorms if you want. Get the feel for what it's like to be a real college student. What'd you think, Walden?"

"I think the kids there are phonies," Walden says.

"Based on what?" Dad asks.

"Just the vibe I got."

"You don't know what you're talking about," my dad says.

"Why, because I think college would be an expensive waste of time?"

"No, because you're too young to be so grumpy and set in your ways."

I pull on my headphones and click on a mix that River made me, full of German electronic bands like Kraftwerk, whose robotic music could be the score from a video game and makes a strange soundtrack to the trees blurring by. My brother and dad's voices fade and obscure as my attention drifts. For a while I tune them out, imagining waking up in my dorm room at BU, going to class, looking out over that busy Boston street while I eat lunch, then meeting up with friends to study. But then Walden's voice rises and he says, "I don't see the point. It's not like Rainey and I have college funds. And we don't need it."

I turn the volume down a little.

"The point is that it's nice to have options," Dad says. "Going to college never even came up at my house. If Mom and I hadn't started playing together, and if we hadn't made it, I would have ended up working construction next to my old man. You know what he did? He poured concrete ten hours a day and had a crooked back. That would have been my life. And if I hadn't liked it, tough shit. Mom and I just got lucky is all. It wasn't destiny. And if you haven't noticed, luck doesn't last forever."

"You and Mom weren't just lucky," Walden says, "and

neither are me and Rainey," to which Dad bats at the air with his hand and starts fiddling with the radio.

He never used to give up so easily.

Mom wakes me up in the darkness, her hands on my shoulders, nudging me and quietly repeating my name—Rainey, Rainey, Rainey—until I open my eyes.

"Honey, I'm taking Dad."

"What? Where?"

"Over to the ER."

According to the bedside clock, it's three-twelve in the morning.

"What happened?"

"I don't know. He just can't breathe right."

I lay there for a few seconds while Mom pads out of the room, then roll out of bed.

"Walden, wake up," I say into the darkness, toward the shape of my sleeping brother.

In the living room, I find Dad sitting on the sofa in jeans that used to fit and his new BU sweatshirt, bent over wheezing with one palm on the coffee table and the other pressed tight across his chest as if he's trying to hold himself together. His respiration sounds like a heating vent with a blanket jammed into it.

"You didn't need to wake her up," Dad says, his voice a broken-down whisper that rises in pitch before trailing off. Through the living room bay window that looks out onto our front yard, there's nothing but blackness.

"C'mon," Mom says, trying to sound calm, shouldering

her purse, slipping on the glasses she wears for driving at night. She comes over to help Dad to stand, but he waves her away.

Walden wanders out in his boxer shorts, his eyes slivered against the harsh light and his fingers hooked into his armpits.

"Want me to come with you?" I ask.

Dad shakes his head from side to side.

"We'll be fine," Mom says. "Go back to sleep."

I sit down on the couch and Walden sits beside me. The Subaru's headlights back out of the driveway, then disappear into the darkness. Silence descends. The room so quiet I can hear the house vibrating and the appliances humming.

"Is he going to die?" I ask, saying the word aloud for the first time.

"What? No," Walden says. He says it so quickly and surely that I want to believe him, but I don't know what to believe, and suddenly, I wish that I'd said goodbye to my dad and told him I loved him. Why didn't I say goodbye?

I lie down on the couch and, eventually, close my eyes. When the phone rings, I fly up like a bomb went off. Frantically, I run into the kitchen and bobble and almost drop the phone receiver. The stove clock reads 5:58.

"Mom?"

"He's stable for the moment," Mom says, "he's okay. But they're going to keep him at least overnight so they can run some tests and make sure he can breathe better. But I need you to go into my room and pack me a little bag, okay? A change of clothes for me and toothbrushes and deodorant for both me and Dad. Can you do that? And then drop it off before school? I can meet you downstairs in the lobby."

She sounds exhausted, far away.

"Yeah," I say.

"And then I need you or Walden to come and relieve me this afternoon so I can go to work for a few hours. I know Walden works this afternoon, but do you?"

"Yeah. But I can call in. I'm sure it will be fine."

"Okay," she says. "I'm sorry."

"It's okay."

"No, it's not. But I don't know what else to do."

Track Seven
Easy There, Cheech

By the time I was fifteen, I'd played over 500 shows in 38 different states and eight different countries. Walden and I used to joke that if you cut us open, little black music notes would come flooding out. Music felt like my past, present, and future squashed into one endless drive. Sometimes after shows, fans, usually older women with bent backs and crispy blue hair would aggressively corner me with something strangely fierce in their eyes and tell me that music was my destiny. I'd wonder: isn't destiny supposed to be something you're moving toward, something you discover, not the only thing you can ever remember doing?

And if something really is your destiny, isn't it foolish to try to escape it? Even if you take an extended detour, aren't you eventually going to be drawn back toward destiny's gravity?

"Am I even making any sense?"

"You've come back from summer break talking in riddles," Mr. Larson says, sipping his steaming mug of green tea and narrowing his eyes at what I can tell has been a meandering journey through my current predicament. "What's this really about, Rainey?"

It's a week or so after Boston and Mr. Larson and I are tucked into the back of his classroom for our first 1:1 check-in of the new school year. Mr. Larson has been my homeroom teacher for the past two years and these check-ins, and the tea Mr. Larson always brews up for us with the little tea kit he keeps on top of his filing cabinet, have become a safe haven.

"Sorry," I say and sip my own tea, peppermint with honey. "How's Matthew?" At the mention of Matthew, Mr. Larson, as usual, peers around the room to see if any of the other students in homeroom are listening.

"You're changing the subject."

"Am I?" I ask. "I hadn't noticed."

Mr. Larson smiles. "Matthew's good. Although his garden isn't doing well and it's all he ever talks about. If I hear another word about heirloom tomatoes or squash beetles, I think my head is going to fly off. And don't repeat this because they'd probably kick me out of the state of Vermont, but I think compost is gross."

We sip our tea. My favorite thing about Mr. Larson is that he's one of the only adults I've ever met who doesn't want something from me. And he never pressures me to talk about anything I don't want to talk about. He just waits. And listens.

I explain about the trip to BU, about Cleo's belief that I could get in and how I might be able to get a scholarship. Mr. Larson is already well versed in *the promise* and my complicated feelings about it.

"How was it being at BU?"

"Everything is so nice there. It's all so clean and organized. But it was kind of weird too."

"Weird how?"

I shrug. "I've never been to a place like that before. Where everyone was doing the same thing at the same time."

"Aside from high school, you mean?"

I smile. "Everyone here is here because they have to be. Everyone there is there because they want to be. They seem to know exactly who they are and what they want to get out of it."

"Trust me, they don't. It just looks like that."

We each have a sip of tea.

"I know the circumstances are frustrating to you, but would going to BU *really* be so terrible?" he asks. "People are known to have fun at college. I did."

"It's four years! That's a quarter of my life so far. Walden says that college is where people go to figure out what they want to do, and that I already know what I want to do. But my dad." Tears well up in my eyes, but I force them down. I'm so mad and sad when I think about my dad right now, that sometimes even saying his name is too much.

Mr. Larson waits. There's this little rock garden on his desk that he lets me play with. I remove the smooth stones and comb the sand with the tiny rake, then re-arrange the stones atop the sand.

"This record company lady has been coming to my shows," I say. "And she came to see me at the coffee shop."

Mr. Larson's face processes this, and he tries not to react. He's always been really good at helping me believe the seriously abnormal life I've lived and continue to live isn't all that strange. I know it's partially an act, but I appreciate it more than I could ever explain to Mr. Larson. The chance to feel normal. To feel okay.

"They want me to come to New York. I think they want to sign me."

"Rainey!" he says, whisper-shouting. "That's amazing. Did you tell your parents yet?"

"Not yet. I know what they'll say. That major labels only care about money. That I'm too young to make major life decisions. That I already promised to go to college first and get a degree. Blah blah blah. But, see. This is what I mean, about destiny and stuff. Plus, and this is the weird part. Cassie, the record company lady, said that they're only interested in me. Not my band. Not my brother and River. I mean, River's going to college, so I don't think he would even care that much, but my brother—"

Mr. Larson nods. He finishes his tea and leans in closer. "Is that what you want? To sign with a record label now? Instead of going to college?"

"Yes," I say. "If I can."

"Then you should tell your family. Soon."

I shake my head, thinking about how I'm supposed to be confirming plans with Cassie to come to New York City this weekend, which seems like a near impossible feat.

"You don't think that your dad would understand if you were truly honest with him?"

"No," I say. "I really don't."

"You've always said your dad is the only person in the world who will always listen to you, who will always take your side."

"He's different now."

Mr. Larson sits back, knocks some dust off the corner of his desk. "How's he feeling these days? Are the treatments helping?"

I do want to tell Mr. Larson about it. About how Dad has been worse than usual the past few days. How they sent him home from the hospital with a breathing mask and a little oxygen tank on wheels. How sometimes he smokes even while he's sucking oxygen, pulling down the mask to take drags. How I'm so mad and confused watching him do this to himself that I want to scream until my lungs bleed. But I don't want to lose it. So I don't say anything.

As usual, Mr. Larson doesn't force it, and just nods. The bell rings and the room erupts with school sounds: bags zipping, feet shuffling, kids yelling, lockers slamming. A muffled voice over the loudspeaker calls a kid named James down to the office.

"Come see me anytime," Mr. Larson says. "I mean it."

"Thanks."

At band practice the next night, River hands me a small baggie of weed, which is inside another baggie to hide the smell, but the smell sneaks out anyway. Pine and musk and a trace of distant skunk. I offer him twenty dollars out of my wallet, but he won't take it.

"My treat," he says, then gets a sleeve of Zig Zags from his guitar case and tries to teach me how to roll a joint.

On tour a few years ago, my dad and I went to a driving range to hit some golf balls, and even though I'm not athletic, it was truly incredible how hard it was to hit that little white ball. It was sitting there perched on the rubber tee like a detached eye, but I could barely make contact or get it to fly straight no matter how hard I concentrated. That's how this feels. I finally finish what feels like a serviceable joint, but when I hold it upright to show off my handiwork, most of the weed slides right out the bottom onto the coffee table because I forgot to twist it shut.

"That was truly pathetic," River says, "I'll buy you a roller."

We're in River's basement, which is where Rainey Cobb the band practices these days. Calling the band my name was not my idea, by the way. But I long ago lost the fight to change it and have even begrudgingly accepted that my name has a slightly "off-beat quality" (River's words). Walden is tuning his drums, cranking bolts with his drum key, then tapping his index finger in the center of each head. I have perfect pitch, but I honestly have no idea what he's listening for. It always sounds the same to me. Evan is in the peach-colored recliner with the grease stain on the left arm, going over his math homework, stealing glances at me and River and giving an occasional disapproving mini-shake of the head.

For a while, I was paranoid about weed. But then River, who is less apologetic about who he naturally is than any person I've ever met, blurted out one day, "We smoke weed, okay," breaking the ice. I know that Evan is positive we're all going to go to jail, but Walden cared less than I thought he would, and even occasionally smokes a little with us.

River and I duck out into the sweaty September night. River sparks the perfect joint he rolled after my abomination, takes a hit, then passes it over to me.

I peek inside at Evan, now bent over a paperback copy of *Dune*. He looks up at us a couple of times, so I slide open the glass door.

"You want to come out?" I ask. "It's nice out. There's lots of lightning bugs."

"No thank you," Evan says. "I don't like the smoke."

I close the door. River rolls his eyes.

"Mr. Delicate."

"Be nice."

"I don't know why he has to come to *every* rehearsal," he says.

"He's our manager."

"He's booked us four shows and designed some crappy posters. We already had the 182 gigs set up, and Walden's posters are way cooler. I think there might be another reason."

"Stop saying that," I say. "He's over it. And it wouldn't matter anyway."

"I'm just saying that the heart is a fickle organ, Rainey. Very fickle."

I shake my head. River always gets philosophical when he's stoned. "Where's Mia?" I ask, taking a hit, then passing the joint back.

"No idea," River says, seeming unconcerned. "Probably

in her room watching *Trainspotting* again or listening to more bands that no one has ever heard of." I haven't quite figured out River's relationship to his older sister. He used to talk about her with tenderness, but since Mia dropped out of school and moved home, he's been more dismissive.

I take another hit, feeling all the tension I've been carrying draining away like water down a bath drain. I know I shouldn't, but I take another hit before giving it back to River.

"Easy there Cheech, we still have to rehearse," he says. "Mia told me she took you to Sullivan Street and told you her master plan."

I nod. River shakes his head.

"Never gonna happen," he says.

"Why?"

"The overlord has deemed it irresponsible."

"You're high," I say and he flashes his biggest grin.

River stubs out the joint on his Chuck Taylors, then slips the nub into the pocket of his ripped jeans. Arching his shoulders forward, he looks like James Dean. I'm not generally attracted to boys, but it's hard not to get a little fluttery around River McRae.

"Why did Mia leave school? She seems so smart."

"She is. I know her grades weren't great, and that she lost her scholarship, which made my parents go rip shit. But every time I ask her, she gets weird and changes the subject. I think something else happened, but I don't know."

He's about to say more, but Walden knocks on the door and points at his watch.

We run a couple originals off *The Treehouse Tapes* and

then "Blister in the Sun" with River on lead vocals doing his best Violent Femmes imitation before we start trying to arrange my new song "Stupid Things" in hopes of debuting it at our show this weekend at Club 182. But by that point I'm so stoned that it's hard to concentrate. It doesn't help that River starts saying everything in a Beavis and Butthead voice, making me laugh uncontrollably.

We try a couple more times, but, eventually, rehearsal devolves into Mario Kart and a family-sized bag of Cool Ranch Doritos, which we lay siege to like invading Vikings.

"I dig that new song," Walden says, breaking the silence mid-way through our drive home. "Would have been fun to play it this weekend."

"Yeah, sorry," I say.

"Since when are you such a pothead?"

"I'm not. I just...I'm not."

The breeze through the open window whirls my hair around. Normally I would yank it back into an elastic, but the rhythm of it feels almost musical.

"Is it Dad?" Walden asks. "Or college stuff? Do you want to talk about it?"

"That's okay." The wind keeps moving through my hair, separating the strands and making them dance. I imagine the wind sliding into my ears and mouth, my body slowly dissolving into tiny particles that drift out into the night until I only exist in the sense that the wind exists, everywhere and nowhere, just the stars and the dust and me.

I hear my brother's voice, hear him saying my name, but it sounds so far away.

My mind drifts to Mia. To the shape of her mouth and

the color of her hair. I imagine her sitting in her room washed in the blue glow of her TV as Ewan McGregor gets swallowed by the worst toilet in Scotland.

When I get home, I climb up to the treehouse, open my massive Case Logic CD book, which I've spent the last two years stuffing with the fruits of my gig money in an endless pursuit of new music, most of it underground indie stuff, and start flipping, wondering what songs sound like the color marigold.

There's a feeling in my heart, a type of wonderful heat, a longing I haven't felt in a long time. Not since Juliet.

It feels so fucking good.

"It's that Cassie person again," Bethany says, handing me the phone.

I duck into the back office with the cordless phone again, leaving Bethany with a growing line of customers, and Walden with a confused look on his face at how often I now get calls at work. My heart is a submarine swimming through an ocean of depth charges.

"Are we still on for this weekend?" she asks.

"Yeah, totally," I say, not thinking, just reacting. I pick a stapler up off the desk and click-click-click a few staples out into the air, then set the stapler back down. "That sounds perfect."

"Is it going to be your whole family? We need to finalize the plane and hotel arrangements."

"Um, no," I say. "Just two of us. Me and my brother, Walden."

It's what comes out.

"Oh," she says, sounding surprised. "Okay. Your parents didn't want to come?"

"No. They do. But they're busy."

"Okay." She hesitates long enough to make me think the jig is up. But then she says, "Write this number down" and recites a 212 phone number, which I frantically scribble onto the back of an old receipt. "This is the number for Rich Bowie, Shore's travel coordinator. Call him. He'll get you all squared away. You won't have to worry about anything."

"Okay," I say. "Rich. Got it. Thanks."

By the time I hang up the phone, I feel out of breath and swirling, wondering how I can get to New York City for the weekend without telling anyone.

Is there a way? There has to be a way.

When I open the office door, my brother is standing there leaning against the wall and picking at his nails, clearly waiting for me.

"Who's Cassie?" he asks for the second time.

My shoulders slump and I know that the bubble just burst.

"Get in here," I say and he steps cautiously into the office. I shut the door behind us, then tell him everything.

Track Eight
The Woman You're Meant to Be

"This is cool," Walden admits, fingering some chords on the Fender Rhodes Stevie Wonder used on his classic run of 70s albums. "This was really Stevie's?" The Rhodes is just sitting there. Not behind glass in a museum. Plugged in and ready to use. Apparently, Stevie donated it. Walden scooches over and I tease out the opening to "Sunshine of My Life," forcing my face to look calmer than I feel.

"I can see why she brought us here first," Walden whispers to me, meaning Cassie. "She's good. How much money are they offering you up front?"

"I don't know yet."

"How many albums do they want?"

"I don't know. We haven't talked about that yet."

It took a lot of convincing, but I somehow managed not only to persuade Walden to come to New York City with me, but to lie to our parents about it. My story is that I'm staying overnight at the Pena Twins' house, Walden's is that he's going with Bethany to visit some friends of hers in southern Vermont. Let's ignore the fact that I've never slept at the twins' house and Bethany has no friends in southern

Vermont. Harder still was persuading Walden to swallow all, or at least the bulk, of his sarcastic comments until we get home.

"I'll try," he said. "But when this all blows up in your face, I'm playing dumb. And then I'm going to laugh my ass off. Deal?"

"Deal," I said.

I even told him what Cassie said about how *you're the one we're excited about*, to which he seemed a little annoyed, but not as surprised as I expected.

"I get it," he said. "You're the star. I'm just dead weight. Any decent session guy can play drums better than me."

"Don't say that! That's not true. And it's not just about drumming. I need you there. I don't want to do this by myself."

"Maybe I can carry your bags," he said.

"Walden!"

"I'm joking. It's fine. Really. Let's worry about it later."

"Are you sure?"

"I'm sure. Stop worrying about me."

Which is how we end up at Electric Lady Studios in Greenwich Village where an up-and-coming soul singer named Brie St. Vincent is strumming a white acoustic guitar and humming the "D'yer Mak'er" melody into the very same condenser mic that Robert Plant used to record Led Zeppelin's *Houses of the Holy*, my favorite Led Zeppelin album, in this very room. A highlight reel of other legendary albums recorded at Electric Lady plays in my mind: Patti Smith's *Horses*, The Clash's *Combat Rock*, David Bowie's *Young Americans*. It's endless. Cassie told me that Brie, who's from Queens, recently signed with Shore. With flawless sepia skin and arresting eyes, Brie has a lordly grace and a mouth like a drunken sailor.

Walden and I assumed our first stop in New York City would be the Shore Records offices on West 54th Street in midtown Manhattan. But after Cassie met us at JFK and hustled us into a waiting taxi, she told the cab driver "Electric Lady Studios," and we were off.

Brie's band is stuck in traffic and she's killing time before her session starts, so I hop on Stevie's Rhodes and Walden gets behind the drum kit and before long, we're jamming on an acid soul vamp in B-flat and Brie is literally scribbling lyrics on the back of a napkin.

"Damn," Brie tells me at one point. "You look like some fuckin' whack ass Emo chick, no offense, but you play like Billy Preston." She turns to Walden. "And you're just absolutely slamming over there. You guys are really Luce and Tracy Cobb's kids? That's some cool ass shit, man."

Saul, the studio manager, shows us the nooks and crannies. "This is where John Lennon and David Bowie recorded 'Fame'," he says, walking us into a square room with egg-foam walls and low ceilings. We see the corner where Jimi Hendrix used to sit on the floor and strum his guitar between sessions, high as a satellite. I'm handed a coiled circle of guitar string that supposedly came when Angus Young broke the high E string on his SG while recording the "Back in Black" solo. Then a framed cocktail napkin whose lipstick kiss came from the lips of Tina Turner. Electric Lady has me starstruck into giddy silence, but Walden seems right at home, peppering Saul with questions about microphones, acoustics, and recording techniques.

From Electric Lady, we're whisked off to the Shore offices where we're paraded down hallways lined with gold records and shelves crowded with awards. You could eat off the floors and the whole place smells like money. Everyone is dressed in expensive business wear except me and Walden. I'm in my typical black (skirt) on black (fishnets) on black (T-shirt) on red (Dr. Martens) on gray (eyeshadow) on purple (lipstick) and I feel like that part in *Pretty Woman* when Julia Roberts first walks into the hotel and realizes she's actually an alien. I overhear one of the executives say he wishes I was "a little less grungy looking," and I try—and fail—not to care.

We sip Perrier from glass bottles through bendy straws. Cassie goes out of her way to introduce me to everyone, but every time she calls me "Luce and Tracy Cobb's daughter," I cringe a little and remember Walden's warning on the plane: *She doesn't really know you. She's just pretending like she does.*

Another executive asks me how I feel about "experimenting with my sound" and exploring my "poppier" side.

With nervous, sweaty palms I shake a million hands and answer questions politely. I hear everything and recall nothing. I'm an actor who can't remember her lines. My mind races with self-doubt.

You shouldn't be here. You're too weird. You're not pretty enough.

Since I was a little kid, I've been fawned at and doted

over by older, admiring people. I know that sounds egotistical, but it's a fact. If I had a nickel for every time some fifty-something gripped my shoulders and pronounced I was going to be rich and famous someday, I'd be able to pay my parents' hospital bills and buy a house on a hill overlooking an ocean somewhere. I was literally born for this moment.

But I'm here, now. This is what I said I wanted and I'm so not ready for it.

From Shore we cab to a brown building with glass doors. An elevator brings us to the second floor. This morning's Pop Tart is my stomach's sole occupant, and I feel lightheaded from all the traveling and small talk.

I see lights on tripods, a rack of clothes, and a European looking guy with glossy, shoulder length hair, oversize tinted glasses, and a massive camera hanging from his neck. There's familiar music playing, which I now recognize as my own voice pouring out of a boombox.

"What is this place?" I ask. "Is someone doing a photo shoot?"

"I thought we'd have a little fun," Cassie says.

I'm guided into a make-up chair and some lady with a blonde coif inspects my face.

"Gorgeous," she proclaims. "That skin!"

I think of the chin zit I popped yesterday morning, of the fact that I have so many freckles.

She unfastens my choker like she's primping a doll who can't talk. "Let's take this out too," she says, tapping my nose ring, which I remove for the first time in two years, feeling naked and confused. My face is lathered with cold cream, then wiped clean. A thick powder is applied to my cheeks with a poofy brush. My eyelashes are teased and pressed. My hair is steamed and styled by confident fingers. In my periphery stand Cassie and Walden. One of them looks very worried.

Cassie consorts with the clothes woman, and I'm handed an outfit I would never wear. I slip into a bathroom stall and take off my clothes, fold them into a little pile, and put on the clothes I was given: a snug baby blue top, skintight jeans, a brown leather jacket, and sandals.

I look in the mirror at a girl I don't recognize pretending to be a woman she isn't. My makeup is tidy and precise, soft Earth shades my mother wears. My hair is styled into an artful tangle I couldn't re-create with a million tries. I look wholesome and trashy at the same time. The crop top reveals my lower belly, and no matter how hard I suck in my gut, a curl of wobbly flesh spills over the tight denim. The crop top lifts and shapes my boobs, manifesting a dark and unfamiliar ravine of cleavage.

Slinking out of the bathroom, Cassie takes me by the hands and hugs me, saying "Oh my God, you look amazing!"

"Gorgeous," the make-up lady agrees.

The photographer voices clear, assertive commands.

I pose on a stool: I hold a guitar. I look this way. Then that. I cross my arms. Lace my fingers behind my head. I touch my face. Make a peace sign. I smile. I stick out my tongue.

Snap snap snap goes the staccato camera shutter.

A stylist slides the leather jacket off my left shoulder,

exposing my pale, freckled flesh. At first, I think it's an accident and pull the jacket back into position.

"No," the stylist corrects, "we want to see *more* of you."

"Super sexy," the photographer coos. "Like that." I feel frozen. "Perfect," he says.

I'm given a short, yellow dress and a jean jacket to change into. The process starts again.

Look natural the photographer says. *So beautiful. Right there. Hold it. That's perfect.*

After I'm allowed to put my real clothes and jewelry back on, we nibble crunchy snacks and sip sodas until Cassie, who disappeared for a while, approaches us holding a glossy, oversize piece of paper, perhaps 12x16. "I had the art department whip this up," she says and rotates the paper, revealing me on the cover on *Spin* Magazine. So real it's almost real. They chose one of the leather jacket off-the-shoulder pictures. I have a sly grin on my face that I don't remember making. My cleavage is aggressively shadowed. My belly obviously soft.

Note to self: if you have mixed feelings about your body, maybe don't put it on the cover of a magazine.

The headline reads *Can Rainey Cobb Have Your Attention, Please?* Fake sub-headlines about Lenny Kravitz and an oil scandal in the Middle East round out the reality.

This is ground control to Rainey Cobb.

"I look so different," I say. What I really mean is that I look pressed and manicured. Injected with sex.

"You look like a slutty Debbie Gibson," Walden says, assessing the mock cover.

"Do you know how many records Debbie Gibson has

sold?" Cassie asks him pointedly, not backing down. "Sixteen million. That's a lot of new RVs."

Walden looks at me.

"I told her about Howard," I say.

"Do you like it?" Cassie asks me. "You're the one whose opinion matters most."

Even though Walden quietly huffs at this, I love the way she says it, as if it's a fact immutable as gravity. Now I just need to make myself believe it.

Do I like it? I have no idea. I'm in awe of it. I'm terrified of it.

"It's so different from how I normally dress," I say. "And do my make-up."

"An evolution in style is part of coming into your own as an artist," Cassie says, mixing the air with her hands. "It's natural to experiment with our dark side when we're younger, but it's time for the next phase of Rainey Cobb. Grown up. Confident. Feminine. Fully in charge."

With very aggressive cleavage, I think, distracted by the size and shape of my own boobs, artificially rounded and more out there than they've ever been in their lives. But Cassie's right. I do look grown up. Feminine. And confident in the way I've always wanted to feel.

"I want to help you become the woman you're meant to be." Cassie taps the *Spin* cover. "And then share her with the whole world."

Later, at the hotel, Walden says, "This is what they do. They change you into someone else. Into who *they* want you to be. I overheard Cassie and the stylist talking about wanting you to start doing sit ups."

"You did?"

"Yeah."

I let this sink in for a second, then force a brave face. "Maybe I want to change," I say.

"Fine," he says. "Understandable. But this much? Overnight? You think your music isn't next? We don't need all this, Rainey. We're doing great. You're doing great. Everybody keeps telling you what you need to do. Dad and Mom with college. Now Cassie with all this. I think all you need to do is keep doing what you're doing."

You just did it too, I think.

Walden flips channels until he finds *Jurassic Park* and sets the remote down. Hungry raptors are stalking children through an empty kitchen.

I retreat into the bathroom and stare and stare at myself in the mirror. My choker and nose ring are back, but my face is still lacquered in Earth tones, so different from the shadowy spaces I like to hide in. I pinch my belly and think about slicing it off with a meat cleaver. Sitting on the toilet, holding the faux-*Spin*, I stare at the woman on the magazine cover.

She stares right back.

Track Nine
The Cinnamon Tape

"Close your eyes," Mia says, swirling a Swiss covered fry through sludgy brown gravy.

I cock my head doubtfully.

"It's not weird. Promise."

We're in our usual corner booth at the Neptune Diner. The coffee caddy and salt and pepper shakers have been neatly arranged. Fresh cream has been procured.

I feel something set into my open palm. I'd know the smooth rectangle of a tape case anywhere. I open my eyes. Another mix. Mia loved my Marigold Tape so much she made me a Sapphire Tape, then I made her a Juniper Tape, after which I requested cinnamon.

Pick a color is fast becoming our secret password.

"Side A is a cinnamon mix, by request of one Rainey Cobb. Side B is *Either/Or* by Elliott Smith because you really shouldn't live without it another second longer."

Mia's made a micro-collage of cinnamon-colored objects cut from magazines: leaves and tree trunks, a fox, a pouting pair of lips. "I can't wait to listen to it," I say, scanning the track names, feeling a familiar buzz at the promise of new music chosen and arranged just for me.

A — DATE / TIME — NOISE REDUCTION ☐ON ☐OFF	B — DATE / TIME — NOISE REDUCTION ☐ON ☐OFF
The Cinnamon Tape	**Elliott Smith Esther/Or**
Ani DiFranco -> Untouchable Face	• Speed Trials
Guided By Voices -> Hot Freaks	• Alameda
Belle and Sebastian -> Get Me Away From Here, I'm Dying	• Ballad of Big Nothing
Cocteau Twins -> Bluebird	• Between the Bars
The Softies -> Hello Rain	• Pictures of Me
PJ Harvey -> Down By the Water	• No Name No. 5
The Sundays -> Goodbye	• Rose Parade
Luna -> Lost In Space	• Punch and Judy
Uncle Tupelo -> New Madrid	• Angeles
Everything But the Girl -> Missing	• Cupid's Trick
Saint Etienne -> Nothing Can Stop Us	• 2:45 AM
R.E.M. -> Find the River	• Say Yes

"You want to hear something stupid?" Mia says a few minutes later.

"Definitely."

"River said he thought it was weird that we were hanging out all the time. Not that four times qualifies as *all the time*. And not that I'm counting."

"Oh," I say, not sure how to respond.

"And now I just made it weird. Sorry. I never mean to do that but it always seems to happen. Good one, Mia."

I sip my coffee and look around the diner. An old man is perched at the counter, his posture bent, his spindly spine visible against the thin cotton of his gray T-shirt. A waiter sets down a slice of pie and the man tucks a paper napkin into his collar.

While Mia gazes out the window, I survey her outfit again: an untucked men's white Oxford paired with a loosely knotted prep school tie and black pants. The two of us dress so different it's like Jekyll and Hyde. The waitress comes by and tops off our coffees. I dump in some cream and three sugar packets. Mia takes hers with cream, no sugar.

In four times hanging out, this is our first real awkward silence, and it lasts a lifetime.

"Have you always liked music?" I ask. I suddenly feel nervous, as if I'm on a date. Wait, am I on a date?

Mia nods. "My dad had this huge collection. Lots of classic rock and jazz. On Sundays, he'd put on the *Godfather*, or some other five-hour long movie, but without the sound, and then listen to CDs while he cleaned. Pink Floyd and James Taylor and Billy Joel. Stuff like that. When he split, he left all his music behind. I never understood that. My mom barely even listens to music."

"Do you still talk to him?"

Mia scratches the top of her left ear, the lobe punctuated by a pair of earrings, one a small golden hoop, the other a spherical turquoise stone set in silver. "On my birthday and holidays. We're not close. And he was a total asshole when he found out I wasn't going to be giving him any grandkids because I am never going near a penis in my life, thank you very much."

She says this while I'm mid-sip and coffee comes spraying out of my mouth in a tremendous woosh. Some even comes out of my nose.

At least the awkward silence is gone.

"Sorry!" she says.

"It's okay," I say, wiping the table, "just, next time, warn me. You were saying?"

"Just that he's my dad. River says he never wants to talk to him again, which I kind of get because he pretty much abandoned us. I guess I can't imagine never talking to my dad again. Speaking of dads?"

I shake my head.

"Rainey!"

"I know, I know."

"You have to tell him. About Shore. About the trip to New York."

"I know. I came close a couple times. It's never the right time. The other day I was working myself up to tell him, but then I found him in the studio studying the BU course catalog and making a list of all the classes he wants me to take."

"You should leave the fake *Spin* cover out," she says. "See how that goes over."

It's been two weeks since New York and I've spent more hours staring at my fake magazine cover than I would ever admit. The whole trip has become a dream I'm still decoding.

"I looked so weird," I say, shaking my head.

"Um, if by weird you mean hot."

I grin at her. "You thought I looked *hot*?"

"That slipped out," she says, obviously embarrassed. She wiggles her chin a little. "But, yes." She shakes her head aggressively like she's re-setting an Etch-a-Sketch, then says, "Okay, mandatory spontaneous subject change. The twins or the one-armed man?"

"What?"

"The twins or the one-armed man. Pick one."

"Uh, the one-armed man," I say.

"Perfect. To the cemetery we go."

I start laughing, then realize she isn't kidding. "Wait, what?"

Mia slides the Cinnamon Tape into her car's cassette deck and drives us through Fairview, past the movie theater and Juan's Tacos and Sullivan Street Jeans. The shimmering guitar of Ani DiFranco's "Untouchable Face" fills the small car like steam.

"So, fuck you!" Mia says, laughing as she sings along with the chorus. In fact, every time Ani sings "Fuck you" we crack up like little kids learning to swear.

As Mia pulls through the wrought iron gates of Fairview Cemetery, I try to act calm, but my stomach knots. I feel like a character at the beginning of a horror movie, the sacrificial teenage idiot who does something so obviously stupid that you don't even feel that bad when they're the first to die.

The passing gray headstones reflect the headlights, pale notches rising from the green grass. Out the open windows, a whiff of pine and woodsmoke.

Mia steers the car off the narrow road, then turns off the engine, but not the headlights, which illuminate the statue of a one-armed man perched nobly atop a pedestal. With a beard and short curly hair, he's dressed in military garb and holding a sword.

"The one-armed man, I presume?" I ask.

The Cinnamon Tape plays on, but quieter now. Songs I don't recognize but yearn to hear again.

Mia kills the headlights, plunging us into darkness.

"Over there," Mia says, pointing to nothing out there in the black.

"Where?" I ask. I can't see anything but dark headstones and silhouetted tree trunks.

"About ten feet behind the statue, to the left," Mia says, "there's a tall metal fence running left to right. He's facing away from us. He hangs out back there."

"Who?"

"General Stockard. The one-armed man. He was from Vermont. He fought at Gettysburg."

"July, 1863. Union casualties 23,000. Confederate casualties 28,000. We studied it in U.S. History last year." I like impressing Mia because I love the way it makes her smile.

"He's walking," Mia says, pointing. "Well, floating. Along the fence line."

I look at Mia, then back out into the darkness. I squint harder. My heart beats faster as the reality of what we're doing fully sinks in. She brought me here to see a ghost. I can't decide if I actually want to see a ghost, or if I just want to see what Mia sees. And then I see it. A human form, slightly lighter than the darkness, hovering several feet off the ground. Oh my God. But as soon as it's there, it's gone, and I'm not sure if I actually saw anything. I squint, but I can't make the vision re-emerge.

"Do you see him?"

"I thought I did, but now I'm not sure. Sorry. I'll keep trying."

I look at her for some sign that maybe she's joking. Or setting a trap to embarrass me. But her face betrays nothing.

"You probably think I'm so weird," she says kind of sadly.

"I've felt weird my whole life."

"Me too."

"I still do."

"Me too."

The acknowledgment of our collective weirdness hangs there for a few seconds.

"When did you start seeing ghosts?" I ask.

"Right after my grandfather died," she says. The mix slides into the next song, a dreamy number with shimmery guitars and a female singer. "We were all standing there at the cemetery while they put him in the ground. I was only six, but they made me wear this black Jackie Kennedy dress. I looked up and there he was."

"Who?"

"My dead grandfather. Floating there. Bluish green and sort of gray. Wearing the suit they buried him in, black with a red tie. He floated around, then drifted away and disappeared. Then I started to see others. I don't know why but it never really scared me. I always found it peaceful and reassuring, that maybe even if you were dead, you weren't all the way gone."

The mosquitoes thicken, forcing us to roll the windows most of the way back up.

Mia reaches past me and opens the glove compartment.

When she does, her bare arm briefly brushes my bare leg, sending a shiver up my belly. For a second, I think she's making a move on me, but then she pulls out a massive bag of Swedish Fish. She shakes a few out into her hand, then hands me the bag. I release the breath I've been holding. *Get a hold of yourself, Rainey.* But I can't deny how much I'm entranced by Mia. How knowing that she's breathed the same breath as another girl makes me feel close to her in a way that's hard to describe.

"I'm addicted to these things. My mom says they're made from horse hooves, but that can't be true, right?"

"Gross," I say and we laugh.

"Are you ready for the *Either/Or* experience?"

The clock reads 9:37 and I should go home. I have homework to do and school in the morning. But I don't want to be a kid who has to go to school tomorrow. I want to seem older than I am, more experienced than I feel.

"Sure," I say, telling myself that I'll get up early and do my English homework.

"First we set the scene," Mia says, and her seat suddenly collapses and sends her flying backward so fast, she screams out in surprise. "Graceful as usual."

I yank up on my seat handle, sending my seat into free fall until it's nearly horizontal. I look over at Mia, our faces less than a foot apart. Electricity pulses through me. I follow the pale curve of her cheek down to her lips, which are small but full. Do I want to kiss Mia? Yes. Right now, I want to kiss her more than anything. But what if I lean forward and I've read the signals wrong?

Mia props herself up on her elbows and flips the tape. "Here we go," she says.

There are a few seconds of tape hiss before a plaintive acoustic guitar plucks the album's opening notes, and I hear Elliott Smith's whispery tenor for the first time.

Either/Or's production manages to sound polished but without sanding down the music's scruffy edges. The acoustic guitars are closed mic'd, the vocals breathy and intimate. The melodies those of a natural songbird born and raised in the wild. Echoes of The Beach Boys, The Beatles, Leonard Cohen, Nick Drake. And yet, it's wholly original. I'm hypnotized, held in place by the power of this singer, these songs.

For what feels like forever, Mia and I lie there drifting through Elliott Smith's haunted dreams, passing the Swedish Fish back and forth until my mouth goes sticky and dry with the sugar.

I wake up to blinding light. To pounding on glass. To sheer panic. I squint against the glare of harsh white light, holding up my hand to shield my eyes.

"Oh shit, Rainey, oh shit, wake up," Mia says. She sits up. "A cop. Oh shit. Holy shit." The cop knocks on the window again, his knuckle rattling the glass. Mia rolls down her window.

"License and registration please," the cop says. "And turn off the music." Only his midsection is visible: navy uniform, brass buttons, leather belt, holstered gun. His voice is ice cold. Mia turns off the stereo, the cassette having flipped back over to the Cinnamon Tape while we were sleeping. She punches the dome light, gets her license out of her purse, then, with shaking hands, opens the glove compartment and rummages until she finds the registration card. He shines his flashlight down and scratches at the license with his thumb.

"My hair used to be longer," Mia says. "And brown. I dye it."

"Any alcohol or drugs in the car?"

"No," Mia says. Then adds, "of course not."

That's when I remember the River-rolled joint in my bag. Luckily, it's inside an Altoids container, but panic grips my body knowing it's there.

"What are you girls doing in here?" the cop says, bending down. With close cropped gray hair and a jowly face, he looks older than his voice sounded. He shines his light around the car. At the dashboard and the lemon-scented air freshener dangling from the rearview mirror. At the seats, still tilted back into a bed. My mind races with what he might be seeing and thinking. I feel utterly frozen with fear.

"Just listening to music," Mia says. "Are we not supposed to be here?"

Her voice sounds measured but calm.

"The cemetery closes at dusk, just like it says on the sign at the entrance, which means you're trespassing. And by the looks of it, that may not be all you're doing."

There's contempt in his voice, but also a disgusting curiosity.

"We're sorry," Mia says. "We didn't know. We're sorry."

"Stay in the car please." The cop walks away and gets into his cruiser.

Mia and I look at each other. The cop is gone for an eternity.

"Why is he taking so long?" Mia asks. "I've never even gotten a speeding ticket."

"Do you think we're in trouble?"

"I don't know. Maybe."

Eventually, the cop comes back and fills the window frame. Then he leans down, his huge body at an awkward angle. He looks Mia up and down, then does the same to me. I feel aware of every scrap of clothing I'm wearing: my short black skirt and fishnets, my purple lipstick, my nose ring. It all feels wrong.

"What's that thing around your neck?" he asks.

I touch my choker. I feel naked. A piece of meat pinned down and dissected.

"A necklace," I say.

"Little tight for a necklace," the cop says. "Looks like it's choking you. And what about the thing in your nose?"

"It's just jewelry." I barely recognize the thin husk of my voice.

The cop's eyes ping pong from me to Mia, back and forth.

"Go home," the cop says, handing Mia back her license and registration. "And next time, be a little smarter about what you're doing and where you're doing it."

"Ok," Mia says. "Thank you. And we're really sorry."

After Mia drops me off, I'm too wired to sleep, and definitely too brain-full to read *Frankenstein,* so I slip into the backyard and climb up to the treehouse. With my nerves frayed and my mind racing, I retrieve River's joint and spark it up with the lighter I keep hidden under the sofa cushions. I suck in a deep pull, then another, sprinting toward oblivion.

Then, with my destination reached, I make a new list in my journal:

Observations From a Truly Weird Night
1.   I may have seen a ghost.
2.   I fell asleep in a cemetery.
3.   Elliott Smith is my new favorite singer.
4.   Mia and I almost kissed. I think?
5.   I officially hate cops.

Finally, I weep silently into my hands. I can't stop, but, eventually, I do.

With cloudy eyes, I write Mia's name once, then again, and a third time. I keep writing it, smaller, bigger, wavier, blockier. Mia. Mia. Mia. Then I write her full name, Mia McRae, not sure what her middle name is or even if she has one, then scramble up the letters to see how many other words are inside her name. I am. Cram. I ram are. I am race. Rim rac. Ira mace.

I draw a little stick figure person, then give it short hair and a tie.

Then, my pen still pressed to the page, the cop's horrible face flashes in my mind and some words stumble into my head. A bubble rising from a lake bottom, they're suddenly there, riding the wave of melody that will carry them. I scribble them down as fast as I can.

Frozen in the high beam.
Stuck inside a bad dream.
This is how it ends. Hey! This is how it ends. Hey!
Hands where I can see em.
Carpe fucking diem.
This is how it ends. Hey! This is how it ends. Hey!
Piggie gets the first swing.
But Jesus wears a blonde wig.
This is not the end. Hey! Nothing ever ends. Hey!

I don't know what they mean, these scrambled images pulled from the cemetery, rescued and rearranged from the swirling dust inside the cop's flashlight. Not yet. Only that Mia has blonde hair and these words ring that weird tuning fork in my chest. The one that lets me know they're the best kind of true.

I take a chance and call Mia, who answers on the second ring.

"I wanted to call you too," she says. "Are you okay?"

"Yeah. I think so. You?"

"Yeah. I don't know, I kind of freaked out when I first got home."

"Me too."
"That was so crazy."
"Yeah."
We talk about everything for a long time.

Track Ten
Grown Up Talk

"I'm coming to town early before your next show," Cassie says. "Let's go shopping."

She picks me up after school and drives me to the mall in Burlington. Before we get out of the car, she asks, "How do you feel about mixing things up a little in the outfit department? Maybe try something different for the show tomorrow night? Something...not black?"

"Maybe?" I say, thinking about how I've barely worn anything but black in two years. Black jeans. Black skirts. Black fishnets. Black T-shirts.

"Do you ever wear dresses?"

"Not really," I say. "Mostly jeans or skirts with tights. Do you think I should?"

"With those legs? Are you kidding? I think you're crazy not to."

"Nobody at my shows really wears dresses," I say. "It's not that kind of crowd."

Cassie turns to me. "A girl lets the world dictate her reality. A woman creates her own."

Every time I walk out of the dressing room, I feel like

an imposter wearing some other girl's clothes, but Cassie's enthusiasm is infectious. When she says I look beautiful, that she would kill for my curves, for my hair, for my freckles, it's hard not to believe her. "The boys are going to go nuts." She gives me a playful nudge. "Maybe the girls too."

It takes a while but we finally settle on two dresses—one, a white knee-length number with tiny yellow flowers and a frilly bottom; the other tighter, shorter and a glossy emerald green. Cassie pairs them with a jean jacket and a shiny new pair of cowboy boots.

"So you can mix and match," she says. "But really, a jean jacket goes with everything."

A quick swipe from her shiny gold credit card pays for it all.

We go for coffee and Cassie tells me stories about Matteo, the Italian guy she just broke up with.

"I was starting to really like him," she says, "and then I saw his back."

"What about his back?"

"Very...furry," she says, and I can't stop laughing. I know that maybe I shouldn't like Cassie so much. That I shouldn't want to please her so bad. But I do. And I want to. I want her to like me, to respect me. I want my taste to rise up to hers, which feels so worldly and effortless. Cassie sees me in the way I want to see myself, and it feels incredible.

That song, "Torn," by a singer whose name I can't remember, comes on over the house speakers, and Cassie grooves in her seat. The song is catchy, but it reeks of the bland, flavor of the month pop music I can't stand. No edge. No risk. Utterly forgettable.

"You should cover this. Your voice would sound so good."

I frown and shake my head.

"Why not?" Cassie asks. "All that screaming you do and all that distortion on your guitar hides how gorgeous and soulful your voice really is." She points up at the speakers where "Torn" is sweeping into the final chorus. "You think Courtney Love can sing this good? Not with a gun to her head. But you can. And way better. I want to put your voice front and center."

We talk about my stage presentation, about not letting my hair cover my face so much while I play, about taking a break from crowd surfing. Cassie suggests making more eye contact. Standing up straighter.

"And you have a really nice smile," she says. "It would be nice to see it on stage once in a while. The angry Seattle thing is kind of over, anyway."

Even though Cassie's suggestions don't always feel right, she's so confident in her vision of me that I find myself agreeing with everything she says whether it rings true or not. I've always made a point *not* to smile on stage, but the fact that Cassie suggests it makes me wonder if she's right. The elephant in the room, though, at least for me, is talking to Cassie about Walden and River and how much I don't want to do this without them.

"About my band," I say as we're setting our mugs and

cookie plates in the bus tub. "Well, mostly about my brother."

"What about him?"

We head outside and get into Cassie's car.

"I just, I really want him to be part of all this. And I keep thinking about what you said that first time we talked. About how I was the one you were interested in. Does that mean you're *not* interested in him? And River?"

"No, of course not. We're interested in them. It's just different."

"Oh," I say, feeling even more confused. "Different... how?"

"Do you think that Walden and River want what's best for you?"

I'm caught off guard by the question. "What? Yeah. Of course."

"Then that's the most important thing. Don't worry so much, Rainey. Let me do the worrying. We're still figuring all this stuff out on our end, and I promise we'll talk more about it when it's time. But you've got a show tonight, so no more worrying, okay?"

"Okay."

Before the show that night, I do frantic sets of sit-ups in the bathroom, feeling foolish and desperate, sweating into the bathmat, then try on the white dress again. Alone in front of my mirror, without Cassie's affirmations in my ear, it feels wrong. The color feels right out of the First Communion playbook, and I hate how pale my legs look without tights. I slip on the jean jacket, then take it right off and, on the verge of tears, quickly change into my usual all-black get up. I hate caring this much about how I look and what I'm wearing, but now I'm in my head and I don't know how to stop.

After the show, Cassie says "I thought you were going to wear one of your new dresses tonight. They're so cute."

I shrug awkwardly.

"Next time, okay," she says, smiling. Her voice is kind, but it's not a request. "And sorry to be a nag, but I thought we talked about you taking a break from crowd surfing?"

"Yeah," I say, remembering the crowd's arms crying out for me during 'Anger Part III.' "I know. But it's part of the show now. I always do it. It feels weird to just stop all of the sudden."

"And what if you get really hurt one of these times?" she asks, gesturing at fresh red scratches on my forearms and the hint of a pale bruise to come above my left elbow. "Plus, don't you think that the risks you're taking send an unhealthy message to your fans? Young girls look up to you."

"They do not," I say.

"Yes, they do. I see the way they look at you. They idolize you, Rainey. And it's time to start acting like it."

For the next show, I squeeze into the emerald green dress, slip on the jean jacket, then pull on the cowboy boots, which manhandle my toes and make my feet throb. I might as well be dressed for a costume party, but I force myself out of the house. At the club, every single person I see comments on what I'm wearing.

"Damn, is it prom night?" River asks. "I left my tux at home."

"Shut up."

"Wow," Evan says, his eyes traveling up, down, and all over my body.

"You too."

"Seriously," River says. "You look amazing, but—"

"She's just getting ready for her close up," Walden says, drawing confused stares from Evan and River. Walden thinks I should come clean to the guys about Cassie and Shore, and I know I should tell them, I want to tell them, I will tell them, but explaining myself right now feels like so much work. Everyone seems to want something from me.

"I want to look nice," I say. "Is that such a crime? Can we move on?"

In the bathroom, after I slam the vodka from my film canister to try and slow my heart down, my bare legs splayed out, it hits me: You can't crowd surf in a dress.

I read the back of the stall door for the hundredth time. *My heart is a thousand years old, I am not like other people.*

The whole show all I can think about is that the kids right up front can probably see my underwear.

I tinker with "Jesus Wears a Blonde Wig," my new song about Mia and the cop. Part protest song, part love letter, it's the heaviest thing I've ever written. An immovable sonic mountain I wish I could hang around that cop's neck, and pretty much the opposite of exploring my "poppier" side. I think about Cassie telling me that young girls look up to me, and how much I'm not ready to accept that. Because if I do, I might start second guessing myself even more than I am. I'm already filled with doubt every time I look in the mirror, and I don't want that uncertainty to corrupt my music.

The muse is never wrong, my dad once told me. "The song that comes out is always the right one. Your subconscious has a mind of its own. You can try to control it, but you'll lose every time. The songwriter's primary job is to be open. And then get out of the way."

Even still, "Jesus Wears a Blonde Wig" feels risky. Dangerous, even.

Dad is thinner than ever and gulps oxygen through a tube as he wheels his little cart from room to room. We look through the BU course catalog together and I pretend to be excited about all the classes I could take. Dad lives in the sweatshirt he bought on campus. My hospital bracelet belt is almost finished.

"My daughter is going to Boston University," he says. So proud it breaks my heart.

"I'm not in yet," I say, but he just smiles.

I try to keep up with *Frankenstein* by reading to Dad during his chemo sessions, but I just fall farther behind. After class, tilted back in her big leather chair, Ms. Ofalko props her clogs up on a metal desk the size of a Volkswagen, and says "This is AP, Rainey. You have to earn your spot. Being naturally bright isn't enough."

I dream about my dad dying.

I dream about being on stage in my underwear and wake up in a cold sweat.

I feel boxed in. Judged. Misunderstood.

A strange anger builds inside of me, hot and unfamiliar.

One day after school I walk downtown to get my paycheck from Cuppa Josephine. I eat a popover and talk for a few minutes with Susie, the owner, who's always been nice to me and has never once mentioned my parents—even though I know she's a huge fan. Then I walk down the block, stopping just short of Sullivan Street Jeans, wondering if Mia is inside. The store name is hand drawn on the street-facing display window, ornate lettering outlined in glitter. On a set of rolling casters, a mannequin stands watch like a security guard, decked out in a shimmery Flapper dress, pearls, and a feathery headband.

An old couple ambles by and I bend down and pretend to tie my shoe. I smell the smoky, burnt essence of roasting coffee beans mingling with the late summer heat.

Out of the corner of my eye, Mia appears. I shuffle backward. If she looked all the way to her left, she would see me, but she's so focused on the display she's arranging: colorful bowling shoes fanned around a shiny purple bowling ball cradled by a stand in the shape of a human hand. Mia's careful, artful even, as she builds the display, adding props to accompany the shoes. A tipped over soda can, some confetti, and a few perfectly messy pieces of popcorn. She ties and re-ties one of the shoe's laces. When it's just right, she nods to herself in approval. It's a small moment, but it also feels like being able to see inside of her, all the way to the warm, secret place where her passion lives.

"Meet the new office manager at Powell, Parker, and June Law Office," Mom says at family meeting one night, making a ta-da gesture with her hands. "I start on Monday."

A real job, she calls it. With benefits and a real pay check, not like the peanuts she earns during her on-again, off-again stints working at T.J. Maxx between solo tours. She's canceled all her fall and winter tour dates. Told her bandmates to find temporary work until the dust clears.

"Just until Dad gets better," she says, her face pinched with the immense gravity of everything.

We're splayed around the living room. Mom and Dad beside each other on the couch. Walden in the rocking chair by the fireplace. Me cross-legged on the floor, leaned back with my palms on the rug and Django's big old head resting in my lap.

Walden tells her she can't. That her new album is too good. That she can't give up now.

"I'm not giving up," she says. "It's just for a little while."

"Why can't you quit smoking and let your body heal?" Walden asks Dad.

"It doesn't really work that way at this point," Dad says.

"Have you even tried?" Walden asks and there's so much pain and hurt in his voice. Without another word, Walden gets up and walks out the front door. Django lifts his head up, then puts it back down.

"What a goddamn mess," Dad says.

Maybe, I think, *you should have stopped smoking while you still had the chance and then none of this would have happened.* Picturing the thousands of times I watched my dad light up a cigarette, knowing he was sucking poison into his lungs and not saying a single fucking word to stop him. He's been killing himself in slow motion and we've all been sitting here watching him do it.

"We want you to be able to live your lives without having to worry about us," my mom says.

"Well, we do worry!" I say-shout, surprised at the volume of my own voice. Django, who's finally had enough of our shenanigans, gets up and goes over to his bed. "Stop telling us what to feel, okay? We're not little kids anymore. And maybe we could help."

"There's nothing you can do, Rainey," my mom says.

"How do you know that?"

"Because they're threatening to stop the chemo treatments." Mom's voice is flat and tired. She's wearing the Yellowstone National Park sweatshirt she always wears at night, the one with the goofy, smiling moose family on it. She leans forward with her elbows on her knees and really looks at me. "Is that what you want to hear?"

"Trace, don't," Dad says.

"The bills are piling up," Mom continues, ignoring him, "and we don't have any health insurance because nobody sees being a musician as a real job, and we're near through the last of our savings. We're in real trouble here, and real money is the only way out. You want to be a grown-up and hear grown-up talk, then there you go. That's the truth."

I move my lips around, rendered mute by her words.

"But between my new job," she says, her voice softening.

"And some memorabilia I think I can sell off," Dad says. "They just opened that Rock and Roll Hall of Fame out in Cleveland and Murph thinks they might be interested in doing a small exhibit someday." I think of the boxes piled up out in the studio, feeling stupid for wondering if Dad was working on a memoir or a scrapbook, not realizing he was trying to save his own life by selling off his past.

"Hopefully, we can get back in good standing with the hospital," Mom says. "But if we don't start paying off what we owe, they'll stop Dad's treatments."

"But then he won't get better," I say. I picture someone in an office somewhere with a big red rubber stamp that cancels somebody's lifeline. "How can do they do that?"

"Because it's a harsh world out there," my mom says.

"How much do we owe?" I ask.

"That's none of your business," my mom says, but I hold my ground, forcing her to take me seriously. She looks at my dad, who shrugs. "About thirty thousand dollars so far," she says softy, then, at the sight of my sinking face, adds, "I should never have told you."

"I had no idea it was that much."

"Without health insurance, medical care is a luxury item," Mom says.

Dad gets up and goes into the kitchen. Mom pads down the hallway into her bedroom. I hear her crying. I listen to Dad running the water, loading the dishwasher.

I do have some regrets, Rain Man.

I lay down on my back and stare up at the ceiling. Above the front door, there's a water damage stain the shape of Kansas. At the junction where the stain meets the wallpaper, the paper is peeling, just enough that you could get a good grip and probably rip the whole sheet off. I think about BU. About why Dad seems to want me to go to college so bad.

It's nice to have options.

Maybe he's right.

Later that night, Walden and I hole up in the treehouse and listen to The Cinnamon Tape while we eat half a box of Oatmeal Cream Pies.

"You okay?" I ask.

"Peachy," Walden says, shaking his head. "I'm just so fucking pissed, you know? How could he do this to himself? To mom? To all of us?"

"He didn't know this was going to happen," I say.

"He didn't *not* know either. It's not exactly breaking news that cigarettes cause cancer."

Sometimes I want to scream and shake my dad's shoulders. I want to blame him for our collective pain and what he's putting us through. But I can't bring myself to hate him the way Walden seems to.

We sit in silence. The music plays. The dreamy space pop of Luna's "Lost in Space" segues into the banjo opening of "New Madrid" by Uncle Tupelo.

"What's this tape?" he asks.

"A mix that Mia made. River's sister?"

"You guys are good friends now, right?"

"I guess," I say.

"Bethany was friends with her in high school. She's the same age as me. Mia, I mean. I would have been in her and Bethany's class if..."

"You ever went to school."

"Right. Do you know why she dropped out of RIT?"

"No," I say, not wanting to hint at how bad I want to know. "Do you?"

"I heard something, but not really."

I want to ask what he heard, but I also don't want to seem too curious.

"I'll ask Bethany," he says. "She knows everything."

I roll my eyes. Bethany does not know everything.

Later, after Walden goes back inside, I sneak the cordless phone up to the treehouse and dial the home number on Cassie's business card. My hands are shaking. She answers almost immediately.

"I hope this doesn't sound rude," I say, "but would there be money? Like, money upfront, if I sign?"

"Yes. We're still figuring some of that out. But yes, there would be an advance."

"How much?"

"Well," she says, "I don't know exactly. Probably twenty-five or thirty thousand dollars. But I shouldn't really talk about it until things are finalized. Are you okay, Rainey? You sound upset. What's this about?"

"Nothing. I'm fine," I say. "I was just curious. Sorry for calling."

"Rainey, wai—"

But I've already hung up.
Thirty thousand dollars, I think.

Band practice is almost over when I tell everyone that I have a new song. Evan looks up from *Dune* with anticipation, candlelight dancing across his pimply face. Mia is in the basement too, having sauntered down an hour ago, asking if we minded if she listened. She's been sitting on the floor, drawing in her sketch book, head bobbing as we play. She looks up now as well, and I feel a little tremor in my belly.

I show River the chords, most of which I borrowed (okay, stole) from "Blitzkrieg Bop" by the Ramones, then play through the rhythm a few times so Walden can hear what I'm going for. Up-tempo. Aggressive. Barely held together. I turn up the volume on my Telecaster, then stomp on my green Ibanez Tube Screamer. With River's help, I've added two more pedals to my guitar set up, a delay and a fuzz pedal, but the Tube Screamer is still my bread and butter, and I always feel a thrill when that clean sound goes gritty and harsh when I stomp the footpad.

"Play that for a couple minutes," Walden says, trying different drum parts, nodding to himself, stopping, starting, until he has a basic pattern.

"I want a lead line over the whole thing that doubles the vocals," I tell River, and I hum the melody while he works out the right notes. "So that it stabs at each word."

"Cool," River says, trying different positions on the neck. "How new is this song?"

"Pretty new," I say, being vague. I still haven't told

anyone about what happened to me and Mia at the cemetery. I was afraid that Walden would find it more than a little strange that I was hanging out in a cemetery in the dark with a girl I just met, and that River would find it even stranger that that girl was his sister. I wonder if Mia has told anyone about the cop.

We play through "Jesus Wears a Blonde Wig," until we start getting a grasp on it. It's one of the simplest songs I've ever written, an in-your-face banger, barely two minutes long, and the structure comes easily. I catch Mia's eyes as I sing "Piggie gets the first swing, but Jesus wears a blonde wig," and by the hint of a smile that plays across her lips, I can tell she gets it. That she knows it's about us. The song comes together unusually fast, and by the time we're into the fourth run through, our instruments have joined together into a Voltron super sound that, judging by everyone's smiles, hits us all the same way. Walden and River even both start chiming in on the word "Hey!" at the end of every line, so that we all shout it in unison like a battle cry.

"Damn," River says.

"You like it?" I ask.

"It's so badass," River says and high fives me. "Nice work, loser."

"It's so awesome, Rainey," Mia says. "I love it."

"Thanks." I try to sound casual, but I love that she loves it.

"We should put this out," Walden says. "As a single."

"Totally," River says.

"A single? Really? How do we do that?" I ask.

"We just do it. We can record it in the studio this weekend. Not the treehouse, Rainey, the studio, so don't even start."

"I know, I know," I say.

"Then, we put it out. People have been begging for new music."

"I can play it on my radio show," Mia says.

"And I know Poser has some other radio connections," Walden says. "Maybe we even do another video. Something fast and raw. Like the song."

"Hold up a second," Evan says, waving his hands. "Are you guys sure? Doing a single and another video sounds cool. But is this the right song? And the swearing? It's kind of..."

"What?" I ask, baiting him, watching him squirm.

"Controversial," Evan says.

"Oh please," Mia says. "It's rock and roll. It's supposed to be controversial."

"That's the point, dude," River says. "I love it. Fuck the pigs." He laughs at how ridiculous he sounds, as if the "pigs" have ever given him a problem in his life.

"If we have somebody film our next show," Walden says, "we can use it as footage for the video. Live footage would look cool with this song. The pit and everything."

"Wait, wait," Evan says. "I thought we wanted band decisions to be unanimous."

"You're not in the band, dude," River says, and I'm surprised at the edge in his voice.

Evan, visibly stung by this, pauses, then continues. "I

know that, but we all agreed that as the manager, I would have an equal say in important band decisions."

"Well, I always thought that was a stupid agreement," River says. "We should have said majority. Not unanimous. Nothing's ever unanimous."

"But we didn't say that," Evan says. "And things totally can be unanimous."

"Yeah, maybe if we're trying to agree that the fucking sky is blue. It's not like it's written down anywhere," River says. "It's just something we said one day, it's not the Bill of Rights."

"Yeah, but—" Evan begins.

"You guys," I say, sort of singing the word *guys*. They both turn and look at me, these two boys who I love with my whole heart, but who could not be more different from each other, and, I now realize, are not really friends themselves in spite of how much time they spend together. All because of me. "It'll be cool," I tell Evan. "C'mon."

Evan thinks for another few seconds. His face softens. "My dad has a video camera I'll bet I can use. I can bring it to the next show. Maybe get Ryan to run the merch table so I can film."

"I can run the merch table," Mia says.

"Okay," Evan says. "Thanks."

I go over and, still wearing my guitar, give him a hug.

"Thanks," I whisper. "You're the best.

"I'm aware," he says.

"I couldn't do this without you."

He grins, and I can tell he's officially been won over.

Note to self: you can never go wrong making boys feel important.

A little later, as I'm packing up my guitar, while River and Evan are bringing some dishes upstairs, Walden already having left to go and hang out with Bethany, Mia comes over to me.

"I've never been in a song before," she says, knocking her shoulder lightly against mine.

"What do you mean? That song is about an article I read in history."

Mia laughs so loud she snorts.

Track Eleven
The Other Team

When I wake up, Walden's bed is empty, and I can already smell a trace of his strawberry shampoo and musky deodorant. I brush my teeth, then yank my sleep-mussed hair up into a bun, say hi to my parents, and bring my coffee out to the studio.

"Morning sunshine," Walden says, "you ready to make some auditory magic?"

"Oh boy," I say. He grins back at me like a giddy little kid.

Mic cables wind across the studio floor like hungry snakes. Three different guitars, including my cherry red Mexican Telecaster, and two electric basses, are in their stands. A pair of Fender tube amps have microphones pointed at their gray bellies.

I sip my coffee while Walden does some more set up. I've learned that it's easier to let him do his thing than to try to help and have him tell me I'm doing everything wrong.

Though the recording side of Paradise Avenue is always clean, the control booth, separated by a curved wall of soundproof glass, tends to be another story. Sometimes it's basically a frat house in here. But this morning, I can tell Dad has already tidied things up for us. The boxes of memorabilia, now far less mysterious, are still piled up against the wall.

Walden fires up the vintage mixing board, which emits a low hum, then sends me over to start smacking drums so he can test the levels. Dad shows up with coffee and half a muffin. He's showered and looks surprisingly fresh in a clean button-down and his favorite flip flops. "Somebody here call a bass player?" he asks, grinning in a way I haven't seen in a while.

Sitting in a circle, we play through "Jesus Wears a Blonde Wig" a couple of times. I mumble sing the lyrics, my voice dipping to a whisper when I say "carpe fucking diem" but Dad just smiles and shakes his head. Dad's playing a blonde vintage Fender P bass, and his playing over the song's simple changes is a little busy at first. When he asks what I think, I simply say "half," which is Cobb Family short hand for: *you're overplaying*. He nods, seeming to agree, and develops a punchy bass part that drives the rhythm without drawing attention to itself.

"I think you got something here," he says. "That's a damn good song."

A huge grin swallows my face. And then we're off to the races.

By lunch, Walden is behind his kit and Dad and I are in the booth listening to playback through the studio monitors. It's a warm September day, and Dad props a metal fan in the corner to cool things off. The late summer air is fragrant with sweet basil and wildflowers.

I record my rhythm guitar part next, tuning up and strapping on my Tele. It's not the fanciest guitar, but I've always loved everything about it, from the thick neck to the scuffed white pick guard to the way the red paint is chipped in several places exposing the pale alder body beneath. The guitar part is simple, but at a 165 beats per minute, it's hard to play it clean all the way through. On my eighth try, I come so close that we decide to use the take.

River shows up around two, staying just long enough to record his lead part, which he tries first on his Gibson 335 but ends up playing on my dad's '57 Telecaster because it has a punchier, more aggressive sound.

"That's a really nice guitar, thank you, Mr. Cobb," he tells my dad, setting the guitar back in its stand. He's long admired my dad's vintage Tele, once named one of Rolling Stone's 100 Most Iconic Guitars in Rock.

"It's not made of glass, River," my dad says, "you don't have to be so careful."

"That's your '57, man," River says, "not sure you can be too careful."

"You would hate to know what I've done to that guitar over the years," my dad says, his eyes full of the beer-stained, long-haul memories of dragging his Telecaster all over the world.

"Yeah." River studies his shoes, then looks back up. "But that's different."

"I guess I know what you mean."

One time, I asked River why my dad made him nervous, and he said, "Um, have you ever *heard* your dad play guitar?" Guitar players are weird. But it's sweet too, to see them like this.

Shortly after River leaves, though, Dad has a coughing fit, one of the bad ones. While Walden runs to the house for the oxygen, I get Dad a glass of water, and as he forces down a few baby sips, I suddenly have the strange feeling that he's simply going to dissolve, like dew off the grass. Walden returns and Dad pulls on the oxygen mask, then cranks open the tank valve and sips a few desperate breaths. Eventually, the panic drains from his eyes.

"I'm okay, you guys," he says, his voice muffled through the plastic. "Carry on. It sounds great." As he walks past me, dragging his oxygen on a small dolly like a man twice his age, he pats the top of my head.

We sit in silence for a long minute before Walden stands up. "C'mon," he says. "Let's get back to work." I nod, feeling deflated but still determined to get the song wrapped today.

We finish with vocals.

"So, I found out why she's home," Walden says into my ear. "Say something."

"Check, check," I say into the microphone, the third one Walden has tried in the last fifteen minutes. They've all sounded pretty much the same to me, but Walden suddenly can't find the sound he's looking for. It's already after three and I'm getting tired. "Who?"

"Duh, Mia," Walden says, looking up at me through the glass. "Say something again."

"Check check," I say. "Really? So?"

"How does that sound to you?"

"It's sounds fine. I think we got it."

"I don't know. Maybe I'll switch it out and try the SM58 again."

"Walden!" I say, actually stomping my foot in indignation. "Tell me what you heard."

"Well, Bethany didn't know the whole story. But she says that she heard from Meg Scolari, this other girl they all went to high school with who went to RIT with Mia, that Mia stalked one of her TAs and then had a breakdown."

"What?" I ask, trying to process this, suddenly hating the way we're talking about Mia. I try to fit together the pieces. Stalking? A breakdown?

"But that's not the best part."

My pulse speeds up. "What's the best part?"

A sly grin spreads across Walden's face. "Well, let's just say that rumor has it that Mia plays for the other team."

"What does that mean?"

"She's a...lesbian," Walden says, saying it like an obscure word from a long-lost language. "The TA was a girl. Honestly, I'm not that surprised. I can kind of see it."

"See what?" I ask, folding my arms across my chest.

"You know."

"I don't, but I'm sure you'll enlighten me."

He cocks his head, trying to read my body language, which has caught him, and me, by surprise. I'm like an animal defending her territory.

"Jesus, forget it. You're the one who wanted to know. I didn't realize you two were best friends."

"We're not," I say, backtracking, trying to turn down the edge in my voice.

"This mic is fine," he says, changing the topic. "You want to try a take?"

"Sure."

The fifth vocal take is the strongest. It's not perfect, and I flub a word on the second chorus, saying "Jesus swears" instead of "Jesus wears," but my voice finally finds the brightly burning, barely controlled aggression that lives at the song's center.

While Walden tinkers with a quick mix of the song, I go into the house to check on Dad and find his blue duffle bag on the dining room table. Bustling into the kitchen, my mom is pulling her long red hair into an elastic. She sees me looking at the bag.

"I'll call you when I know if we're staying or not," she says.

I nod and then watch the car slowly back out of the driveway to the sound of grinding gravel.

A few minutes later, Walden and I are at the twin desk chairs in the control booth, a rough mix of "Jesus Wears a Blonde Wig" pouring from the studio monitors. I haven't told him about Mom and Dad going to the hospital yet. I close my eyes and listen, feeling myself being pulled into the music, into the web of a song that both scares and thrills me.

After the fade out, I look over at Walden, who's grinning and tapping the control desk. I feel almost in awe of what we just made, but I can't stop thinking about what Cassie will think.

"We should put this out right away," he says.

"I'm not sure," I say.

"What? I thought you wanted to. That was the whole point. It's so good."

"I kind of want to play it for Cassie first."

Walden stands up, looking shocked. "No way. Screw that."

"Just to get her opinion."

"And what if she says don't put it out?"

I shrug. I haven't thought that far ahead.

"Rainey, you're talking crazy. A month ago, you didn't even know this lady. She's already giving you fashion advice, and now you want her approval on your music? She's not even a producer. She's some A&R rep with dollar signs in her eyes."

"She's smart about music," I say. "And she cares about my future."

"She cares about *her* future."

"The two can't be connected?"

"Rainey, listen to the track we just recorded. It's alive because we made it come alive. This is all we need. Just us. Like it's always been. They'll only mess things up."

"Mom and Dad made their first four albums on Elektra, Walden. Not some indie label."

"Yeah, until their album sales dipped this much," he says, measuring a tiny distance between his fingers, "and then the label tried to get them to go New Wave or some bullshit, to trade in the sound they'd worked for fifteen years to develop for what was trendy, and when Mom and Dad pushed back and stuck to their guns, Elektra hung them out to dry."

I shrug, knowing this is an argument that I can't win. And that he's right.

"She's messing with your head," he says.

Thanks, Captain Obvious.

Track Twelve
Everything Used to Scare Me

It's a clumsy exchange to begin with. The cordless phone held up to the studio monitors in Paradise Avenue, my heart jackhammering while the song plays, wondering what Cassie's face is doing on the other end. Knowing Walden would strangle me if he was here right now.

Cassie waits so long to respond that I think we've lost the connection.

"Hello? Cassie?"

"That was...interesting," she says.

"In a good way?"

"What's the title again?"

"Jesus Wears a Blonde Wig," I say. "But I could change it if—"

"Rainey," she says, audibly exhaling, "it's a cool song, but I want you to think long and hard before you release it. In fact, I think you shouldn't. Let's get you together with a producer and we can start talking about the sound and feel for the next album. In fact, we should have done that already." She pauses. Silence so loud I can hear her thinking.

"I see your music heading in a totally different direction than this. More vocal driven, the way we talked about. Less heavy. To a place where we can expand your audience. I want your music playing on every radio station in the country."

"So do I," I say.

"Good. But parents are not going to want their daughters listening to Rainey Cobb if her new song bashes cops and has a cross dressing Jesus in it. And they certainly won't want them buying her new album, or going to her show and buying her T-shirt."

"That's not what it's about!" I tell her the story about the cop and the cemetery. About how my friend, Mia, has blonde hair. "It's a metaphor about how this friendship showed up at a really important time for me. I'm not even religious. It's also about how that stupid cop—"

"It won't matter," Cassie says. "All that will matter is what people choose to hear. This song will create controversy and controversy always comes with a cost. I love music that takes a stand. Public Enemy is one of my favorite bands of all time. But that's not what first made me interested in you. It's not why I keep coming to your shows."

"Why do you?" I say, starting to wonder.

"Because your voice makes me feel something I've never felt before," Cassie says, sliding inward, softening. "There's this amazing power and freedom in the way you sing. And from the first second I heard it, I knew I had to work with you."

"Just not on this song, or with my band," I say, unable

to hide my anger. Or the hurt from how much I wanted Cassie to love my song. I also feel embarrassed by how badly I misjudged the situation.

"Believe it or not, this is part of the process, Rainey. Working these kinds of things out. Sometimes it's easy, but sometimes it's hard."

She's so calm and composed I almost want to throw the phone across the room to hear the sound it will make.

"Just think about what I'm saying, okay? Will you promise me you'll do that?"

I promise.

Later, when I tell Walden, he gives me the biggest *I told you so* look of all time.

"What now?" he asks.

I shrug. "I'm not sure yet."

"She's being melodramatic. Art is elastic. It's there, then it disappears."

"Cassie said that parents aren't going to want their kids to buy my music," I say.

"That's stupid," he says. "Our music isn't for kids anyway." He frames me with his fingers.

"What are you doing?"

"Portrait of the artist as a young conformist."

"Shut up, that doesn't help," I say. "Do you really think she's so wrong, though?" Reluctantly, I've started to see some of the truth in Cassie's words.

He shrugs. "I don't care what she thinks. She's not the artist."

The muse is never wrong.

But what if it was this time?

I tell Walden to wait. To sit on the song. For now.

Operation Cheer Up starts with a large pizza in downtown Burlington. Sausage, mushrooms, extra cheese, and three root beers each. We lick sweet sauce from our fingertips and wipe grease smears from our happy cheeks. Followed by massive ice cream sundaes from Ben & Jerry's, then double espresso shots from Uncommon Grounds to bring us back to life.

"You have to hold it like this," I tell Mia, cradling my demitasse, my pinky up in the air, slurping loud enough to draw agitated stares and sending the both of us into hysterics.

Giddy and overcaffeinated, we go to the arcade and play games until our eyes hurt and our fingers ache. One of the games is a punching bag that gauges your power with each punch. Mia feeds it tokens five different times, punching a little harder with each swing, a fierce and determined look in her eye.

Emerging from the bowling alley, it feels like days have passed.

"How long were we in there?" I ask.

"Three years," Mia says.

In the western sky, the sinking sun suggests a glorious pastel sunset.

Mia drives us to a quiet stretch of beach on Lake Champlain where we walk barefoot through the sand, then lay out a blanket from Mia's trunk. We share a bag of

Swedish Fish while we listen to the gentle surf and watch the sun go down down down. We've been talking non-stop all night—music, movies, books, food—carefully avoiding the subject of Mia's mom and the bank loan she won't co-sign that inspired Operation Cheer Up in the first place. But while the colors mutate from orange to purple to whisper pink, we gaze in rapt silence.

"Feel any better?" I ask.

"A little. I'm just so sick of people telling me what to do."

"I think maybe your parents and my parents should get together and go bowling," I say, digging my toes into the cooling sand.

"Nice."

Darkness settles. Deepens. The world seeming to contract in the light's absence. The few other sunset gazers around us have long gone. It's an unusually warm night and the dark rolling water looks strangely inviting. I imagine its cool touch on my toes, my legs, my face. An impulse strikes me.

"Wanna go swimming?" I ask.

Mia turns to me in the darkness.

"Now?"

"Well, yeah."

"We don't have any bathing suits."

"We can just go in our underwear," I propose, feeling unusually bold. "I won't look."

"Then our underwear will be all soaked," she says.

"Good point."

"We could skinny-dip."

My belly tingles with nervous excitement. I look around again. We are utterly alone.

"Seriously?"

"I will if you will," she says.

Mia goes first. I hide behind a tree and swear I have my eyes closed while she undresses and hurries into the water. Feeling nervous and excited, I slip off my shorts and tank top, then take off my underwear, and while Mia promises her eyes are closed, I run as fast as I can and splash into Lake Champlain naked as the day I was born. The bracing water slaps and enlivens my bare skin, colder than I expect, but exhilarating.

Bobbing there with only our necks exposed, our naked bodies concealed only a few feet from each other's eyes, neither of us can relax at first. We keep nervously laughing. But it also feels intensely exciting, as if we've pulled a secret storybook moment out of thin air and written ourselves into it. The pale crescent moon softly lights Mia's face, her ruby lips, her yellow hair and plush cheeks, though the dark water conceals other things I wish I could see. I'm naked in the moonlight with a beautiful girl. I feel tingly and alive. Anything is possible. Back on shore, our troubles are waiting for us, but not out here. Out here, this stolen moment is ours and ours alone and we savor and soak it up.

A shooting star dashes through the night sky.

"Look," I say, pointing.

"Shooting stars used to scare me when I was little," she says.

"Really?"

"Everything used to scare me." Her voice has grown wistful.

The shooting star trails off. Its absence so inky black it's like it was never there.

"I thought when it disappeared it was because it had hit someone's house." She shakes her head. "Stupid, I know. My whole life I've been afraid. I was afraid of letting my parents down. Of getting bad grades. Of not being a good enough daughter. Of not being athletic or girly enough. I was afraid of wearing the clothes I wanted to wear." Her words have grown slightly labored from the effort of talking while treading water. "And then, when I realized I was gay, I was afraid there was something wrong with me and everybody knew it. Like I was letting everyone down."

Mia wipes at her eyes.

"Now my mom won't help me because *she's* afraid I'm only going to own a store the rest of my life and never amount to anything. Jesus, at least I know where I get all my fear from."

"This probably won't help," I say, circling my arms to stay afloat, "but I used to be afraid of The Incredible Hulk on TV."

Mia chuckles and looks back up at the sky, maybe hoping to see another shooting star. "Thanks for tonight," she says. "I needed this."

"What, being naked in public?"

Mia splashes me and I splash her back. The grin on her face is impossibly cute. I want to kiss her so badly my body aches and vibrates with the yearning. I want to wrap my arms around her and feel her skin against my skin.

"I needed this too," I say. "You're the only person I can be myself around lately. The only person who isn't up my ass about everything."

"Me too. That's how I feel, too. About being around you. But not the ass part."

"I guess we should keep being around each other then, huh?"

"Guess so."

It's already after eleven when Mia drops me off, so it's a shock to find both my parents sitting on the couch in silence looking like somebody died. It's a school night and I suddenly remember the homework I haven't done. Not to mention, my hair is still wet from the lake and I panic, wondering how I'm going to explain myself—what I was doing, who I was with—but they don't seem to notice.

"Come sit down," my mother says, clicking off the muted TV. Her posture is ruler rigid.

"Oh-kay," I say. I ease into the rocking chair. My dad kneads his chin with his fingers.

"Is everything okay?" I ask. I have a horrible feeling.

"We had an interesting phone conversation earlier this evening with Cassie Plimpton from Shore Records," Mom says, shaking her head.

Houston, we have a problem.

"Cassie called you?"

"She wanted to apologize that she hasn't met us in person yet, and to tell us how excited she is to be working with our daughter on plans for her next album."

I open my mouth but my mom cuts me off before I can speak.

"You went to New York City and met with a record company without telling us? And did a photo shoot?"

"Walden came too," I say stupidly.

"Oh, we've already spoken to him," my mom says. "He told us this Cassie person is also the one who bought you those dresses, the ones you said you bought yourself? What else have you been lying to us about?"

I stare at my hands.

"*Look* at us," my mother says, and I look back up to where my parents' sad, defeated faces advertise how much I've screwed everything up. "What else?"

"Nothing," I say, pulling my wet hair away from my neck.

"I don't even know what to say, Rain Man," my dad says, shaking his head. With sunken cheeks and deep-set eyes, he's a shell of himself. He's wearing his BU sweatshirt and is on the verge of tears. As usual, his jeans are speckled with patches of sawdust from a recent carving. "I thought that we had this all figured out. What about college? You've been so excited about it."

"No, Dad, *you've* been so excited about it."

"But we've been picking out courses."

"You've been picking out courses. I've just been sitting there."

"But we had so much fun at BU. Didn't we?"

He sounds so broken and confused I want to cry. How can he be so naïve?

"We did, I know, but...this is what I want." My voice is almost too soft to hear.

"Speak *up*," my mom says.

"This is what I want," I say, a bit louder. I want to tell her about the money, about my plan to use the advance to pay the hospital bills, but the words won't come. A vast gulf seems to have opened between us.

"Well, you can forget it," she says. "You're going to college. Just like we've been talking about. Just like you promised."

"It's my life."

"Yes," my mom says. "And pretty soon you'll be free to make all the poor choices you want to. But as long as you're living under this roof, and as long as you're under eighteen, it's still our job to help you make good decisions. And this conversation is over."

Track Thirteen
A Meaty Chunk of My Right Cheek

A week later. I'm touching up my makeup in the dressing room at 182. Thick mascara. Dark eye-shadow. Purple lipstick. Fuck-you hair.

Cassie's dresses are neatly hung in my closet and I'm back in black.

Across the room, River tunes his guitar, calm as an empty church. Evan nervously fiddles with his dad's gigantic video camera, panning it around the room like Spielberg Jr., mumbling to himself: "Extra batteries, check, extra video tape, check, lens cap, check."

"I told Poser to spread the word we're filming a video for a new song," Walden says.

"You did?" I ask, whirling around.

Walden side-eyes Bethany. "Was I not supposed to do that? I thought it would help make the crowd look extra excited in the video."

"I don't want people to think it's weird," I say.

"That we're filming a video? They'll think it's cool, especially if they think they're in it."

Five minutes until showtime. Four. Three.

I scurry down the short hallway that leads to the stage, trying to muffle the heavy footfalls of my red Doc Marten boots. The crowd's anticipation is an electric hum in the air. Easing back the black curtain, I confirm what I already suspected. Cassie isn't here. Of course she's not. My mother forbade her from even talking to me. Told her thank you, but we're not interested in Shore Records.

I had no say in the matter. No voice. Just a piece being move around on a board.

But tonight, I do have a voice. And a microphone. Tonight, my voice feels ready to scream.

In Cassie's usual spot stands a short guy with John Lennon specs wearing a white press pass and a fancy Nikon with a long telephoto lens.

I slip into my lucky middle stall in the bathroom and pop the cap on my film canister, full to the brim with Popov. Maybe it's because I haven't eaten much today, or because River and I ripped a joint in the back of the RV on the way over, but tonight the vodka makes me go mushy like a piece of overripe fruit.

Pushing out of the stall, a bit wobbly, I meet my reflection in the bathroom mirror.

"What are you looking at," I say. There's a glint in my eye, something wily and a bit crazed, and for half a second, I don't recognize the brazen girl staring back at me. Who knows what she might do?

On my way out, I scrunch past three girls who whisper, "That was her!"

In the dressing room, the four of us all lean down and put our heads together. I read the story of our shoes: my

Doc Marten boots, then Evan's brown bucks, followed by River's black Chuck Taylors, and Walden's gray Nikes. You could probably write an entire story about people by only describing what's on their feet. With my left arm around Evan and my right around my brother, I feel grateful for the safety of these people, this band. Nothing can touch me. Not here.

"Let's fucking destroy these people," Walden says.

And we do. Two songs in and I can feel it. Something extra. I've always been at ease on stage, more comfortable on it than off of it. But tonight, I feel bigger than myself. I feel dangerous and invincible.

The sell-out crowd is speckled with faces strange and familiar, including the Pena Twins, a couple of teachers, and a handful of kids from school. I'm surprised to see Clive Brewer, the quarterback himself, standing way in the back with his perfect ass and his even more perfect girlfriend, who is a foot shorter than him and is blowing aggressive bubbles with a huge wad of pink gum.

During "Ordinary Girl," River does that thing with his hair that gets all the girls screaming.

"He's single," I joke when the song is over, then switch to keyboard for a pair of ballads, "Everysecondeveryminute-everyday" and "A Quiet Place," both from *The Treehouse Tapes* and both about Juliet, the girl who changed my life and broke my heart, a fact that nobody, not even Mia, knows but me.

Somewhere during "A Quiet Place," I notice the photographer again. Lurking stage left, he's finding the angles, squatting down, craning up, close enough that I can read *Burlington Tribune* on his press pass.

"You guys ever feel angry?" I ask the crowd after "A Quiet Place," which roars back its approval at the now familiar segue into The Anger Suite. Two girls on River's side of the stage, both wearing Rainey Cobb T-shirts, start jumping up and down. Evan, perched right in front of me, leans forward, and for a quick second, I'm reflected in the lens of his dad's video camera. Imagining my parents' disapproving faces and remembering Cassie's warning that I shouldn't release "Jesus Wears a Blonde Wig," anger surges through me. A liquid tremor of boiling rage. Then I remember that my parents, who casually snapped my dream in half like a twig, are up at the hospital again tonight because my dad couldn't catch his breath. Something slips loose inside of me. It's all too much.

I sling both middle fingers dramatically at the camera, then raise them up to the crowd, who give theirs right back to me. A collective *fuck you* to all the forces conspiring against us. "Sometimes you need to let it out, right?" I ask. The salivating crowd shouts its agreement. If I told them to run out into the streets and lay siege to downtown Burlington they would gladly do so. "Sometimes life backs you into a corner and you feel trapped. And anger is the only way to deal with it. So, let's get fucking angry!" And with that, we tear into "Anger, Part 1," snapping into action like a motorcycle springing to life.

Our music buzzes with barely contained recklessness. I sing so hard my throat burns, smashing my mouth against the microphone's curved body, metallic and moist against my lips.

River poses on Walden's drum riser, then jumps, landing perfectly on the beat before flying into his solo in "Anger, Part II." I widen my stance and head bang while I crank away on my Telecaster, letting my hair vine over my face. Time slows and stretches, suspending us in an endless moment, as if this is all we've ever done or ever will do. Segueing into "Anger Part III," the lighting guy washes the room in tones of pale pink, casting a dreamy pall over the two hundred sweaty bodies gathered here for this strange and necessary form of worship. The ceiling fans are useless and the room has swollen to ninety degrees or more. My black tank top is a wet rag.

Toward the end of "Anger, Part III," I take off my guitar and drop it with a thud that reverberates through my boots. Normally, I walk to the front of the stage and fall backward into the crowd for surfing, but tonight, I run and hurl myself like a careless diver jumping into a pool. For a long moment, I'm floating, weightless and free, wondering if I'll ever come down, before what feels like a thousand hands catch me.

What nobody tells you about crowd surfing is all the people that touch your butt. I mean, your butt is pretty much in their face and they have no choice but to get up in there. In the heat of the moment, it's not as weird as it sounds. But tonight, someone actually squeezes my ass, gripping a meaty chunk of my right cheek. The same hand slides around my ribcage and fondles my boob, getting in a few squeezes before I swat it away.

"Hey, what the fuck!" I shout, dipping my head back to see who grabbed me. And that's when something, probably an elbow, pile drives into my right eye socket. Vision blurring with dancing white specks, I start to pass out, then snap back into awareness. Panic sets in. I kick out and flail, desperate to be on my own two feet. And then I'm falling through the pink darkness. When I land, my tail bone smacks against the unyielding floor and a tremor of pain shatters up my back. For a second, I can't move and I'm afraid I've really hurt myself. But my vodka-soaked adrenaline overrides the pain and panic. Confident hands whisk me to standing.

A voice shouts, "Fuck yeah, Rainey!"

With moshing kids in motion all around me, I bang my head and stomp my heavy boots against the floor, ricocheting off bodies, pistoning my arms up and down. The mass of us some great machine set in motion.

Eventually, I work my way back to the front where a couple of huge guys, along with Daryl, the security guard, toss me back up onto the stage. Picking up my guitar, I join in with River and Walden as we finish "Anger, Part III," the final notes raising a holy roar from the crowd.

River puts his face right next to my ear and shouts. "Holy shit, are you okay? Your eye looks really fucked up."

I nod yes and give a thumbs up to Walden, who looks completely freaked out. My feet are wobbly. For a second, I'm sure I'm going to spray vodka and pretzel mush all over my boots.

"Rainey, are you okay?" River asks again.

I nod again and furiously shake my head. "Let's do Jesus."

"Really?"

I turn to Walden and say, "Jesus."

"Are you sure?"

Cassie's face briefly flashes in my mind. If she was standing at the bar right now in She-Terminator mode, I might not have the guts to go through with it, but Cassie, and the chance of signing with Shore Records, are long gone and I don't care what happens.

I step back to the microphone. "You guys want to hear a new song?" I ask. The crowd shouts back its excitement. "Here's one hot off the presses. Help us out, okay? You'll know your part when it comes. And don't forget to smile for the camera."

At this, kids mob Evan, mugging for the awaiting lens.

I tune up my guitar, then look at Walden, who's worried but still seems willing to trust his most unlikely field general. Four times he clicks his drum sticks to set the tempo, then we erupt into "Jesus Wears a Blonde Wig."

I scream out the first verse.

Frozen in the high beam.
Stuck inside a bad dream.
This is how it ends. Hey! This is how it ends. Hey!
Hands where I can see em.
Carpe fucking diem.
This is how it ends. Hey! This is how it ends. Hey!
Piggie gets the first swing.

But Jesus wears a blonde wig.
This is not the end. Hey! Nothing ever ends. Hey!

Just as I'm hoping, by the second verse, the audience has found the pattern, raising their fists and shouting out every time we get to "Hey!"

The song is so short, but I don't want it to end, not yet, so I repeat the first verse. I want to play it faster, harder, louder. Then, riding a rogue wave of manic, angry adrenaline, I take off my guitar, holding it by the neck like an axe, then bring it above my head and swing it downward as hard as I can. When the body of my red Telecaster hammers against the stage, it fractures right at the neck joint, and when the weight frees itself from my grip, I recoil, then realize that I'm now only holding the guitar neck itself. The heavy red body is now a corpse lying dejected on the floor.

"Thanks a lot," I tell the crowd, then drop my guitar neck and walk off stage feeling like Attila the Hun.

"What the fuck, Rainey?" Walden says, storming over to me. He looks scared and furious. "What the hell happened?"

"I got elbowed in the eye. I'm okay. How do I look?"

"*Not* okay," Walden says. "Your eye is super swollen. And your guitar, Rainey. Jesus. You broke your fucking guitar!"

Then Evan is there, looking horrified, the video camera in his left hand.

"Did you get all that?" I ask.

He nods and holds up the video camera.

Poser comes over and inspects my face, gently placing his palm against my cheek and examining my eye. "That's one way to get their attention," he says and lays a baggie stuffed with ice chips over my right eye, which at this point, I can barely see out of.

"I'm fine," I say, having no idea if what I'm saying is in the least bit true, knowing I'm in a moment I'll have to make sense of later. "I'm good."

The crowd is still out there stomping, calling out for more. We almost never do encores at Club 182, but tonight, I'm struck by a whim. Hurrying to the dressing room, ignoring the mirror, I click open River's acoustic guitar case and pull out his Guild D50.

When River sees me with his acoustic, he says "No way! That was my grandfather's."

"I'm not going to break it. I'm going to play it."

"You're not going back out, Rainey," Walden says, his voice unusually authoritative. "The show is over. Do you hear me? Over."

I shake my head, then turn to River, who, looking flabbergasted, throws up his arms. "I think Walden's right. What the hell are you going to play anyway?"

"I haven't decided yet," I lie, then walk back out into the spotlight. The crowd goes absolutely wild.

"We love you!" someone shouts.

"Are you okay?" yells someone else.

"You should see the other guy," I joke, then quickly tune the Guild. "Thanks again for coming." Then I start playing G to G Major 7 over F# to E minor, the opening chords to "Say Yes," the impossibly beautiful final song on *Either/Or.*

"This is by Elliott Smith," I say.

Before I sing the opening lines, I make eye contact with Mia, out there behind the merch table, a nervous smile spreading across her beautiful face.

Track Fourteen
I've Never Worn Purple Lipstick Before

"How we doing?" Poser says, poking his head into the dressing room where I'm kicked back in the purple La-Z-Boy icing my right eye. Evan is sitting next to me, propped on the edge of the couch. Looking like the aftermath of a horrible accident, the body of my broken Telecaster sits in two pieces next to him.

"We're...decompressing," Evan says.

"I'm okay," I say, not mentioning that I've spent much of the twenty minutes since the show ended puking my guts out in the bathroom, then furiously brushing my teeth with an extra toothbrush and toothpaste I keep in my gig bag. Surprisingly, puking made me feel a little better.

"Let me know if you need anything," Poser says.

When I finally wander out into the empty club, Poser is spritzing the counter and wiping it down with a white rag. Miles Davis purrs softly from the house speakers. Walden and Bethany are packing up Walden's drum kit for the journey home.

Over in the corner alcove by the front door—two couches in an L shape and a big round table in the middle—

someone is picking up trash and straightening throw pillows, and that someone turns out to be Mia.

"Oh my God, your eye!" she says, bringing her hands to her mouth.

"I'm okay. What are you doing?"

"Just helping out." She gestures over at Poser. "In high school, Poser let me in for free if I helped clean up after. I didn't have a lot of friends."

"I figured you left with River."

"He drove himself. Hanging with his drop-out sister is not good for his image."

"Why didn't you come back to the dressing room?"

"I wasn't sure if it was okay," she says. "I figured you guys were processing the show, or whatever. Is that what bands do, process? Thanks for the encore, by the way. Not that you played it for me or anything. That's not what I mean. I just love that song."

"I did play it for you."

"Oh," she says with a girlish grin. "Well, it was amazing." Her eyes continue inspecting my face.

"Is it that bad?"

"How bad do you think it is?"

"*Night of the Living Dead*?"

She smiles. "It's not quite that bad. I got hit in the eye by a baseball once. It kind of looks like that. Although, that bruise is going to get worse. It's always darker the second day."

"Awesome. Because people at school definitely don't stare at me enough."

Mia chuckles. "I'm leaving soon. Do you need a ride home?"

"Um, let me check."

I walk over to Walden and tell him I'm going to catch a ride home with Mia.

"Really?"

"Aren't you staying at Bethany's anyway?"

"Well, yeah," he says. "But we can drive you home first."

"It's cool. She said it's no problem."

He looks over at Mia, and I think about his joke that Mia *plays for the other team*. For the millionth time, I wonder what he'll think when he finds out that I play for them too.

"That was crazy tonight," he says.

"Yeah."

Walden and I have been around shows our entire life. Most of the time, you forget them and move on to the next one. But once in a while, you have this feeling after a gig. The whole world seems different somehow. Tonight feels like that.

"The song still isn't officially out, just because we played it once," he says. "We don't have to...I don't want you to feel pressured."

Walden's never been great at apologizing, but I know it takes a lot for him to say this. To see how much I need some understanding. Some patience. I wrap my arms around him.

"You're nuts," he says, gripping me tighter, his voice betraying how scared he was during the show when he saw me get hurt. I grip him back. Neither of us seems to want to let go.

Mia drives us through the dark silent streets of Fairview and winds up my long gravel driveway. It's one in the morning, but feels far later.

"Everybody is asleep," she says, gesturing at the dark house.

"No, my parents aren't here," I say, images of my dad in a hospital bed, my mom dozing in a chair by his side. I'm so mad at them, but I also feel so guilty at how caught up I've been in my own stupid life, which feels insignificant in the face of everything else.

"My parents used to go out all the time. Or they'd have their friends over and they'd all get wasted and go in the hot tub. Now my mom never goes anywhere."

"It's not that," I say. "They're not *out* out. They're at the hospital."

"Oh no. Again? I'm sorry. They've been there so much."

I don't want to say anything else because I know I'll start crying. I turn to Mia, and then, before I can stop myself or out-think my instincts, I lean forward and kiss her. She kisses me back, at first, before stopping.

"Rainey, I don't know if we should do this."

"But..."

"I know."

"I thought that—"

"I know. And I do. A lot."

"So do I," I say.

"But."

"What?"

"I'm just, there's a lot you don't know about me."

"I don't care."

And then we're kissing again. Harder, more passionately. Her tongue slides into my mouth and mine into hers, slippery, tender, and strong. I have so little experience, and yet, my body knows exactly what to do. Mia smells sweet, a mix of root beer and summer sweat, and her cheeks are perfect little pillows. Her breath is warm as she kisses my ear, making me shudder, and I run my fingers through her hair, soft and pale blonde as corn silk, gripping the back of her head while she nibbles my ear lobe. My heart is pounding, and though we don't go very far, my body sparkles and soars under Mia's touch, like I'm levitating two inches off my seat.

I don't know how long we kiss, but it's long enough that I disappear all the way down into the deepest part of myself, down into us, wishing I could stay there forever and never come up. That I could sail away from everything but this feeling.

"I've never worn purple lipstick before," she jokes when we finally stop. The clock reads 2:15. Mia yawns, and so do I. "I should get going," she says. "I have to work in a few hours."

"Okay," I say, then reach for the door handle.

"Wait, Rainey?"

"Yeah?"

"Am I your first? Girl, I mean."

"No," I say, suddenly amazed we've never talked about it. "Second."

She cocks her head coyly. I can tell she's surprised.

"You'll have to tell me about her sometime."

"I'll tell if you will."

"Fair enough," she says, laughing in a knowing way. "Hey, pick a color."

"Ooh," I say, colors firing in my mind. "How about watermelon?"

"Have you ever noticed that we always choose objects that suggest a color, instead of the colors themselves. Marigold. Cinnamon. Watermelon. Isn't that weird?"

"That's what makes it ours," I say, then kiss her one more time.

When I get inside, the full weight of my day finally smashes into me like a wrecking ball. I heat up some water and drop in a chamomile tea bag, but standing there in the kitchen I'm so dead on my feet I can barely move. For entire lifetimes, I stare at the kitchen cabinets, drifting to the clock's metronomic click-click-click. But I can also still taste Mia on my lips, and the memory of kissing her finally knocks me out of my reverie.

I drink my lukewarm tea and gobble some cold cheese pizza, then bring my gig bag into my bedroom so I can take a closer look at my broken guitar. But first, I pee and wash my bruised face with warm water. The swelling has gone down, but my right eye is ringed in vibrant colors from dessert beige to plum purple.

Mia's description was right. It looks like I got hit in the eye with a baseball. Or maybe a softball. Maybe twice. In the bedroom, my guitar bag is still waiting for me, but I feel too tired to open it up, so instead I lay down and cradle its broad, cushioned body. When my dad gave it to me two summers ago, he told me that nobody trusts a guitar player with a brand-new guitar. I knew exactly what he meant. I also knew he was giving me a small part of the part of himself that means the most to him. And now I've broken it like a careless child.

What's wrong with me?

On the nightstand, the monster on the cover of *Frankenstein* is still pondering himself in the water's reflection, my bookmark still several chapters behind. Beside the book is perched a hummingbird in flight that my dad carved from a hunk of butternut and gave to me when I was little. I lay back on the bed, wrap my body around my broken guitar, and close my eyes.

I have some regrets, Rain Man.

I wonder. Can you avoid regrets? Or are we all destined to do things wrong so we can learn to do things right? And what if we never learn at all? What if we never figure it out?

Asking for a friend.

Track Fifteen
Major Loco

"You're a freaking crazy woman!" says Rachel Pena, setting down her pink plastic lunch tray with a clack.

"Caa-raaa-yyy-zeee," says Clara, swiping a fry through a dark river of salty ketchup.

Eyes big and hands in motion, the twins are even more fired up than usual.

"But, sorry to say, you may have blown it with Clive Brewer," Rachel says.

"Ka-blam-o," Clara adds.

"Last time I checked," Evan says, not looking up from his mayonnaise-smothered chicken patty and his copy of *Dune Messiah*, "Clive Brewer has been dating Mandy Thompkins since fifth grade." Though he's sitting right beside me, Evan and I haven't really spoken since the show two nights ago. I haven't even asked if he's watched the footage because I'm terrified to see it. Since we don't have band practice on Sundays, Evan and I usually get together to play video games or listen to music in his bedroom, but his call never came yesterday, and I felt too shy to pick up the phone. I slept most of the day anyway, finally waking up around three in the afternoon when my parents got home from the hospital.

"That's technically true," Clara says, "but last time I checked, Mandy Thompkins is a dumb ass cheerleader with an IQ of eighty-two, and we were hoping Rainey here could break them up and show him how much better he can do."

"You really think his IQ is much higher than that?" I ask.

"Girl, when you look like that, you get a free pass in the IQ department," Clara says. "And Clive is actually really smart. He just seems dumb because he's so hot."

"I doubt that very much," Evan says.

"Whatever man," Rachel says.

"Yeah, whatever," Clara says.

"The point," Rachel continues, "is that rumor has it he was a little freaked out and thinks you might be a devil worshiper, which probably means no go in the dating department."

I roll my eyes, then steal a look over at Clive and Mandy's table. Clive is laughing at something the boy next to him said. Mandy is moving the lettuce around in her salad with a plastic fork. She looks bored. She catches me staring and I lower my eyes.

"What happened, Rainey?" Clara asks. "Getting hurt? Smashing your guitar and everything else." She makes a swirly motion around her own eye to indicate mine. "You kind of went loco up there, girl."

"Major loco," Rachel says. "Everyone's talking about it."

I have a bite of my cheeseburger, wishing I had been

able to convince my mom to let me stay home from school today. I rarely beg, but I laid it on pretty thick, faking a sore throat and a fever before finally breaking down into anxious tears over the stares my bruised face was going to inspire. "Actions have consequences," she said. And that had been that.

What happened up there? I think about how to answer this question. But the list is too long, the reasons too complicated. There's something else, too. And that's that I'm not totally sure what happened up there. I keep thinking about that moment when I smashed my guitar, and the more time that passes, the more it feels like someone else did it. I almost can't even remember doing it.

"Not to mention you look like you got beat up by Mike Tyson," Clara says.

"Okay, the black eye was not my fault," I say. "Somebody grabbed my butt *and* my boob while I was crowd surfing and when I leaned back to see who did it, I got elbowed. And the other thing, I don't know. I'm not the first person to do it. Pete Townsend from the Who used to do it all the time. And Jimi Hendrix. And Kurt Cobain. And it wasn't even that nice a guitar." Evan looks over at me. He knows how special my Telecaster is, but for once, he picks up the cues and goes back to his book.

"There's some crazy rumors going around," Rachel says.

"What, that I worship the devil? Give me a break."

Rachel shrugs, seeming hesitant, but then adds, "One says that you got in a fight with some biker chick and she cold cocked you with a chain or something. Another one that you lit your guitar on fire. But the craziest one is that you wrote your name in blood on the stage."

"That's insane," I say, feeling a little angry. "There wasn't even any blood."

"Hey, don't shoot me, I'm only the messenger," Rachel says. "I know you're just a fierce as hell, badass mamma-jamma. But people like to talk some bullshit, that's all I'm saying."

Clara makes a talk-talk gesture with her hand.

The next morning, I'm halfway through my bowl of Honey Nut Cheerios with frozen blueberries when my mom drops the *Burlington Tribune* in front of me with a thud.

"Your paper, Mr. Townsend," she says, slipping in an earring and buttoning up the top button of her white blouse, which she's wearing with a burgundy skirt and black heels.

I can barely believe my eyes. It's me. On the front page. A blurry version of me, shot from the side and at an upward angle. The picture has me in rapid motion, caught the second before my guitar collides with the stage of Club 182, my hair flying out like a rainbow and a crazed look on my face.

The caption reads: *Local teen rocker Rainey Cobb performing at Club 182.*

The picture is a teaser to a story in the culture section, which I rapidly flip to.

The writer details the packed crowd, the sweltering atmosphere, the "infectious" energy.

Picking up where her legendary parents left off, Cobb is an electrifying performer, a combination of raw musical talent and natural stage presence. Continuing to play, and in fact debuting a new song, all with a fresh black eye she picked up while crowd surfing, was one of the most brazen acts of showmanship I've seen in over fifteen years covering the local music scene.

And that was before she went full Pete Townsend on her guitar.

Watch the music calendar, folks. Because when Rainey Cobb takes the stage again, who knows what will happen.

"Well?" my mom asks when I'm done reading.

"They liked the show," I mumble, but she only shakes her head.

"That's all you have to say? They *liked* the show? Is this really how you want to be known? A crazy girl who gets black eyes and breaks her guitar like a lunatic?"

"I don't know."

"You don't know?"

"I talked to Dad about the guitar," I say. "He said he didn't care."

"That's not what I'm talking about. And you know better than to believe that."

She sits down across from me and clinks her wedding ring against her coffee mug. I notice she's wearing blush and eyeliner. Her nails are freshly painted. She smells like soap.

"Rainey, you have to use your head," she says. "Once people see you in a certain way, it's hard to change their minds." Her voice is wistful and memory-tinged. "I don't want you to get hurt. Or do anything you'll really regret."

"As if it even matters."

"What does that mean?"

"It means who gives a crap what I do on stage? In a few months I'll be in some classroom and nobody will even care."

"Rainey, we've been over and over and over this. College is—"

"A safety net so I don't ruin my life," I say mockingly. "I know."

"It's so much more than that. I just wish you could see it. You will. I know it's hard to believe, but you really will. The music industry will promise you the world, and it will make you feel like everything is going to be easy and perfect, but it won't be there for you when things don't work out. It chewed us up and spit us out and I won't let that happen to you. When college is over, you can—"

"You're just jealous," I mumble.

"Excuse me?"

"That's why you want me to stop playing. You don't want me to be bigger than you guys were." It's the meanest thing I could possibly say to her, cruel and cutting and deeply unfair. My mother's face pinches with sadness.

"Do you really think that?"

"No," I say, but it's too late. I already said it. And I already hate myself for saying it.

For a long time, we're both silent. Mom clinks her mug some more. Django wanders in and nudges me for a scratch, then wanders away. I wait for the tsunami, wait to hear how ungrateful and selfish I am, but instead, Mom turns the paper around and scans the article.

"You're writing new songs?"

I nod. "A few."

"Must be nice," she says, standing up and smoothing her skirt. "I can't even remember the last time I wrote a new song."

"You look really nice," I say, meaning it.

"Thank you. It's my first day. I'm hoping that looking the part will distract them from how much I don't know what the hell I'm doing."

She pauses on her way out of the kitchen. Without turning, says "It means so much to him, Rainey."

"I know."

Track Sixteen
I Can't Believe I'm
Actually Asking You This

Since my mom has to take the Subaru to South Burlington for work, Walden drives me to school in Howard the Duck. I make him park down the street so no one gets a good look at the aging, rusty touring vehicle that we basically grew up in. At this point, poor Howard looks like something that needs to be donated to a demolition derby.

I draw a figure eight on the thigh of my black jeans.

"Want me to talk to them again?" he asks.

I shrug. "It won't matter."

"You don't actually have to go. You know that, right?"

"Yes, I do. It will kill Dad if I don't. Sorry. I don't know why I said it like that."

"I know what you mean," Walden says. "But Dad's not going to hogtie you and drag you to Boston. The world will keep on spinning if you don't go to college. It's your life."

"What am I going to do instead, work at the coffee shop? Cassie probably never wants to see me again after talking to Mom."

"I'm sure Debbie Gibson's parents were no picnic," he says.

"Shut up."

Walden grabs his backpack from behind the front seat and starts ruffling through it.

"What are you doing?"

"Hold on," he says, flipping pages in his sketchbook, which he then hands to me, revealing a pen and ink drawing of a fat tree with a treehouse nestled among its branches. I recognize Walden's crosshatch style, the slightly wobbly curve of his line. Beneath the drawing it reads: Treehouse Records.

"What's this?"

"Our record label," he says. "Forget college. Forget Cassie. Forget all that shit. We can do everything together, exactly the way we want to. We have the studio. You have the songs. Rainey, we can do it ourselves."

When Walden gets excited about something, he talks with his whole body. His eyes go wide and he gestures grandly with his hands.

"You make it sound so simple," I say, handing him back the sketch book.

"It is that simple. I even know what our first release is going to be."

"This isn't a game, Walden! It's my life."

"It's my life too."

"I know, I'm sorry," I say, knowing that I sometimes forget how much energy and time my brother has put into my music. How he never stopped pursuing any of this. I did.

I grab the door handle, then let go.

"I wanted to help," I say.

"What do you mean? Help with what?"

"Cassie said they would give me an advance. When I sign."

"She did? When? You never told me that."

"I called her after I talked to Mom and Dad about the hospital bills. I was going to give them the money."

"How much?"

"Cassie said twenty-five or thirty thousand."

Walden shakes his head.

"Rainey, you shouldn't—"

"It's most of what they owe the hospital."

Walden smiles and touches my shoulder.

"They would never take your money, you know that, right?"

I nod, feeling myself about to cry.

Walden points at the clock.

"You're late," he says.

After third block, River and I skip homeroom and duck into the woods to rip a quick joint, then hustle back inside so we're not late for fourth block. I only took two puffs to make sure I don't feel too stoned, but just as we're about to walk into AP English, I realize I forgot to borrow River's Visine to make sure my eyes aren't bloodshot. I'm literally halfway through the door when panic seizes me. I hiss out River's name, but he's too far away. The bell rings, leaving me standing half in, half out of the room with Ms. Ofalko looking over at me.

"To enter or not to enter," she says, "that is the question."

For a second, I almost turn and walk right down the hallway, but of course, I can't do that, so I walk to my seat with my head down.

"I forgot Visine," I whisper to River, who sneaks the Visine out of his backpack and passes it to me while Ms. Ofalko's back is turned. I jam the tiny plastic tube down into my pocket and ask if I can go to the bathroom.

"Class literally just started, Rainey, so no." Ms. Ofalko sounds agitated.

I keep my head down during the free write, and I'm grateful to River when he volunteers to share his writing, which should help draw attention away from our left-central quadrant of the classroom. But when Ms. Ofalko tells us to circle up for discussion, I get nervous. We were supposed to finish *Frankenstein* for today and I'm barely halfway through.

Ms. Ofalko is always introducing topics from the real world to help us make connections to the books we're reading, and today we're talking about Dolly the Sheep and the ethics of medical cloning. When I'm called on the first time, I'm able to fudge a vague but semi-smart sounding response about the problematic nature and potential snowball effects of scientists playing God, but a few minutes later, when Ms. Ofalko asks how this topic relates back to the themes in *Frankenstein*, then circles back to me for a response, I know I'm cooked.

"Because that's what Frankenstein was sort of doing," I say, my voice soft.

"Yes, but be more specific, please. Make a connection to the book."

My heart is a drum. My mouth a desert. I tap my pencil eraser on the top of my desk. "Frankenstein was so caught up in whether or not he could create the monster—"

"That he didn't think about whether or not he should," Ms. Ofalko finishes. "I've seen *Jurassic Park* too. But that's still not very specific, is it? Any of us could invent a general response, but only someone who has actually read and sufficiently considered the text can make a meaningful connection. So, please be more specific."

"I can't. I haven't finished."

"I see," she says, then looks around the room. "Someone, please jump in and rescue this dying conversation."

After the bells rings, Ms. Ofalko asks me to stay after. The unused tube of Visine presses against my leg. She shuts the classroom door, then gestures for me to sit down.

"I saw the article in the paper," she says, pointing at my eye. "Does it hurt much?"

"Not really. It just looks bad."

"It must feel incredibly strange to look down at the paper and see yourself looking back," she says. "I don't think I'll ever know what that feels like."

I shrug.

"Rainey, I don't really know what to say to you. In two years of having you in class, I've never once seen you unprepared, and now here we are, several classes in a row where you walk into my room without your work done. Not only that, you seem disinterested and distracted. Doesn't what we're doing in here matter to you?"

"Yes."

"Would you please look at me when I'm speaking to you?"

I look up at her and she calmly studies my face. My eyes. I can see her brain working, calculating.

"Rainey," she says, rotating her coffee cup in a counter clockwise circle. "I can't believe I'm asking you this, and I wouldn't ask unless I felt sure, but are you sober right now?"

"What?"

"Let me be more direct." She leans forward. "Are you high right now?"

"No," I say, my voice flat and unconvincing.

"Are you sure about that? Please think carefully before answering. I care about you a great deal, Rainey, but there are also protocols in place that put certain responsibilities on my shoulders in spite of that."

An elaborate silence hovers between us. Five, ten, twenty seconds. I've already looked away, but I can still feel Ms. Ofalko's eyes boring a hole through the side of my head. My heart beats in my ears, the hot, heavy slap of my pulse against my brain. I know my silence is closer to an admission of guilt than a denial, but I feel mute, paralyzed. There's something else too. In the strangest way, I want her to know. I want to be caught.

Eventually, she goes over to a phone attached to the wall and dials a number.

"Hi, Mr. Larson, it's Ms. Ofalko. Yes. Hey, I've got

Rainey here, and we're wondering if you're free to come up and chat with us for a minute."

An hour later, after the principal has called my mom at work to tell her what happened, after I've been forced to get on the phone with her and she's told me how angry and disappointed she is but also that it's her first day at her new job and she can't just get up and leave, so I need to see if my brother can pick me up, I dial my home number, praying Walden answers instead of my dad. Mercifully, he does.

"I need you to come and get me," I say.

"What? Why? I have to go to work."

"Just. I have to leave now, okay. Can you come? Please?"

He must be able to hear in my voice that something isn't right because he doesn't probe further or complain, only says, "I'll be right there."

I wait outside alone for Walden, who pulls up in Howard the Duck. We drive in silence for a while before he finally asks what happened. Feeling too embarrassed to speak, I almost make up some stupid elaborate story. But he's going to find out anyway, so I tell him the truth. That I got busted being stoned on school grounds. That I'm suspended from school for three days. That it was my favorite teachers who collectively lowered the axe, telling me they had no choice, and that it was for my own good. That they've both been worried about me since the start of school and are hoping I can use the next three days to reflect and reset.

What I don't tell Walden is that Mr. Larson was fighting back tears as he walked me down to the principal's office. That he hugged me before he left.

"Do you want to talk about it?" he asks.

I know this is it. The part when I should start crying. That this is the pivot into catharsis, where I can finally let it all go. But I can't.

Because I can't really feel anything.

Side Two
Puddle Jumping
October, 1997–September, 1998

Track One
Who Are You?

"This one is my favorite," Mia says, handing her grandma a massive oak leaf, it's body candy apple red and freckled with black dots.

"Oh, that's a good one," says Grandma Rose, her liver spotted hand lightly trembling as she studies the red leaf, rotating it by the stem so that its color goes blurry like a bird flapping its wings. "Can you believe it? It looks like a huge piece of candy. We used to jump in big piles of leaves when I was younger. My father would get so mad."

All the leaves we collected are arranged on a tray on wheels so that Mia's grandma can examine them without having to get out of bed.

"I think these are even prettier than the ones we brought last week," Mia says. "They're changing colors so fast. I can't believe it's already October."

"When did you come?" Grandma Rose asks. Her blue eyes are the color of faded jeans, surrounded by a web work of deep wrinkles. "You were here?"

"Last week," Mia says. "We played checkers."

"Oh, I think I would remember that," Grandma Rose

tells Mia. "Who are you? You look like a girl but you dress like a boy."

Mia, who's wearing a rugby shirt and a logo-less ball cap, fights not to laugh at this, and so do I. "Mia, Grandma. I'm Mia, your granddaughter."

"Huh?" Grandma Rose says.

Mia repeats herself, speaking loudly and over enunciating.

"Oh, that's right," Grandma Rose says, shaking her head softly from side to side. "Mia. You're the one who broke your mother's heart."

The blood practically drains from Mia's face. "What?"

"When you dropped out of college," Grandma Rose says, her face growing somber.

"She said that? My mom said that?"

"Oh yeah," Grandma Rose says, "all the time she says it. You really hurt her feelings. You should go back. And try harder next time."

"What can I say, I'm doing my best," Mia says, her voice quavering. She looks at me and rolls her eyes.

Grandma Rose's face softens back into its drifting gaze. "I wonder when they're going to bring my lunch," she says, examining the door.

"You ate lunch earlier," Mia says, "remember? You had a tuna sandwich."

"I did?"

Mia nods.

"Tuna's good."

"Yeah," Mia says.

"Don't ever get old, I tell ya," Grandma Rose says. "It's

no fun. I can't seem to remember anything. These golden years aren't all they're cracked up to be." I think about what Mia told me the first time I came with her to visit her eighty-three-year-old grandmother, who has dementia and lives in a nursing home in South Burlington. How Grandma Rose could be casually cruel, but that you couldn't take it personally. How she could be completely confused one moment, not knowing what day it was, but then remember other details with striking clarity. Surprisingly, the further back in time she reaches, the sharper her memories become. Last time we were here, she told us about meeting her first husband at a silk mill in Derry, Pennsylvania in 1931. Moments later, she forgot her granddaughter's name.

Even though it scared me at first, I like being around Grandma Rose. All my own grandparents are dead. And in spite of the sudden twists in conversation, talking to a woman who has over eight decades of life inside of her yanks time into perspective. I look at her and I think: *this person was born the same year World War I started. Before the Great Depression. Before Hitler and Hiroshima. Before television and The Beatles. She's raised three children, buried two husbands, beaten breast cancer, and lived all the way from there to now.*

In the face of all that, maybe my own problems aren't actually the end of the world.

Mia tacks a few leaves to a corkboard, which features a patchwork of family photos and art by Mia's sister, including a vibrant watercolor of two figures, one big and one small, holding hands beneath a golden sun. Across the top it reads *Sunrise with Grandma Rose.*

"Grandma, Rainey brought her guitar," Mia says, nodding to me.

"Who?"

"My friend," Mia practically shouts, pointing at me. "Rainey. She's a musician. She brought her guitar. Maybe you might like to hear some songs." We're sitting on opposite sides of Grandma Rose's bed. On the far side of the room, her roommate, who has hair as white as Mrs. Claus and is cradling a Cabbage Patch Doll, stares straight ahead, her face a soft and placid mask, as if she's sleeping with her eyes open.

Grandma Rose turns to me.

"Who are you?"

"I'm Rainey," I say. "Mia's friend."

"Hi honey," she says, smiling as if she's never met me before.

"Hi."

"You're really pretty. But you shouldn't wear so much makeup."

I chuckle and look over at Mia, who simply shrugs. I'm glad I'm not wearing a skirt and fishnets or she'd probably tell me I look like a prostitute. Instead, I'm wearing what I've been pretty much living in lately: old jeans, white T-shirt, and the light blue cardigan Mia gave me from Sullivan Street Jeans. It's loose and cozy with oversize buttons, somewhere between Mr. Rogers and Kurt Cobain. River has started calling me and Mia the Slacker Twins. But every time I wear it, I can feel my sense of style evolving in a way I like.

"What should I play?" I ask, taking out the acoustic guitar, a Gibson J-160, which my dad told me I could borrow as long as I promised not to break it over anybody's head.

"It doesn't matter," Mia whispers. I can tell she's fighting not to let the hurt show.

I play "Fly Me to the Moon," the first thing that comes to mind, and then "Two of Us" by the Beatles and "Angeles" from Elliott Smith's *Either/Or*, which I have listened to approximately a million times, every nook and cranny of it now seared into my brain.

As I play, Grandma Rose's face fills with absolute wonder. Not because I'm so good or anything. I think it's that music is magic. It seems to temporarily free Grandma Rose from the burden of constant forgetting and frustration, cutting all the way through the fog of her dementia to something childlike that lives inside of her. Inside all of us, maybe.

"What about 'You Are My Sunshine?'" Grandma Rose asks. "Do you know that one? It's my favorite song."

"Um, I think so," I say, humming the tune in my head and working out the chords.

As I sing, Grandma Rose whispers along, at first just mouthing the words, and then when it gets to the chorus, actually singing, remembering every line. Soon, all three of us are singing together. It sounds so beautiful.

Mia merges onto I-89 South and sets her cruise control for

58 MPH, hands perched at ten and two. I can tell she's up there in her head somewhere.

"Are you okay?" I ask.

"Yeah," she says. "I know she wasn't trying to be mean. Sometimes she's just a parrot, repeating things without thinking about what they mean. It's not her fault."

"But your mom? She's never said that to you?"

"Not those exact words. I've gotten *I'm disappointed in you*, but not *you broke my heart*. Maybe it's the same thing."

While Operation Cheer Up was a smash success, Operation Convince Mia's Mom to Co-Sign on a Small Business Loan has been an utter failure. Pam McRae is just as convinced that her daughter should go to college as Luce Cobb. And she's holding her ground.

"I probably already told you this, but my mom never finished college," Mia says, fiddling with the radio before turning it off. "She got pregnant with me halfway through. I know she meant to go back, but then she and my dad got married and then they had River." I've never heard this part of the story before. "My dad became a lawyer and my mom became a housewife. She says her only regret in life is not finishing college, so it's always been really important to her that I get my degree. I was going to. Maybe I still will someday." Mia grips the wheel hard. "It's fucked up how parents put their own stuff on you, as if you're some kind of project they're working on and not an actual person." She could be talking about me. Mia shakes her head. "What's so wrong with being a person who owns a clothing store instead of someone who works in some stupid office doing some stupid job they don't even like?"

"Nothing," I say.

"Most people go to college and get some random degree, and then get funneled into a middle-class life that's totally underwhelming, just so they can have a midlife crisis and wish they'd pursued something they actually cared about. Adolescence is this big lie that pretends to get you ready for being an adult but doesn't actually do anything to prepare you for the real world. But if you don't follow the pack, you're some kind of cautionary tale."

"Yep." Her words feel true enough to be carved into stone and it's such a relief to hear a perspective that justifies my skepticism about college and the so called real world.

"See, you're the only one who gets it," she says. "This is why I need to spend all my time with you." She looks over at me and grins. "That, and you're cute as hell."

My mouth spreads into a grin that doesn't do much to hide how vulnerable I feel when she looks at me with those green eyes. Why does Mia make me feel so powerless? So exposed? Like I've left a window open inside myself and the whole world can see how I feel about her.

I feel other things too, though. I feel guilt and unexpected shame about my secret relationship. About the way Mia and I hide what we are. One day I called us liars because nobody knows we're a couple, and we pretend we're just friends.

"We're not liars," Mia said. "We're magicians. It's a magic trick. People only see what they want to see. And anyway, it's not our fault. Blame a culture that's stuck in the stone age."

River and Evan both suspect something. Duh. But Mia

and I have agreed to say we're just good friends. At least for now. I think Walden wonders about it too, but he doesn't ask, so I don't tell.

Behind closed doors, I feel completely at ease, but when Mia and I are in public, I get nervous. That stupid cop ends up back in my brain, shining his flashlight in our faces. I make sure not to laugh too loud at Mia's jokes or stand too close to her. I worry that people can see something in the way we are together. An electricity between us that can't be denied. Whatever it is, it's something I'm not ready to have seen. Something I'm not ready to share.

It doesn't help that I hear the word "gay" used as an insult on a daily basis.

It's an amazing word, actually. The Swiss Army Knife of slurs that seems to be a synonym for just about anything bad. Stupid. Embarrassing. Ugly. Unfashionable. Immature. Gay can happily stand in for all of them at a moment's notice. Never mind that you're insulting thousands, and probably millions, of people. I'm sure we'll be fine.

I hate that I'm so scared of people finding out, but I can't help it. How do you find the courage to show who you really are when the whole world is a billboard screaming that who you really are is wrong? And stupid? And ugly? And embarrassing?

Mia says I need to listen to more Ani DiFranco. That I need to scream "Fuck you!" a little louder and keep being exactly who I am. She also says that coming out to her family was terrifying, but that it was the most liberating thing she's ever done.

"How did you know it was the right time to tell them?" I asked her.

"I didn't. I just couldn't take it anymore. And I realized that I couldn't control how they were going to react. I could only control me. Letting go of that fear changed my life."

Mr. Larson and Matthew live in a big yellow farmhouse with a wrap-around front porch and a small creek running through the backyard. Using the key Mr. Larson gave me, I unlock the front door and Roxy the pug runs over and yips happily as we pet her and tell her what a good girl she is. I fill Roxy's bowl with fresh water and give her a treat.

"Pugs are ugly and adorable at the same time," Mia says.

"Don't listen to her, Roxy," I say, scratching behind her ear. "I don't think you're ugly."

"*And* adorable. But c'mon, they're so wrinkly and sneezy."

On cue, Roxy lets out a wet, nasally sneeze that sends her scampering backward.

With Roxy at our heels, Mia and I walk around the house, scanning Matthew's huge movie collection and admiring Mr. Larson's model ships, a small fleet arranged on shelves and mantles. There's sailboats and schooners and a massive gray replica of the Bismarck.

The house has modern furnishings and everything is tucked into its right place. Mia slides her finger across the coffee table, then holds it up, completely dust-free.

"Now this is a level of cleanliness I could get used to."

"They have a cleaning lady," I say.

"Where are they again?"

"At a wedding in Florida."

"You guys must be really close if he's asking you to come into his house."

"Yeah," I say. "We are."

For the record, I never blamed Mr. Larson for my three-day suspension six weeks ago. Even still, things have been a little weird between us. I know he had no choice but to bust me, and it was my fault, but I can tell he feels like he let me down somehow. I think asking me to let Roxy out this weekend was another in a series of olive branches he's been extending in my direction, along with stocking up on Werther's candy and my favorite chamomile tea for our check-ins.

Mr. Larson also made me promise to stop smoking pot. He said that it wasn't actually making my problems go away, only hiding them. River still smokes, and it's hard to resist, but I've managed to keep my promise. So far.

In the basement, we find a treadmill and colorful dumbbells on a metal stand. Old movie posters line the walls: *Vertigo. Casablanca. 8 ½. Citizen Kane.*

Back upstairs, we peek in the bathroom, guest room, then the master bedroom.

"That's where the magic happens," Mia says, jerking her thumb at the massive four-poster bed, neatly made with a striped duvet and heaps of throw pillows.

"Oh my God, stop right there."

"Boys are so sex crazed that I'll bet gay men have sex every twelve minutes."

"Leaving now," I say, plugging my ears and saying la-la-la-la over and over again. Mia may come across as painfully shy, but she's a total horn ball. I have trouble even dealing with the word sex. It's not that I never think about it. Just that I don't know what I think about it.

While I play fetch with Roxy, Mia tuns on the television and casually flips channels.

"Hey, I know that girl," she says.

The video for "Jesus Wears a Blonde Wig" is mid-way through on KEXB, the local cable access channel. I'm standing at the microphone, screaming away. Evan's camera work is wobbly, but there's something undeniably raw about the footage, which was cut together by Walden's friend Steve. Video me drops her guitar and hurls herself into the crowd like an insane person, then, thanks to the magic of editing, body slams her Telecaster against the stage.

"My friend Lucy who works for KEXB says it's been the most requested video for four weeks in a row," Mia says.

"Really?"

"She also said they got another angry phone call saying it should be banned. Some lady said they should be ashamed to be playing God-bashing music."

"I'll add that to my BU application," I say.

Mia crawls across the carpet and climbs on top of me. I smell the rose water she spritzes on her cheeks every morning. She kisses me.

"I never thought I'd get to kiss a real live rock star," she says.

I roll my eyes. "Rock stars don't go to college. Or get grounded."

Mia chuckles. "If you were my daughter, I'd probably insist on a little break in the routine too."

She's referring to the fact that my mom has forced me to take a break from playing live, so I can prove to her that my incessant lying and school suspension were one-hit wonders.

Mia kisses my neck. She knows it's my favorite spot. A moan slips out of me.

"We're in my teacher's house," I say.

"So."

"So, it's weird."

"I think it's kind of sexy," she says and begins sliding up the hem of my shirt.

"Mia."

"Mia's not here right now," she says, her hand now on my bare belly, gradually trailing up my midsection. "Please leave a message after the beep. Beep."

When she gets to the bottom edge of my bra, I say, "Okay, Cassanova. I gotta get to the hospital pretty soon."

She wrinkles her nose, visibly disappointed. Mia never pushes me, but even still, I'm always the one who hits the brakes in these situations.

"What's the girl version of Cassanova?" Mia asks.

"Cassaneva?"

"Cassawanda?"

"Cassamandy?"

"Gross," she says. "I hate that name."

"I got it," I say. "Cassa*mia*."

"Oh my God, that's perfect. You're perfect."

"Hardly."

"Definitely," she says.

Track Two
50-50

Dad is tipped back in a wide-armed cozy chair with his feet up and a striped blanket over his lap. If not for the IV sticking out of his arm and the chemo drugs slowly drip-drip-dripping into his body, he might be enjoying a lazy Sunday at home.

He smiles when he sees me, and when he pulls his headphones down, I catch a few bars of Louis Armstrong's "Potato Head Blues" before he clicks the music off.

Mia and I stopped at Dunkin Donuts on the way to the hospital (maple frosted for me; chocolate frosted with sprinkles for her) and I put the paper bag on the table next to him. When he sees the apple fritter inside, he smiles like a little kid.

"You know me too well, Rain Man," he says. His voice is soft. He breaks off a tiny nibble of sugary donut and slides it past his dry lips. He's thin and pale and his skin has a slightly bluish tint, as if someone injected a minute amount of dye inside of him.

But he's here. That's what Dad keeps saying. *I'm still here, Rain Man. I'm still here.*

And it's what I've learned to try and focus on.

I hold his hand. "How are you feeling?" I ask.

"Like I'm losing the fight but winning the war."

I break off another small piece of apple fritter and hold it up to him, but he shakes his head, so I pop it into my mouth.

"Hey, Rainey," says Claire, walking into the room with two paper cups. Similar to all the cancer nurses I've met, she looks like a normal person, but is actually a saint in disguise. Giving. Selfless. And eternally calm. I can't even imagine what it must do to your humanity to watch people suffer day after day, but Claire walks around like she has the best job in the whole world. Maybe she does and I don't know how to see what she sees.

"Hey Claire."

"You're almost done, Luce," she says, lightly flicking his IV bag. "Fifteen more minutes and you're a free man. You want some more ginger ale?"

"No, I'm good."

"You warm enough?"

"Yeah, thanks Claire," he says, adjusting his beanie.

"Is your chauffer here able to drive you home?" Claire asks.

"Yeah."

"No hot rod stuff."

"Please," my dad says. "She drives even slower than I do. She even wears a seatbelt."

Claire smiles at me, and looking at her gentle, hopeful eyes, it's easy to forget that these treatments have put my parents so far into debt, they probably won't ever claw their way back out, or get my mom's solo career off life support. It's easy to forget that they've been unable to kill his tumors, which still inhabit his lungs like a conquering army enjoying the spoils of war.

It's easy to pretend that the doctors haven't given him a 50-50 chance of survival.

When I first heard the number a week ago, I felt so numb I couldn't even cry. But Dad didn't seem discouraged.

"50-50 is a coin flip," he said. "I'll take those odds. Sounds a lot like life."

There's a beeping from across the room, and Claire glides over and pushes a button on a machine hooked up to a completely bald fifty-ish woman who's reading *People* magazine with the recently deceased Princess Diana on the cover.

"How's your day been?" Dad asks.

"Good. Mia and I went to visit her grandma at the nursing home, and then to Waterbury to let Mr. Larson's dog out."

"She's a good egg, that Mia. A little quirky, maybe, but I like that."

For a moment, barely a millisecond, I wonder what it would feel like to say: *She's my girlfriend.* But then the moment's gone.

"What's the latest on the store loan?"

"Still DOA," I say.

"Her mom won't budge, huh?"

"Nope. She says that if Mia doesn't go to college now, she might not ever go."

"Smart lady," Dad says.

I roll my eyes and Dad grins. "Just doing my job. Speaking of that, remind me I have to call your school and let them know you're out tomorrow."

"Okay." Something in my voice must betray my lack of enthusiasm.

"I thought you were excited?" he asks.

"I am."

Dad waits. "You sure?"

"Yeah. I can't wait. My mind just wandered."

Dad ponders this for a moment. "Cleo says he set you up with an amazing engineering student named Nina. Supposed to be almost as smart as you."

"Cool," I say, thinking, *engineering*?

Dad shivers and puts a palm to his chest. "Gonna close my eyes for a minute," he says.

"You need anything?"

"Nah. I got my donut. I got my daughter. What else could a man ask for?"

"Your health?"

"Let's not get greedy," he says.

Track Three
Let's Go Scuba Diving

The prosthetic arm, detached from a body and hooked to a thin metal stand, appears almost floating. Elbow straightening, easing forward, the hand closes around a bright yellow tennis ball perched on a plastic stand and lifts it into the air as if plucking an apple from a tree. I watch, transfixed, as the hand's metal digits tighten around the ball, after which the arm pivots back, then rapidly forward, throwing the ball a few feet before it hits the ground and bounces off the concrete wall.

Nearby, a tall girl with elegant fingers and skin the color of toasted almonds, writes something down on a clipboard, then walks over and picks up the ball and sets it back on the plastic stand. Only then does she notice the three people who have been watching her.

"Oh my God," she says, bringing her hand to her chest. "Sorry. Hey, Dr. Brown."

"Hey Nina, sorry," Cleo says, holding up his hands in apology. "Didn't mean to startle you. Nice to see you so focused."

"I haven't had enough coffee," she says, laughing, then

comes over and confidently shakes all of our hands. She seems to have no idea who my dad is, which is always a check in the plus column.

"Wanna tell us about what you're up to?" Cleo asks, motioning at the metal hand.

Nina explains how as part of her internship with Dr. Finney, one of the biomedical engineering professors who specializes in prosthetics, she's testing grip strength and throwing distance. The goal is synergy between the two to emulate human instinct and action.

"It doesn't look very impressive, I guess," she says, "but we are making progress. And our two test subjects are really excited with the results. Eventually, we want to improve fine motor capabilities to be able to perform more advanced functions."

"Which is a fancy way of saying hold a pencil," Cleo says.

"Exactly," Nina says, chuckling.

Within moments, my dad and Cleo have left, something about "let's get out of the way so these two can get acquainted," leaving me and Nina very much alone in the lab: bright white walls, low fluorescent lighting, and lots of fancy looking equipment. Dad is hanging with Cleo for the day and spending the night with him and his wife, so I won't see him again until tomorrow morning. Hands deep in my pockets, I don't know what to do or say. The prospect of spending all day and night with a college girl I don't know both thrills and terrifies me. I wonder if I've made a huge mistake in agreeing to this, but there's no going back now.

Noticing the clock, Nina says, "C'mon, we gotta book

if we're going to fuel up before Dr. Simon tries to put us back to sleep."

I trail Nina through crowded hallways, trying to match her rapid pace.

"Do you have a class this morning?" I ask, realizing too late what a dumb question it is. Of course, she does. That's the whole point. *Good one, Rainey.*

"Introduction to Engineering Design," she says, "followed by Multivariate Calculus, which is even more nauseating than it sounds, and that's saying something. But nothing happens at BU without caffeine. This place runs on espresso. You'll see."

At the café, Nina orders us cappuccinos, which she pays for by swiping her student ID, and we wait while the barista pulls espresso shots and steams milk. *Bang. Hiss. Plunk.* The café buzzes with chatter and bodies in motion. Everybody seems to be going somewhere.

"Bio or engineering?" she asks.

"Huh?"

"Your major?"

"Oh. I'm not really sure yet."

"Wait, I forgot, Dr. Brown said you're an amazing musician, or something? And that you might want to major in English? Wonder why they paired you up with a science geek for the day."

"Maybe he doesn't know any English majors," I say, not really sure if I'd want to major in English, but I love books so it sounded true enough when Cleo asked me. "But this is cool, too. I kind of want to try something new."

"Well, this is the place. Overachievers thrive here, so you're going to fit right in."

"What makes you think I'm an overachiever?" I ask, wondering if this description fits me.

"Takes one to know one, I guess. C'mon, we gotta go."

We hustle across a courtyard where dueling car horns battle in the late morning traffic, walk into another building, then down a long hallway and into Nina's design class. We plop down in the third row next to a guy with shaggy chestnut hair pulled into a bun. He's wearing baggy cargo shorts and beat to hell Birkenstocks.

"Rainey, Miller, Miller, Rainey," Nina says.

"Nice to meet you, I'm Nate," the guy says, reaching across Nina to shake my hand, which he holds a fraction of a second longer than necessary. "Everybody calls me by my last name, though. Do you go here?"

I shake my head. "Not yet."

"She's shadowing me," Nina says. "And she seems cool, so make a good impression. Meaning don't, you know, be yourself."

Miller whispers something into Nina's ear, which she shakes her head at.

"Miller thinks you're cute," Nina tells me. "But if I was you, I'd pretend I'm busy until the year 2,000. And remind him that you're still in high school."

"I can't believe you just did that," Miller says, looking bashful, but not necessarily embarrassed, as if he's glad I know he thinks I'm cute.

"It's BU engineering, dude," Nina says. "Girls gotta stick together."

I don't find Miller very cute in return, and not because he's a guy, but all the same, the attention makes me flush with excitement.

After Nina's morning classes, we grab a late lunch in the dining hall. Nina spreads lab results on the table and studies them while we eat taco salads. Some dressing from Nina's salad drips onto one of the papers, leaving an oily imprint. "Oops," she says. "I don't think Dr. Finney will like that."

I zip my lips closed and Nina grins.

"Looking good Nina," says a guy with a moustache, walking by and high-fiving Nina without stopping.

"Hey, Todd," she says, then side-eyes me after he's gone. "Stay away from that one, too. These boys, I swear to God. They think their feet don't even touch the ground."

I love the pace of Nina's day, the way it whisks her along. No bells. No hall passes. No supervision. I love the way students eat together, coming and going as they please, clustered in corners reading books or consorting with professors. The idea of college has always felt so foreign to me, but now that I'm actually here among the students, it's hard not to picture myself hustling to class, waving to friends across the courtyard, immersed in and swept away by this world. And unlike high school, Nina's classes all have purpose, and give her meaningful problems to solve directly connected with what she wants to do with her life. Ten years ago, Nina's little brother lost his arm in a bad car accident, and she's been determined to work with prosthetics ever since.

"I know I'm supposed to be a good little capitalist and

scheme about how to make my first million or whatever," she says. "But honestly, I just want to get involved with something that makes people's lives better. Hell, maybe I should join the Peace Corps."

"You'll have less debt," I say.

"You got that right."

After popping by Nina's dorm room to feed her red beta fish, Homer, who has a swirly tail and lives in a tiny bowl with a tiny house and an orange gravel floor, we go to the student center where Liquid Fun, Nina's improv troupe, is having their weekly rehearsal.

"Improv?" I ask. "As in...comedy?"

"I know it seems insane and so different from my major," Nina says on the walk over. "But engineering is stressful. I'm always putting on a brave face, but half the time I'm just trying to keep up. The courses are super hard, and the competition for internships is cutthroat and professors pick favorites early. Everyone here is really smart. And, if you haven't noticed, it's mostly guys and they tend to be easily threatened by our kind. As if we didn't give birth to their dumb asses. Anyway, I did a lot of theater in high school and I miss it. I don't perform with the troupe yet, but the rehearsals are a fun way to unwind and get out of my head."

A loose assemblage of students, perhaps fifteen in total, is milling about, making small talk. Though Nina says they come from all different kinds of majors, from medicine to communications, they all seem to know each other well.

"Y'all this is Rainey," Nina announces but no one is listening.

"*He's* here?" I ask, noticing Miller, the Birkenstocks guy from Nina's morning class.

"Oh, yeah. I forgot to warn you. Miller and I dated for five minutes freshman year. That's how I heard about Liquid Fun."

Miller glides over to us. "I'm glad you came."

"Thanks," I say.

"Give it a rest," Nina tells him, but he only smiles bigger. I can't help the way it makes my heart flutter. The look on Miller's face is not so different from the way Evan, or other guys at my school, look at me, but Miller is older and more experienced, and his attention feels like a more precious gift.

Rehearsal starts with a game called *Yes, Let's*.

"Let's go scuba diving," shouts a girl in overalls. "Yes, let's!" everyone choruses back and starts slow-motion air swimming and making silly fish faces. I'm headed for the corner to sit and watch when Nina grabs my arm and shouts "Let's play air guitar" then starts ripping an epic solo. "Yes, let's!" the group calls out and starts pretending to play. I'm frozen and embarrassed, but it's so ridiculous, and I'm the only one not doing it, so, reluctantly, I make a guitar shape with my arms and start fake playing. Before I know it, Miller hops in front of me, and starts going full Kurt Cobain, headbanging in my face until I smile and start laughing.

"That's better," he says.

From there, the group plays a number of improv games, mostly involving having to react on the spot to a ridiculous story suggestion.

"I'll be the caller," Miller says, starting a new game. "Every time I say ding, everyone switches from English to complete gibberish, but still has to be just as convincing. Ding again and you go back to English. Who wants to play?"

"We will," Nina says, standing up and dragging me with her.

"No way," I say.

"You got this."

"No, I really don't. This is why I do stage crew."

"Just go with it."

We're joined by two boys and assemble in front of the group, who are all splayed out in beanbag chairs like a hippie commune. My heart is absolutely pounding, but it's all happening so fast I almost don't have time to be afraid.

"You two," Miller says, gesturing at us, "are trying to sell these two a high-tech new vacuum cleaner. Go."

"Well, Sally, if we don't sell this here vacuum by close of business, we're gonna get fired for sure," Nina says in a bizarre southern accent, jumping into character. She elbows me hard and says, "So try and hide that limp and let's go."

I fake hide my fake limp while Nina fake knocks on a fake door, which is fake opened by one of the guys.

"Howdy there, sir, if I can just have one moment of your time, I'd like to talk to you—"

"Ding," Miller calls, at which point Nina switches to gibberish while she wheels in our fake vacuum and starts going over its fake, but still very impressive, features. Kneeling down, she points and gesticulates at nothing, somehow making it look and sound amazing even though she's only stringing non-sensical syllables together like the world's smartest baby.

"Ding," Miller says again.

"And right now," Nina says, "I'm going to turn it over to my assistant, Darla, who will finish our demonstration, including my favorite feature, the side blender. Our signature innovation. That way you can whip up a healthy fruit smoothie while you clean your floors." Nina looks at me.

Having no choice, I start talking. "That's right," I say, "the side blender is truly a wonder to behold, and makes the tastiest fruit smoothies you ever did taste," and then, suddenly, I'm doing improv comedy in front of a group of strangers, something that this morning I wouldn't have committed to doing with a gun to my head. And yet here I am.

What was it Mr. Larson said? *People are known to have fun at college.*

By the time we get Nina's mail from her box in the student union and walk back to the dorm, it's already eight-thirty. Nina and I are both exhausted. We'd talked about going out for Mexican food with Miller and some improv people who were going to a fajita place that makes guacamole right at the table and never checks IDs, but Nina asked how I felt about take out and bad TV instead.

"I have a bit of a day tomorrow, and I kind of just want to chill," she says. "Plus, I didn't want Miller to completely turn you off of ever going here. He's honestly not a bad guy, if you can get past the being a guy part. I swear to God, lesbians are on to something."

We have Indian food delivered and devour containers of Chicken Tikka and Saag Paneer in our sweatpants while we watch *The Real World* on MTV. Nina seems to know all the characters and fills me in on the various mini dramas. We laugh at the stupid fights they have. I love that Nina is a serious engineering student but still isn't above some truly bad television. Growing up in a house without cable, it's the kind of show I've never really gotten to watch. The sort of all-American, brain-rotting schlock my parents persistently denied us.

"You like ice cream?" she asks, pulling a pint of Ben and Jerry's out of her tiny freezer.

"I'm from Vermont," I say and she chuckles.

Sitting on her small sofa, we pass the Cherry Garcia back and forth, sharing the same spoon, until it's totally gone.

"Good thing it's low fat, huh?" Nina says. "Ah, whatever, we earned it, right?"

"Right."

I follow Nina to the shared bathroom and we brush our teeth at adjacent sinks.

"I win," Nina jokes when she finishes brushing before me, then says, "see you back at the room," and slips out.

The room, I think, loving the sound of those two words.

Two girls saunter in mid-conversation and keep talking as they enter side-by-side stalls, at which point I slip out and walk back down to Nina's room. I curl up with an extra blanket on the sofa and Nina clicks off the light. The glow from a Boston street lamp seeps around the window shade, putting a soft yellow filter over everything. I feel tired, but buzzed from the day. From who I'm with. From all of it. It's all been so much more fun and exciting than I expected.

I try to go to sleep, but I just lie there, staring at the Einstein and Fugees posters on Nina's wall, wondering what posters I would put up if I had my own dorm room. How I'd decorate things. What I'd order for takeout and what TV shows I'd watch at the end of my long days. A whole other life has begun to reveal itself, full of promises I never knew existed.

"I know this might sound crazy," Nina says, her voice surprising me in the darkness because I assumed she was asleep, "but would you maybe want to room together next year?"

"Really?" I ask, sitting up on my elbows. I'm shocked, but excited by her question.

"I know it's forever away, but I'm losing this single next year because they rotate them around, and, I don't know, you're easy to talk to and I think we would have fun. Don't you?"

"Yeah."

"There's a lot of people here with huge egos and I don't need all that drama. You're so down to Earth."

"Cool," I say, wondering if I really am down to Earth, or if I'm just good at pretending I'm down to Earth. "If I get in and I decide to—"

"You'll get in. But why wouldn't you go here? Are you looking at other schools?"

"Something like that," I say, knowing it would be impossible to try to explain my life to Nina. To almost anyone, really. To tell her that I'm considering coming here because my parents won't let me sign a contract with a major record label.

"Just promise me it's not Tufts," she says, yawning. "Those assholes rejected me."

"It's not," I say, laughing.

In the morning, we trade phone numbers and addresses, and Nina gives me a huge hug before heading off to class.

"How was it?" Dad asks me when we meet back up.

"Not bad," I say, grinning.

"I'll bet. I know that face. Not bad. I can read you like a book, Rain Man."

Wearing his BU sweatshirt, he looks so happy. So proud.

On the way home, Dad and I stop off in Concord, Massachusetts to visit Walden Pond.

"Since your brother's not here," Dad says.

Dad's always had this deep fascination for Henry David Thoreau, his experiment to live alone in the woods, and the book he wrote about his experiences—*Walden.* Yet, somehow, even in all our family travels, I've never been to Walden Pond before. Dad says it's time.

We wind through the woods to the verdant, glimmering shores of Walden Pond, which is smaller than I thought it would be, a kettle pond formed by a melted hunk of orphaned glacier. On a map, it's the shape of a lima bean with a periscope. A park ranger shows us the wooded site where Thoreau's original cabin stood, its size and shape suggested by an outline of waist-high stone columns strung together by a chain, explaining where his desk and chair would have been. Where he would have stacked his firewood and where he would have written his essays. Nearby, there's an actual replica of the cabin and after the park ranger steps out, Dad scurries over and lies down on Thoreau's bed.

"Quick," he says, tossing me his camera.

I take one where Dad pretends to be sleeping, then one where he has this goofy grin on his face, then one where he has his arms and legs kicked out like a dead cat.

The small, one-room cabin is humbling in its modesty, precisely how its builder and sole occupant planned. Thoreau knew exactly what he wanted when he came here. Or at least he was good at pretending he did. What would it have been like to spend so many hours, days, and months alone with nothing but birds, books, and your own busy thoughts for company? If your life's ambition began and ended with the progress of your garden? With your communion with the local wildlife? With a satisfying line in your journal?

Dad makes me sit at Thoreau's small desk and pretend to be deep in thought while he takes my picture. Then we walk down to the pond and watch ducks gliding by in the early afternoon sun, its reflection so bright off the pond's glassy belly that it almost hurts my eyes. My dad asks a fellow tourist to take our picture. I smile with abandon.

"He stood right here," Dad says, looking out at the pond, the trees, the sky, excited as a kid at Disneyland. He puts his arm around me and pulls me in tight. "Pretty cool, huh?"

"Pretty cool."

Track Four
You Have to Jump

"Cuppa Josephine," I say.

"Rainey?"

It's a voice I haven't heard in almost two months, but one that immediately raises familiar goose bumps down the lengths of my arms. It's late Saturday morning, and Bethany and I have been slinging lattes, heating popovers, and pressing panini sandwiches non-stop. My apron is milk smeared and crumb dotted. I smell like cheddar cheese and vanilla syrup.

"It's Cass," she says. "Am I catching you at a bad time?"

Trying to play it cool, I look over at Bethany, who is wiping down the counter. I take a few baby steps further away.

"No. It's okay."

"Cool. I'm in town visiting my friends and I wondered if you want to take a walk later, when you get out of work. Catch up."

"Oh," I say.

"What time do you get off?"

"Three," I say, looking at the clock, which says it's 11:45.

"Perfect. I'll swing by. Cool?"

I should say no. Of course, I should. My parents have forbidden me from having any contact with Cassie or anyone from Shore Records, at least until I turn eighteen next May, so I should hang up the phone right now. Not only that, in the days since BU, I've finally started to accept the fact that I'm going to college. And thanks to Nina, I'm even warming up to the idea.

But as usual, I'm completely disarmed and undone by anything and everything to do with Cassie Plimpton, both by her and by the Technicolor alien world she comes from, so I simply say "Cool," as if someone else is controlling my voice.

When I walk out the door at 3:05, Cass is perched on the bench that faces the front door with her legs crossed and her elbows hooked over the back. "Hey, stranger," she says.

"Hey," I say, feeling self-conscious about my espresso-steam frizzed hair and the smell of roasted coffee on my clothes. About what it would mean if my parents happened to drive by right now and see me with Cassie. After some very tense weeks, things have gradually gotten smoother with Mom and Dad and I'd like to keep it that way.

I steer Cass away from downtown, and we take a winding walk through Fairview neighborhoods. Over the past week, most of the remaining leaves have fallen from the trees, littering lawns and decorating sidewalks with their jagged color. Halloween is in a few days, and we small talk about our favorite candy bars and the most embarrassing

Halloween costumes we wore when we were little. Twix and Pippi Longstocking for me. Snickers and Oscar the Grouch for her. Cass tells me about how she used to visit relatives in the Midwest every fall and how they rode ponies and played hide and seek around giant hay bales.

"One time I got lost and instead of trying to find my way back to the house, I stood there and cried until my dad found me," she says. "I still don't know why I was so scared."

As usual, it's easy talking to Cassie. So easy that in another reality we might be sisters. But the conversation isn't the problem. It's everything we're not saying.

We turn off Maple and up Brook Street. At the house on the corner, a boy with golden hair is throwing a ball for a black poodle that's running so fast across the yard its body is blurry with speed.

"Are you writing any new songs?" she asks.

"A couple." I explain how I've been playing lots of acoustic guitar and some mellower songs have emerged. Not exactly ballads. "Like Elliott Smith songs," I say. Of course, I don't tell her that both of my new songs, "Two Doors Down" and "The Magicians," are about a girl named Mia and the things she does to my heart.

"I think Elliott was the shyest person I've ever been around," she says.

"You *met* him?" I'm impressed, baffled even. In my mind, Elliott Smith has become more of a myth than a real person.

"Just for a few minutes. He's a genius. But kind of tortured."

Cass kicks at a small pile of colorful leaves, which

flutter and dance around her red Chuck Taylors. "I'm back with Matteo," she says.

"How's his back?" I ask. I know it's a little weird that Cassie talks to me about her boyfriend, but I like it too. That same feeling as when my parents first started letting me watch R-rated movies with them.

She laughs. "Still furry. But he's handsome and sweet enough that I've decided to adjust my priorities," she says. "God, I've missed talking to you!"

"Me too. I'm really sorry. About by mom and how everything worked out. I never meant for any of that to happen."

"She's just doing her job. I had no idea you hadn't told them. Obviously."

We both laugh, which helps to break the awkwardness.

"So, college, huh?" she asks.

"Yeah," I say. "I spent a day shadowing this girl at BU recently. It was pretty cool. I went to classes and stayed in the dorms and stuff."

"Is that what you really want?"

"I liked it more than I thought I would. And I promised my parents, so—"

"And they obviously have your best interest at heart, but..." she says, trailing off. Every conversation with Cass is a dance and I haven't quite learned the steps, leaving me feeling clumsy and behind. "Rainey, I know I may be overstepping my bounds, but I like you too much not to be honest with you. In the music business, four years is a lifetime. In this industry, you have to jump when your moment comes or you might lose it forever. And this, right now, this is *your* moment. If you wait, I can't promise it will be waiting for you. Are you really willing to take that chance?"

The question hangs there, unanswered. The different ways my life could go lay themselves out in my mind like roads on a map, forking from this very point and winding away in opposite directions. One to the mountains, one to the sea.

We stop at Deke's Ice Cream where Cass buys us each a Creemee, chocolate and vanilla twist for Cass, maple and raspberry for me.

"Why is it called a Creemee?" she asks, having a lick. "It's just soft serve."

"It's a Vermont thing. I've never seen it called that anywhere else."

Cass looks at her watch.

"I gotta go in a few," she says. "I know it's probably risky, you being out with me. We don't want to push our luck."

"Oh, okay."

"There's one more thing, though," she says, taking a tiny nibble from the top of her cone, then wiping her mouth with a paper napkin.

"Okay."

"If you sign with Shore for three albums, instead of an advance, we'll pay for the rest of your dad's chemo," she says. "And pay off what your family owes the hospital."

My mouth turns to sand and I can barely speak.

"How did you know about my dad?"

She smiles. "Luce Cobb may be out of the spotlight,

but he's still got one of the most recognizable faces in music. Word gets around."

I hate the idea of people knowing about my dad's illness. Of seeing him so sick and vulnerable. But I try to stay focused. "You'd really do that?" I ask.

"Yes."

"Really?"

"Yes. But from here on in, I need you to trust me. That goes for new music. After you put out your 'Jesus' song, I had to fight hard for you. It wasn't easy. More than a few people wanted to pull the plug."

"Sorry," I say, but I'm not sure if I should be. It's just a reflex. My mind is swimming.

"Rookie mistake. But if we're going to do this, we have to be a team. I can give you everything you want, Rainey. But only if we work together. And only if you meet me halfway."

"Okay." I want to bring up Walden again, but I know it's not the right time.

"Now the hard part is up to you." I know she means convincing my parents.

We head back to Cassie's car, which is parked in front of the coffee shop. We're about to walk past Sullivan Street Jeans when the door opens and, suddenly, there's Mia.

Time stretches, then stops.

"Oh," I say, "hey." I hate how weird my voice sounds, breathy and forced, but the juxtaposition of these two women is too much for my already swirling brain.

"Hey," Mia says cautiously.

I turn back to Cassie. "This is my, uh..."

"Friend," Mia says, making a face at me, then accepting and shaking Cassie's hand.

"Friends are good," Cassie says, clearly confused. "Be in touch, Rainey."

"I will."

And then Cassie is off to her car and gone. I turn to Mia, who furrows her brow at me.

"Sorry," I say. "I didn't mean for that to be so awkward. I didn't expect to see you."

"Wasn't that the record company chick?"

"Yeah."

"The one you're not supposed to be talking to?"

I nod.

"The one your parents would blow a gasket if they knew you were talking to?"

I nod again.

"Wait, what were you about to say? Before? About me? This is my..."

"I have no idea." I rub my forehead. "She makes me forget how to use words."

"She is pretty hot," Mia says, looking up the street where Cassie drove off.

"It's not that. I mean, she is. But we just had the craziest conversation."

"Neptune debrief?"

"I'm gross from work," I say. "And I smell like coffee."

"As if I care about any of that. I want to hear everything."

Track Five
I Want to Live in That World

We slide into our normal spot and order what we always order. A You Cheddar Believe It for me. Fries with melted Swiss and a side of gravy for Mia. Bottomless coffees for both of us, with fresh cream, of course. We get the same waitress as always, a tough and buxom lady with shoulder length black curls and a red nametag that reads Pat, which is exactly what you would name a diner waitress if you could choose any name in the world.

On the drive over, I brought Mia up to speed on Cassie's offer and the now near bottomless depth of my confusion over what to do next.

"You know something," Mia says, tidying up the condiments and coffee caddy (salt and pepper neatly aligned, cream pitcher handle at 6 o'clock, ketchup and mustard label out). "You have the most interesting problems of anyone I've ever met."

"Happy I can provide the entertainment."

"Sorry," she says, "it's just, holy shit, Rainey."

"I know."

"I mean, holy shit!"

"I *know*."

"Holy steaming pile of goat shit with whipped cream and cherries on top."

"Gross!"

And then we're both laughing hysterically at this ridiculous and truly disgusting image, but also at the absurdity of it all, and it feels so good to let it out. With tears streaming down my face, the tension ball in my gut begins to loosen.

Our food comes. I steal a couple of Mia's fries and she steals a bite of my grilled cheese.

"They might still say no," Mia says.

"Shore? I don't think so."

"No, your parents. They're probably going to be really pissed that you were dealing with Cassie without them. And, I know it's amazing, but it's also a little sketchy. Isn't it?"

I've been so overwhelmed by the implications of Cassie's offer that I haven't thought as much about this part of the equation.

"Not to mention, pretty manipulative."

"No, it's not," I say. *Wait, is it?*

"Rainey, I'm sorry, but it totally is. Take it from someone who's easily manipulated. I know this would be amazing for your family, beyond amazing, and how much stress the bills are causing, but they're totally using your dad being sick to pressure you into signing."

The realization finally stings me. She's right. I've just been too blinded by my excitement to see it. But if they're actually going to pay for my dad's treatments, do I even care? This would get my family out of debt. Maybe save my dad's life. If your house is on fire, you don't stop and worry about where the water comes from.

Pat comes around and tops off both our coffees.

"I wish this wasn't so hard," I say.

"Yeah," Mia says. "But that's also how you know it's really important. All the great characters have to go through hardship in order to figure out their true path in life. Luke Skywalker. Frodo. What's her name from that Russian book by that one guy."

"Anna Karenina?"

"Exactly."

"She died at the end."

"Okay, bad example. You know what I mean. It's the classic hero's journey."

"Joseph Campbell," I say. "Junior year. Ofalko's American Lit Seminar."

"Exactly. Best teacher ever. And when they write books about *you* someday, this will be the pivotal chapter. Moving out of darkness into the light and all that stuff."

I shake my head.

"And it was over a grilled cheese sandwich late one afternoon at the Neptune Diner that Rainey Cobb figured out exactly what she was going to do," Mia says in a dramatic narrator voice, using her spoon as a microphone. "But she couldn't have done it without her trusted friend and confidant, Mia McRae. Though history has long forgotten this incredibly beautiful, splendidly witty, albeit minor figure in the life of the great musician, she's the true unsung hero of Cobb's story."

I giggle. "Thanks for listening to all my bullshit."

"That's my job," she says. "And it's way more interesting than my bullshit."

"You're the only one I can talk to about it."

Mia smiles.

"But you're not a minor figure in my life," I say.

"Oh really?"

"Really."

Mia picks some crusted Swiss off the edge of her plate, then reaches across the Formica booth top and takes my hand. She slides it gently toward her so that our hands are a centerpiece, cradling my hand as a girlfriend or boyfriend would, like it's not just any other hand. Not just any other fingers. Not just any other skin. But fingers like a piece of art. Skin like a temple. "I love your hands," she says. "I love what they can do."

I giggle.

"That's not what I meant," she says. "I'm talking about music, you perv."

"I know. It just sounded funny."

Not wanting to risk anyone seeing us, I pull back, but Mia gently tightens her grip, just enough to hold me in place, and gets a coy look on her face.

"What if we could just hold hands and nobody would care?" she asks. "What if two girls, or two guys, could just sit here in a stupid booth in a stupid diner in some stupid town and hold hands, which by the way is what people who care about each other are supposed to do, and nobody would even care enough to notice? I want to live in *that* world."

"I'm not sure that world exists," I say.

"A girl can dream."

The cash register dings, drawing my eyes left. Most of the time, I don't recognize who's standing at the register, usually some old couple or a family with kids. But this time I very much recognize who's standing there because it's Clive Brewer and Mandy Thompkins. Clive is sliding his wallet into his back pocket and repositioning his toothpick when our eyes lock. I yank my hand out of Mia's and look away from him.

"Oh shit," I say.

"What?" Mia asks. She looks over toward the register.

"Don't look."

"What, do you know those kids?"

"Yeah, they go to Green Valley. Stop looking, okay. I think they saw us."

I hate how my voice sounds, an impatient director barking at his actors.

"Rainey, they're thirty feet away, I'm sure they didn't see anything, and even if—"

"Just shut up, okay."

I block my face with my hand like a little kid closing her eyes during a game of hide and seek, imagining that if I can't see them, they can't see me either.

"The coast is clear," Mia says a few seconds later, "you can come out now."

I look at her.

"Sorry," she says.

I want to tell her it's okay, but I don't believe that. Not if Clive Brewer saw us holding hands and he tells Mandy, who will then tell all her friends, who will then tell the entire world. *See, we always knew there was something weird about her!* By tomorrow morning the whole school might know. I'd love to pretend I don't care what anyone thinks about me, especially the jocks at my school who I'll never see or speak to again after graduation, but the cold heavy feeling in my gut knows it's not that simple.

"I have to get going," I say. "I'm tired. And I need a shower."

"Okay."

We sit in heavy silence while we wait for Pat to drop off the check. Mia tallies up our cash and puts the bills face up in a neat pile in ascending numerical order, a ten on the bottom, then a five, followed by four ones and three stacked quarters.

"You didn't have to tell me to shut up," Mia says, lifting, then dropping the stacked quarters over and over again, straightening out the pile each time. Her voice aches with hurt.

"I'm sorry. It just came out."

She nods. "I'm sorry too. But I didn't like that."

Track Six
A Simple Arrangement

Some brothers and sisters go to the movies; my brother and I hit the recording studio. It started when I was playing my new song "The Magicians," believing I was home alone, only to look up and find my brother in the doorway with that look on his face, the one that says he's itching to be in the studio.

"That's not bad," he says. "New?"

"Yeah."

"Wanna lay it down?"

"Sure," I say, remembering my promise to share all my new music with Cassie, but knowing this is just for fun.

"The Magicians" is one of the most complex songs I've ever written, full of 6th and 7th and half-diminished chords and a slippery key change toward the end. Because of this, Walden says the arrangement should go in the opposite direction.

"A complex song," he says, "needs a simple arrangement."

We record it with acoustic guitar, bass, drums, and a single harmony vocal. Then, at the last minute, Walden suggests adding in musical saw, whereby you pin a length of saw vertically between your legs and bow it as if you're playing the cello. I can barely get a sound out of it, but Walden, who I've never seen touch one before, makes it sing as if he's been playing it for years, teasing out a high-pitched, ethereal ache. At first, I worry the saw will sound too weird or folky, but Walden tucks it into the mix just right. It sounds like a distant, mildly depressed angel is singing backup. I never would have thought of it. Nobody would have but my crazy, brilliant brother.

"It sounds so good," I say.

"See," Walden says, his legs propped up on the edge of the mixing board as we listen to playback, enjoying our traditional post-recording Cokes and Oatmeal Cream Pies, "this is why we should do it on our own. Treehouse Records, sis. I'm telling you. Those idiots at Shore would have murdered this song. Big label people don't know how to keep it simple. Let us never forget what Phil Spector did to 'The Long and Winding Road,' an offense that is long overdue for criminal prosecution."

"You could be on the label too, you know."

"What are you talking about?"

"Cassie came to see me," I say.

"What? When?"

"Last weekend."

"Jesus, Mom and Dad are going to freak if they find out."

"It's not my fault. She called me one day while I was working at Cuppa. And then she just showed up when my shift was over." This isn't an entirely true version of events, of course, but the white lie feels harmless and makes me look a little bit better.

"She's got balls, I'll give her that," Walden says. "What did she say?"

I swallow.

"They offered to pay for the rest of Dad's chemo. And all the hospital debt we owe."

Walden's mouth opens all the way. "She actually said that?"

I nod.

"If you sign?"

"For three albums."

Walden stands up and stomps around the room. "Three albums! Rainey, that's the next ten years of your life."

"I know."

"They think money can buy everything."

"Well, in this situation, it can. They're offering us a lifeline, Walden. For Mom and Dad. For all of us."

My brother shakes his head from side to side. He looks so far away. So sad. "This isn't how it should be," he says.

"Well, this is how it is. But I'm going to tell them I won't do it without you. Or without River, if he wants."

"Oh, give me a break. Have you even told River about any of this?"

I shake my head.

"I wonder why that is," he says.

"I'm going to tell him. And, you know what, it's not that crazy. Nirvana kept the same lineup after they signed."

"Who cares? That was different."

"How? How was that different?"

"When Nirvana first signed, Kurt Cobain wasn't Kurt Cobain yet. He was just the lead singer of Nirvana. He only became Kurt Cobain after. It's different with you because you're already you. That's why Shore only wants you. And remember the *Spin* cover that had only you on it? Because I do."

I swallow the last bite of my Cream Pie and wipe away some sugary crumbs.

"I'm going to tell Cassie," I say. "I'm going to sign. I have to."

"Go for it," he says. "Tell Mom and Dad too. It won't matter. They'll never take Shore's blood money. And in the meantime, you're going to get grounded until Christmas."

The next night, I borrow the family Subaru and make the rounds.

I start with Evan, who, after I trounce him in Mario Kart, lapping his Bowser with my Peach, not once but twice, turn to him and say, "I have to tell you something."

"You're not gay, are you?" he asks.

"Gee, that just gets funnier and funnier."

"I know, but it's my only joke. What is it?"

I swallow. I think back to the first day of school, when I almost told him in the hallway, wondering if I should have. Have I betrayed him in waiting this long?

"You know that woman who was coming to our shows over the summer?"

"The old one at the bar? The journalist?"

"She's not old! And she's not a journalist."

"Okay, okay," he says. "Yes. I know who you mean." He seems to read something in my face. "She's from a label, isn't she?"

I nod and smile meekly. "I knew it!" he says, slapping the couch for emphasis. "I totally knew it. Which one?"

"Shore."

"What? That's amazing!" He hugs me and shakes my shoulders in excitement. "But wait, what about BU and the promise and all that?" He puts "the promise" in air quotes.

"I'm working on it."

"You're going to need a new manager," he says.

"No. Not yet. There's still time."

"C'mon Rainey," he says. "I don't know how to navigate any of the stuff you're going to be dealing with. Record contracts and lawyers or whatever." Evan eats a few Ruffles out of the bag we're sharing, licks crumbs from his fingers, then puts them right back into the bag. "Besides, nine months from now I'm going to be eight hundred miles away anyway."

"What?" I say, leaning forward in excitement. "You got in?"

Dimples form in the corners of his cheeks as he smiles, tightening his freckles into bunches. For weeks now, he's been nervously waiting to hear from Notre Dame, his top choice for college. It's where his dad went and he's always dreamed of going there too.

"I wish it didn't mean having to be so far away from you," he says.

"I know."

"But you can come visit me when you're on tour."

"I'll probably be in Boston, in college," I say.

Evan shakes his head. "No way. You'll figure it out. You have to. And then you can get me free tickets to shows and I'll brag to everybody we used to be best friends."

"*Used* to be best friends?"

"Are best friends."

It's going to be so strange not to have Evan around. Not to see him every day. Not to have him look at me the way he does, as if my face is the answer to a riddle. Two years ago, I looked up from a piano that lived in a side hallway behind the auditorium stage to find him standing there listening to me play, nervous and awkward and achingly sweet. In a lot of ways, Evan is the first really good friend I've ever had. I don't want to lose him.

"You wanna know something," he says. "Becker isn't even an Irish name. It's German. Do you think that will work against me at Notre Dame?"

"You're so weird," I say.

"Oh, I'm the weird one. That's rich."

River, who I invite out for a walk, doesn't take the news as well.

"That's obviously very very cool, but why did you wait so long to tell me?" he asks, slipping some of his long blonde hair behind his ear. "Who else knows?"

"Walden. Evan. Mia."

"So, literally everybody else," he says.

"I'm sorry."

"You barely even know Mia."

I shrug, thinking about how untrue that is, how maybe River just hasn't been noticing how much time his sister and I spend together. "I felt kind of weird about telling you," I say.

"That's stupid, why?"

"It seems like they may only want to sign me," I say.

"Instead of the band."

"Yeah, but I'm going to tell them I won't sign without you guys."

"And blow up your dream in the process? That's really dumb," he says.

"Plus, I know you're still waiting to hear from colleges. I'll probably be in Boston next year anyway, but I didn't want to put any pressure on you or make your life more complicated."

River ponders this for a long moment.

"I can't believe you told Mia before me, you loser," he says again, circling back to what is clearly the most important part of the story to him, sounding annoyed, but a bit less wounded, as if he's already starting to forgive me.

"We talk a lot."

"So do we," he says, gesturing between us. "At least we used to. Remember, I'm the guy you trusted enough to come out to before anyone else."

"I know," I say.

"There's something going on with you and Mia, right?"

"Yeah."

"And yet another secret reveals itself. Do you actually work for the CIA or the KGB or something? Is your name really Natasha?"

"I said I was sorry," I say.

"Friends tell each other stuff, Rainey. Especially good ones. They don't keep secrets about major life shit."

"I'm surprised Mia didn't tell you. Or that you didn't ask her."

"She and I don't really talk," he says.

"You should."

"Yeah."

We walk in silence through the suburban streets of River's well-manicured neighborhood. Stretch after stretch of oversize homes with basketball hoops in the driveways and groomed dogs parading through the bright green lawns. Smells of cut grass, barbecue, chlorine.

"By the way, I don't care that you're dating my sister."

"You don't?"

"No," he says. "I didn't care that you were gay. Why would I care about this? I love you both. I want you to be happy. And it's nice to see her smile again."

River has this amazing way of making everything seem so easy, so simple.

"Thanks, that means a lot."

We complete our normal loop, and start back toward River's house.

"You could be a little more excited for me," I say.

He stops and turns to me, then wraps me up in a huge hug.

"Fuck. I'm sorry. I'm such a jerk. I am excited for you. It's incredible. You're incredible. I mean it. I got caught up in my own shit there for a minute."

"So, what do you think?" I ask, once we start walking.

"About us maybe signing with a label? Provided I can somehow hypnotize my parents into forgetting they want me to go to college instead and then convince Shore it's all of us or nothing."

"I think you should send me a postcard from the road," he says.

I punch him in the arm. "I mean it," I say. "You could, we could—"

"Okay, first off, there's no way I'm going to let you blow up your dream because of something so dumb. Second, my sister already dropped out of college and my mother would spontaneously combust if I said I wasn't going. Besides, this is your ride. It's always been your ride, Rainey." River gives me one of those grins. "I knew that from the first second I came to band practice sophomore year and heard you play 'Ordinary Girl' for the first time. God, Evan was still playing drums then. Remember that? He couldn't keep a beat to save his life. But I remember standing there, listening to you sing, trying to play it so cool, thinking I'd stepped into a dream or something. Your voice gave me goosebumps."

This level of vulnerability and directness is unusual for River, who's always so aloof and detached, and I find myself surprisingly moved by his words, by the way he remembers when we first met and started playing together. It's sometimes hard to know what you really mean to people, and once in a while, when they do tell you, it's almost too much. They're pouring words into your heart, filling it up with so much love that it feels like it's going to burst.

As we pass a broad willow tree, ravens caw out at us

aggressively, followed by a pair of squirrels dashing through the road, and then a trio of barking dogs.

"It's wild kingdom out here," I say.

"Nature is a fickle thing," River says, putting his arm around me, "very fickle indeed."

Track Seven
A Coin Toss

Dad's line dips into the water, then rises back out, sending a thin curve of ripples across the pond. This one, near my house, is far smaller even than Walden Pond. Too small even to have a name, I guess. We've always just called it The Pond.

"Here we go," Dad says, leaning forward to brace himself and beginning to work the line, gently loosening his finger grip to let out some more, then yanking back quickly, hoping to hook the fish good and fast. "Got em," he says.

"I think it's a big one," I say, watching Dad struggle to reel in the fish, blowing on my hands and rubbing them together against the early November cold.

"You should feel him pull. I think we're gonna need a bigger boat."

When Dad finally hauls in the shimmery perch, it's about ten inches long with a golden yellow body and orange lower fins striped with vertical bars. Like all just-caught fish, it's wriggling in a chaotic, mid-air dance, its eyes bulged and wild with fear. I get so excited when we catch a fish, but then I always get scared by the animal panic in their eyes.

"Can you unhook him?" Dad asks. Even though the temperature is in the fifties, Dad's face glistens with sweat. He's had a horrible few days. High fever, nausea, and I know he hasn't been sleeping. He looks pale and sunken, his breathing labored as the engine of an old Chevy.

It's been two weeks since BU. A week since Cassie came back into my life. I'm growing ever more desperate to tell my parents about everything, but it's never the right time. Either dad is in crisis, or Mom is rushing out the door to the law office or working the phones, talking to the hospital or selling off memorabilia. In the meantime, I've spent my evenings at the kitchen table filling out financial aid and scholarship paperwork. As of this morning, all the papers have been signed, sealed, and sent out to the powers that be.

I shuffle forward on my knees, trying not to rock the row boat, and grab the fish where he's dangling off Dad's line, squeezing just tight enough to keep him from flopping around. Dad taught me that a firm grip not only calms the fish down, but makes him easier to unhook.

The hook comes out easily enough, but the fish's body is so scaly and slick that I lose my grip and drop him into the hull. He hits the gray metal with a dull, dense *thwack*, then starts sputtering like a drop of water in a hot pan.

"Oh shit!" I scream.

"Just pick him back up," Dad says. "It's okay. You can do it."

I try, but the fish's movements are so sporadic and

violent, I can't time it right. Finally, I get a hold of him, but he twitches suddenly, jabbing his fins into my flesh and I drop him again. I keep trying, but I can't seem to do it. Though a fish can be out of water for several minutes, a stressed fish will die far quicker. And this is one very stressed fish. Eventually, grimacing in pain, Dad wriggles forward, and with a few confident movements, has the fish calmly in his grasp.

"There you go big guy," Dad says, stroking the fish with his thumb. "Somebody wants to get back in the water, doesn't he."

Dad looks up at me, but doesn't acknowledge my embarrassment. Instead, he smiles, as if it's all going according to plan.

"He's a beaut, isn't he? Look at the coloring."

"Yeah."

I feel so ashamed knowing that if Dad hadn't been here the fish probably would have died that I almost start crying, but I manage to hold back my tears.

"Let's get you back in the water," he says. "Goodbye fish."

"Goodbye fish," I say.

It's what we always say to the fish before we set them free. Dad lowers the fish into the water. It's perfectly still at first, perhaps still in shock, then kicks a few times and swims away. We sit quietly listening to the birds and the wind off the water. Dad drinks some coffee from the thermos, steam rising from his cup, and we eat blueberry muffins wrapped in tin foil, the berries still oozy from the oven, the sugary top crunchy between my teeth. The light overhead is a flat gray—no clouds, no sun—and the trees look naked and spindly with all their leaves gone and their bark wet from recent rain.

I blow on my hands and pick some lint off my cardigan, knowing I should have brought my fleece along. I started the day in a good mood, but not being able to pick up that stupid fish, and watching Dad have to do it, is messing with my head. Reminding me there's a 50-50 chance that this could be our last time ever going fishing together. I know it's crazy to think that way, imagining each moment could be the last, but how am I supposed to stop? How am I supposed to accept that my dad might die?

"Did I ever tell you that your mom almost got disowned because she decided to marry me?" he asks.

The question is so out of the blue that I look up at him confused.

"What? Really?"

"We were still in high school when we got engaged. Seventeen. Same as you."

I know this fact as a part of Cobb family lore, of course, but I'm not sure I've ever thought about what it really means. How impossible it seems that two people could be the same age I am now and think about committing to each other for the rest of their lives. To embracing forever together.

"Why did you? Decide to get married so young? You were already playing music together. Neither one of you was going anywhere. What was the hurry?"

He smiles, then shivers against the chill air, crossing his arms over his chest.

"Let's just say we weren't as careful as we should have been," he says.

It takes me a second to figure out what he means, but then it hits me. I'm too shocked to be grossed out. "Mom got *pregnant*? At seventeen? While she was still in high school?"

Dad nods, and wrinkles his mouth. He looks away from me before looking back.

"She'd kill me if she knew I was telling you this," he says, a guilty smile on his face.

I picture my mom at my age, realizing she's pregnant. How scared and unsure she must have been. Then I do the simple math in my head, realizing that this would have been before Walden was born, which has me really confused.

"Getting married was what you did in that situation. At least back then it was. Even if you were too young. But your grandmother wasn't having it. She said I was a loser and that if Mom married me, she wasn't her daughter anymore. She threatened to kick her out of the house." Dad lets out a heavy breath. "But of course, we got married anyway, because like all seventeen-year-olds, we knew everything. But then about a month after the wedding, Mom lost the baby."

"What?"

"Miscarriage," Dad says. "Just one of those things. A fluke. We were sad, of course, but we were pretty relieved if I'm being honest."

"Did Grandma ever find out? About mom being pregnant?"

Dad shakes his head. "Nope."

"I always thought you and Grandma were so close," I say. There are tons of pictures of my dad and my mom's mom together smiling, and I grew up hearing about how she and Dad used to dance to Hank Williams records and play cards while they drank Wild Turkey.

"I won her over in the end. We all lose our heads sometimes, especially when we're trying to protect the people we love. She realized I wasn't such a bad guy, and that she'd probably overreacted a little bit. And maybe not given us enough credit for how much we really loved each other. How committed we were to making music together."

"Wow," I say.

"You're probably wondering why I'm telling you all this," he says.

"Sort of. I'm glad you told me, but—"

"I guess it's my clumsy way of saying that I'll love you no matter what."

"No matter what-what?"

"Whether or not you go to college."

"Oh," I say, letting these shocking words sink in. "You mean—"

"It's your life, Rain Man. And you have to do what feels right in your heart. Whether that's college, or reaching back out to that lady at the record label, or neither. That's fine too."

"But all this time you've been saying that—"

"I've been saying a lot of things," he says, shaking his head. He flicks something off the leg of his jeans. "I've been told I need to do a lot more listening." I can only assume he's referring to something my mom said to him, which is even more surprising, given how stubborn she's been about things. He looks out over the water. "Why didn't you tell me how you really felt?"

"I thought I did."

Exhaling, he says, "I know I haven't made it easy. You and your brother have had to take on so much. I know you're under a lot of pressure. I want you to have a great life. A life with options and flexibility. But you're old enough to start charting your own course and I need to accept it. It's hard, though. The dad training manual doesn't come with advice for the moment when you realize your little girl's all grown up."

The wind picks up and pushes our little boat across the water.

I've been so sure for so long about what I do and do not want, but things feel so complicated now. "How will I know if I'm doing the right thing? How did you and mom know?"

"You won't," he says. "And we didn't. But that's life. It's a coin toss, remember?"

And then I do start crying. It's all too much. The weight of everything. The threat of losing him. My heart has cracked open and spilled everywhere. I find myself telling Dad about Cassie coming to Cuppa Josephine. About the offer to pay for his chemo. About how I want to help so they don't have to worry about the money anymore. I'm so tired of holding things inside.

"I want to help," I say. "I'm so tired of sitting back and feeling powerless."

He nods when I finish, but he doesn't look surprised. Which is surprising. I assumed the news about Cassie would come with fireworks, and some kind of reprimand. Dad has the last slurp of his coffee, then rinses the cup in the pond and screws it back on top of the thermos.

"You knew already," I say.

"Yeah." He flicks a water droplet off the rim of the boat.

And then it hits me. It wasn't my mom who said he wasn't listening. It was Walden. Walden told him about Cassie and the money.

"But don't blame your brother, okay. He loves you, and remember what I said about protecting the people you love. But whatever you do, you need to do it for *your* reasons. We're fine with whatever you decide. And we'll sign the contract with you if that's what you really want."

"You will? You would?"

He nods. "I talked to Mom. It took some convincing, but she agrees with me that we shouldn't stand in your way. Not if it's what you really want. It's your life. Your dreams. But it can't be about their money and the hospital bills. If you signed just to get us out of this pickle, we couldn't live with ourselves. I can't carry that weight, kiddo. Do you understand?"

"Yeah," I say.

"I love you, Rain Man."

"I love you too."

"I'd hug you but I'm pretty sure I'd tip us over and I don't want to go swimming," he says, so we hold hands and cry and drift along wherever the gently moving current takes us.

Track Eight
Dress Up Day

"'Maybe Forever,' take four," Electric Lady's sound engineer says into my oversize padded headphones from behind the soundproof glass that separates us. He's sitting in a leather swivel chair next to a producer named Bruce who has a Steven Segal ponytail. Beside him are Cassie and the executive from Shore who said the thing about exploring my "poppy" side. Tucked into the corner like strange wallpaper, arms crossed, sits my brother.

The "Maybe Forever" backing track starts up in my ears. Again. Bubbly guitar. Punchy synth. Tambourine on two and four. Programmed drums. I open my mouth. Again. I sing some ghostwriter's words. Again. I'm stuck in the world's strangest-ever karaoke routine. Again.

I'm a comfy sweater
You're a fancy shirt
I'm a little bit Ernie
You're a little bit Bert
We got nothing in common
But baby that's why it works

Pre-recorded harmonies swell in my ears as the music pivots into the chorus.

So maybe I'll hold on
Just a little bit tighter
So that maybe our love will burn
Just a little bit brighter
Maybe give me your whole heart
And maybe I'll give you mine
Maybe forever came just in time

A key change signals the outro and I belt out the refrain.

Maybe forever came just in time
Maybe forever came just in time
Maybe forever came just in time

When the backing track cuts out, my voice echoes off the foam-covered walls for a split second before silence envelops me. I wipe sweat off the back of my neck.

After every take, I'm reassured that "it sounds great" and that "your voice sounds even better in person." I've spent countless hours in recording studios over the years, singing into microphones while the tape rolls, delivering the goods when it's my turn to deliver them, but this feels so different. I came here to sing my own music, to step into the major label world as a songwriter to be reckoned with, but it turns out there were other plans.

I pull the headphones down around my neck and sit on

the stool they gave me. Everyone is looking at me through the glass. Now I know how a goldfish feels. The door opens, and Walden walks slowly into the room. Entire novels are written in his big brown eyes.

"Don't," I say softly. "Just...don't." I'm not in the mood for what I know he'll say. *You're better than this bubble gum crap. It's not worth it. We don't need them.*

"I just wanted to give you this," he says, handing me a bottle of water.

"Oh. Thanks."

That day, after I went fishing with my dad, I called Cassie, who immediately sprang into action like somebody had plugged in her power cord. Within thirty-six hours, she'd not only engineered my return visit to New York, but had somehow snuck us into Electric Lady for what's called a "test" session. "Not to mention," she said over the phone, her voice full of motion and positive energy, "I heard back from legal, and we *finally* have a contract to show you."

I buzzed with excitement at the idea of finally holding a real record contract with my name printed in ink. At the prospect of recording my music at historic Electric Lady studios. At taking the first step in a journey I've been dreaming about for so long. To prepare for the session, Walden and I worked out an arrangement and even recorded a rough demo of "Two Doors Down," one of my other new songs. Walden meticulously packed his stick bag, and even carried his cymbal bag on the plane because, like all drummers, he wants to marry his cymbals.

After Cassie picked us up at the airport, she took us to

a fancy brunch place where we ate Eggs Benedict and drank fresh-squeezed blood orange juice.

For a few minutes, it was all exactly as I pictured.

"Today," Cassie said, popping the yolk of her poached egg and sending an oozy yellow river into a fortress of home fries, "we're going to have a little fun."

That was the moment the picture began to blur and distort. Because the last time Cassie said those words, I ended up on a fake magazine cover with aggressive cleavage and more confused than I've ever felt in my life.

Note to self: Be careful what you wish for. You just might get it.

After Walden leaves, Cassie comes into the room. I sip some water.

"You sound amazing," she says. "Beyond amazing. Everybody thinks so." Her voice oozes excitement—love even.

"Thanks," I say, studying my shoes.

"You don't think so? Is it the song?"

Um, yeah, it's the song. Bert and fucking Ernie?

"Kind of," I say.

"I know it's not poetry," she says, smiling huge, "but it's catchy as hell. You can't imagine hearing this on the radio?"

"No, I can."

"Try not to overthink it and have fun. Remember today is just an experiment."

"To figure out what, exactly?"

"What shape you are."

"This song doesn't sound anything like my music," I say.

"Rainey, you're seventeen, how do we even really know what *your* music sounds like? Your creative journey just started. But I hear you, this may not be the song."

My head moves up and down.

"Do you trust me?" she asks, taking my hands in hers, squeezing. "I need you to trust me."

"I trust you."

It's not a lie. I do trust Cassie. It's just that trust is turning out to be more complicated than I expected.

After "Maybe Forever," we record a reggae-tinged pop song called "Pineapple Tree" and then a club drone called "All Night" that's basically an R Kelly song. All were written by the hired gun songwriters that Shore keeps on retainer, and whose vast catalogs of future radio hits await the next big thing. I haven't touched my guitar all day. Walden hasn't touched a drum stick. Our demo of "Two Doors Down" is still in my backpack. I'm not sure what the hell is going on.

"Think of it like dress up day," Cassie says on our lunch break while we window shop along busy Greenwich Village streets and eat Cuban sandwiches from a local deli. Walden, seeming lost in his thoughts, wandered off alone somewhere to brood. My parents were supposed to come on this trip, but as we were getting ready to leave for the airport, suitcases piled by the door, Dad couldn't catch his breath and ended up in tears while Mom forced him into the Subaru—and back to the hospital.

"I'm sorry," he said.

"It's okay," I said, trying to mask my disappointment. "It's not your fault."

"We'll come next time," Mom told me, cradling my face, touching my nose with hers. "I promise. Knock em dead."

Walden and I took a cab to the airport.

"When I was in high school," Cassie continues as our reflections blur past in an art gallery window, "my friends and I used to go to Filene's and have dress up day. We'd try on a million different outfits and laugh until we peed our pants. Most of the time we didn't buy anything. But it was fun to see how we looked. How we felt. That's what today is like."

I get what she means, but this analogy is not working with me. I have no desire to play dress-up day with my musical identity. "But I'm a songwriter," I say. "I thought you liked my music."

Cassie exhales slowly, like a teacher trying to figure out the right way to break down a complex equation to a student who probably won't get it. A man walks by us walking a cat on a leash, followed by two women in fur coats.

"Rainey, I do. I think your music is awesome. I love your music. But I think it's your voice that's going to put you on the cover of *Spin* for real."

"Alanis writes her own songs," I say.

"Alanis writes radio ready hits," Cassie says, her voice rising, sharpening. "One after the other. And even she doesn't do it alone. Glen Ballard helped write every song on *Jagged Little Pill*. But you bring us songs as radio ready as 'You Outta Know' and 'Ironic' and I'll stop talking."

"'Jesus' has been getting lots of requests. So did 'Ordinary Girl.'"

We pass a young man sitting on a stool outside a fruit stand, elegant piles of mangoes and melons perched to his left.

"On indie stations and cable access," Cassie corrects. "Your audience is passionate, but they're underground. And Grunge is dying."

I laugh contemptuously. "I'm not Grunge," I say.

"Then what are you?"

"I don't know. I don't think about it like that."

"I know you don't," she says. "But I have to. It's literally my job to think about it like that. We want you on mainstream radio and MTV so that when your songs come on, it's not dozens of people listening, but tens of thousands. And that means evolving your sound. That's what Bruce is here for. He's a genius at this. I've never seen anyone better at pairing artist and material. But it takes time. It's a bit like falling in love."

Everything Cassie is saying makes a certain kind of sense. It sounds right. So why does it feel so wrong?

"My sound *is* changing," I say, starting to feel both defensive and desperate. This whole time I've believed it was my music that Shore and Cassie loved. But it turns out what they really love is my voice. "My new songs are different. Less heavy."

"Honestly, Rainey, we're a little nervous about your music."

"Why?"

We weave through a cluster of young women carrying big white shopping bags and talking at top volume, then turn right at the next block. I couldn't find my way back to Electric Lady if you paid me.

"Remember when you played me 'Jesus Wears a Blonde Wig?' Remember what I said?"

"You said it would cause controversy," I say.

"And that controversy always comes with a cost. Well, this is part of what I was talking about. Every indie station that plays that song gets complaints, and you've got a bit of a reputation as a loose cannon. Everyone knows you're a good songwriter. And everyone knows you are off the charts talented and that you're the only white girl on the planet who can sing like Etta James. This process is about finding the sound that will make you pop, while still being authentically you. And that process takes some trial and error. When the album comes out, it will still say music and lyrics by Rainey Cobb. And you will have input every step of the way. We're not going to ignore your ideas or throw you to the wolves. I promise. You'll see."

My head is swirling and I'm finding it hard to organize my thoughts or come up with any rebuttal. Expectation and reality are having a street fight in a back alley in my mind, and at the moment, expectation is lying on the ground in a pool of blood.

Cassie buys us iced lattes from a coffee shop—hazelnut for her, vanilla for me—and we sip them at a small bistro table for two. Cassie crosses her long, tanned legs and scratches at her short, dark hair, artfully styled and crispy with product.

"We need to talk about my band," I say. "Well, really about my brother."

Cassie nods. She can see where this is going. The cash register dings. A steam wand hisses to life.

"I love your brother. He's smart and talented. You're going to need him around to help keep you grounded. And if you want to keep him in your touring band, we can talk about that."

"But the contract?" I ask.

Cassie sips her latte. Her silence says it all.

"I don't want to do this without him."

"Rainey," she says, reaching out and taking my free hand, "he's going to be with you the whole time. You're starting to see me like a monster or something."

"No. I'm not."

"I'm on your side one hundred percent," she says.

"I know. But what if I said I wouldn't sign without him?" I ask.

"Then things would get more complicated. And probably slow way down. Really, I think you're making too much of this. Walden loves you. He's not going anywhere, whether his name is on a piece of paper or not. You must know that."

After lunch, we're back at Electric Lady, splayed around the sound booth. Bruce cues up a rough demo of an R&B song called "Backseat Kiss." My ears immediately perk up. Good backbeat. Live drums. Stax style rhythm guitar. It's the first song that sounds anywhere near something I might sing.

Sensing my enthusiasm, Bruce says, "Hey Mikey, I think she likes it."

"I recognize the singer," I say, trying to place it until I

realize it's the sultry, smooth voice of Brie St. Vincent, the soul singer we jammed with last time we were here. The one who called me a whack-ass Emo chick who played like Billy Preston.

"It wasn't quite right for Brie," Cassie says.

We set up in one of Electric Lady's larger recording rooms. Bruce plugs a black Fender Strat into a vintage Twin Reverb and teases out a few licks. Walden hops on the house drum kit. We carefully carry Stevie Wonder's Rhodes into the room and I mess with chord voicings as Bruce teaches me the song. He offers me the printed lyric sheet, but I shake my head.

"You sure?"

"Yeah. I got it."

He ponders this for a moment, then says "You're like one of those waitresses who can take an order from a table of ten without writing anything down, aren't you?"

"Something like that."

"I knew I liked you."

Within a few minutes, we're running takes. Walden lays down a perfect pocket and cracks his first smile of the day. Before I know it, we're off to the races. I tap into the soulful register in my voice. Shades of Aretha and Dusty Springfield. It's the best I've felt all day.

It's still not my song. In fact, it's far closer to something my parents would write. But it's at least music in which I can recognize my reflection.

"I'm still not convinced R&B is the right platform," the Shore exec quietly tells Cassie after we pile back into the control room to listen to playback. "It's more naturally limiting. And I definitely don't love her stuck behind a piano." He could be talking about furniture. *I don't love the coffee table next to that window. And this painting doesn't really go.* He obviously has no idea I spent my entire childhood behind a piano. That I feel naked on stage unless I have my hands on an instrument.

Walden's voice is in my head. *They don't know you. They're just pretending to.*

"She won't play it live," Cassie assures him. "And I agree. But we're getting closer."

"We've only got a little time left before they kick us out of here for the day," Bruce says, looking at his watch. "You brought in a song, right, Rainey?"

"Yeah," I say, suddenly feeling self-conscious about "Two Doors Down." With finger picked acoustic guitar and slow-burn vocals, it's the sonic opposite of everything we've been playing all day. More delicate. More personal. And way less radio ready.

Bruce slides in our burned disc and my acoustic guitar and voice fill the room like a scented candle whose aroma doesn't quite fit the mood. As the song plays, I catch the exec and Cassie trading micro looks.

"Good song," Bruce says during the fade out.

"Thanks," I say.

"Who's the lucky guy who lives two doors down?" he asks.

"Nobody," I say, wondering what he would say if he knew it was about a girl with mushy pea green eyes who works two doors down from me and smells like rosewater.

What any of them would say. Especially Cassie. "It's just made up."

"It's quite a departure from everything else, don't you think?" the Shore executive asks.

"Or maybe everything else is a departure from this," Walden says, chiming in for the first time. In his voice, I can hear the coiled tension he's been holding back all day.

"I'm just saying—"

"I know what you're saying," Walden says. "But this is *actually* her music. Unlike the bullshit you've been having her sing all day."

And, scene.

"Who writes these things?" I ask, the record contract's words washing over my eyes and eluding my understanding.

"Lawyers," says Walden, popping a handful of Smartfood and swigging from a Dr. Pepper.

Note to self: Being offered a record contract is more fun than reading one.

On the hotel TV, Bruce Wills is fighting terrorists with bloody bare feet.

After the session, Cassie took us back to the Shore offices for more meeting and greeting, then out to a sushi restaurant whose aqua colored walls were lined with enormous tanks teeming with exotic fish. I ate octopus and eel. I had a tiny sip of Cassie's warm sake. I fumbled my chopsticks. As we were hugging goodnight, Cassie handed me an envelope.

"Ta da," she said.

"Is this?" I asked, bringing my hands to my mouth like a girl being proposed to.

"Go over it with your parents," she said, nodding, smiling. "Take notes. Write down any questions you have. And then we'll talk next week."

She hugged me. I hugged her back.

"I know today was a lot, but you were amazing. It gets easier."

What gets easier? I thought. *Pretending to be somebody else?*

By the time we got back to our hotel room, I felt wrung out like a wet rag.

The contract's most salient points are easy enough to comprehend. A three-album commitment. A twenty-five-thousand-dollar advance against future profits, making me wonder about the extra thousands they were prepared to spend on my dad's medical bills and how often details are left out of contracts. But the other five pages of tiny type, broken into sections and sub sections and sub-sub sections, not to mention a comprehensive array of footnotes, might as well be written in Swahili. I wish my mom was here to help me go through it. To tell me that it's totally normal to be excited and scared and confused all at the same time.

"What does that mean, against future profits?" I ask.

"An advance isn't free money," Walden says. "It's a loan to live off while you make the album and then pay back when the album starts earning money. But you don't get any more money until the advance is paid off. In other words, don't blow it on a sports car because you might need it to buy milk."

"What if the album doesn't earn as much as the advance?"

"No clue," Walden says. "But I wouldn't worry about that."

I twiddle my thumbs and eat some Cool Ranch Doritos and drink my Coke. Bruce Willis shoots one of the bad guys and then jumps through a window. I have so many conflicting emotions about today. So many things I want to say.

"I asked Cassie what would happen if I refused to sign without you," I say.

"Really?" he asks, sounding genuinely impressed. "And?"

I shrug. "She said things would get more complicated. And slow way down."

"In other words, it's totally not worth it."

"I don't know. Maybe. It didn't sound good." I shrug. "Sorry," I say.

"Yeah."

"I don't know what to do."

He's lying on his stomach on his bed, facing away from me, but now he turns toward me for the first time. I brace for one of his patented *I told you so* diatribes, but instead he only throws a piece of popcorn that hits me right in the eye.

"Ow."

"That didn't hurt."

I throw the popcorn back at him and he smiles as it misses his face by a foot. I'm so grateful for my brother right now that I feel like if I tried to explain all the reasons why,

I would crack into a million pieces and float up into the ether.

There's a knock at the door and Walden and I look at each other nervously.

"Room service," calls a voice.

Walden pads over and opens the door where a sharply dressed hotel employee is standing with a basket. Inside are a bottle of sparkling cider wrapped in a bow and chocolate covered strawberries packaged in an elegant gold box.

"Who's it from?" I ask.

Walden hands me a small card and I read it aloud.

"Here's to a bright and successful future together. Welcome to the family. Everyone at Shore Records."

"Man, the big time is a really weird place," he says, chomping on one of the strawberries.

"Surreal," I say.

"Want some bubbly?" he asks.

"Definitely."

Track Nine
Can You Sign This?

I wait for the strange aftertaste of my bizarro-world day at Electric Lady to grow sweeter with time. But it doesn't. It turns sour, and a little bitter.

Pretty much everyone—Mom, Dad, River, Evan, Mia—agrees with Walden's assessment that Cassie and Shore are a bunch of "blood sucking leeches," a description that's way too harsh, but one I don't correct. Mom says I need to be more assertive in telling them what I want. With my sound. With Walden. She makes it sound so easy. As if I can flip a switch and bend Cassie and the entire situation to my will.

The only person who thinks I'm being shortsighted is Murph, my parents' best friend and longtime manager, who I invite out to lunch without telling my parents and swear to secrecy in exchange for her honestly. "Sounds about right to me," she says when I walk her through my experience in New York. "It's showbusiness, Rainey. What did you expect? There are always tradeoffs. Nobody gets out with their purity entirely intact. Certainly not your mom and dad, so let me pop that bubble for you right now. You should have heard some of the arguments I had with Elektra back in the day about your mom's hair and clothes. About your dad's drinking. His weight for Christ's sake. About whether or not they should be more affectionate on stage. And that was before we started arguing about the songs. You can't blame Shore for wanting to get the most out of their investment. You can't afford to be that naïve. And your voice really is that good."

"But I want to use it to sing my own songs," I say.

Murph shrugs as she stirs two Sweet'N Lows into her iced tea. "They're in the record selling business, first. The art making business second. Contracts are all about compromise."

"You're saying I should sign?"

"Not necessarily. I'm saying you shouldn't hold out for the fairy tale or you'll end up waiting forever. If you do the first album their way and it goes well, think of the leverage that will give you for the second."

"What about a smaller indie label?"

Murph pops the last of her burger into her mouth and licks some ketchup off her thumb. "More integrity, way less money. They may let you make the record you want to make, but they won't have any money to distribute it so good luck getting into Tower Records, let alone paying the bills. For every indie band that makes it big, Nirvana or whoever, there's a million dead bands by the side of the road with their guts hanging out."

I tell her about Walden's plan to start our own label and do everything ourselves.

"That's what your parents did fifteen years ago when

Elektra wanted them to change their sound too much," Murph says. "Going it alone comes with even fewer guarantees. And no support. You'll have your integrity, but you may not have much else."

"I'm really glad I called you, Murph," I say.

"Sorry, kid." She signals for the check. "My back hurts and I'm entirely incapable of bullshit."

A few days later, I get a postcard in the mail. It's from Nina in Boston.

Yo! I meant to write by now, but classes have been crazy. Just wanted to say you <u>better</u> still be coming to Boston next year. We are going to RUN this place. I'll keep the Cherry Garcia on standby.

Something about her excited tone makes me feel excited too. And the memory of my day with her in Boston is still one of the only lights in a series of dark tunnels. For the first time, going to college and giving myself a few years to figure out my life begins to make sense. Would it really be so bad? I dig out the BU course catalog and flip pages. I look at the list of majors and wonder which one is me. *This is good*, I think.

I make a list.

Potential BU Majors:
1.   English
2.   Environmental Science
3.   Communications
4.   Sociology
5.   Teaching
6.   Journalism

7.   Radio and Television
8.   Biomedical Engineering
9.   Anthropology
10.   Physics

Within a couple of days, though, my mind drifts back to Shore and the contract. Maybe Murph is right. Am I really going to throw out a record contract with one of the country's biggest labels because my artistic integrity feels threatened? What kind of childish thinking is that? But then "Maybe Forever" starts playing on a loop in my head, or I re-read Nina's post card, or I think about the executive saying, "I don't want her stuck behind a piano," and I'm right back on the merry go round.

Two weeks later, River and I are working on a new song after school when Walden brings in the mail. River and I put our guitars down and walk into the kitchen. Walden hands me an envelope postmarked from Boston and stamped with the BU logo. The envelope feels thicker than one page, which I've heard is a good sign. Rejections are always short.

I crack the seal, pull out the pages, and start reading.

"I got in," I say. "And my scholarship was approved. It will cover about half my tuition."

"Try not to sound *too* excited," River says, picking up the metal Tom the Turkey off the counter and tossing him up in the air like a football, then setting him back in position between his decorative gourd body guards. Tom has puffy white feathers and a wry grin on his face, as if he's not about to be butter basted and roasted with herbs. It's not much, but even any level of holiday-themed decorating is a major feat for my mom.

"I am," I say. "Excited."

"But…"

"She already knew she was going to get in," Walden says, getting a Coke out of the fridge and cracking the seal. "She just doesn't know what the hell she wants to do about it."

"Ahh," River says, holding up his index finger, "the age-old question man has been struggling to answer since the dawn of time. Whether to take the scholarship to a top university or sign the deal with a major record label while you're still in high school."

"Don't be a dick," Walden says. There's not much force in his voice, but I can't help but grin. I secretly love it when Walden sticks up for me.

"I'm just saying you pretty much can't go wrong."

"And yet, somehow that doesn't make it any easier," I say.

River picks Tom the Turkey back up and positions him atop one of the gourds like he's a cowboy and the gourd is his horse, then moves Tom back and forth in little up and down riding motions. While Tom has his ride, River whistles the Lone Ranger theme song, lost in his own little world. Walden and I exchange glances. Walden rolls his eyes. River already admitted he smoked a joint in his car on the way over, but this routine speaks for itself.

"Can we stay focused here?" I ask.

"Sorry," River says, then snaps his fingers and gets an excited look on his face. "Wait. I got it. Do you have any envelopes? For mailing letters?"

"I think so, why?" Walden asks.

"I have an idea," he says. "Go get the contract."

When I come back from my bedroom with the Shore contract, I find Walden rummaging through a couple of drawers in the kitchen until he comes out with two plain white envelopes. River takes the envelopes from Walden, then puts the folded-up contract in one, and the BU acceptance packet in the other. He licks and seals both envelopes.

"What the hell are you doing?" I ask.

"Destiny is a fickle thing, Rainey," he says.

I start shaking my head, fighting not to laugh.

He puts the envelopes behind his back, moves his hands around as he sings, "*Mixing up the letters, mixing up the letters, I'm mixing up the letters, yeah!*" He then pulls them back out and holds them out to me, one in each hand. To the naked eye, it's impossible to tell which is which. It's actually quite startling how completely the envelopes hide their contents.

"Choose your fate," River says. "But choose wisely, young Jedi. The balance of the entire universe depends on it."

He's being ridiculous, but there's something so tantalizing about the prospect of choosing one of them, of letting chance take the wheel, that my heart starts to race. I reach out for the one on the left.

"Not that one!" River shouts, scaring the crap out of me, and we both crack up.

Walden is having none of our shenanigans. "This is so stupid," he says, and heads toward the back door. Before he closes it behind him, he says "I'll be in the studio."

River hands me the letters.

"Well," he says. "It was just an idea. In case you get really desperate."

"I am really desperate."

He shrugs. "I have another joint in my bag. Always helps me think."

"Yeah, about whether there's life on other planets, or which Jimmy is better, Page or Hendrix."

"Page all the way," he says. "Wait. No, Hendrix. Shit. They're both so good!"

"River!"

"Rainey!"

He's so infuriating, but somehow so sweet that I literally stomp my feet.

"C'mon," he says. "I have a freshly-rolled think machine sitting there in my backpack. I'll go get it, we'll light it, inhale it into our bodies, and the answer will magically come to us."

I shake my head.

"I promised."

"You know he will never find out unless you're stupid enough to tell him, right?"

"I might be that stupid," I say. "And that's not really the point. I'll still know."

"And then you'll feel guilty?"

"Yes."

"You always do things the hard way," he says.

"I do not."

"Okay." He picks up Tom the Turkey to do God knows what with him. "My mistake. I must be thinking about somebody else."

"Here's what I don't understand," says Rachel Pena, pushing up her sleeve and popping a fry into her mouth. "Why would you go to college if you could be a rock star instead?"

"Yeah," Clara says, tearing open and swigging from a carton of chocolate milk, "that doesn't even make any sense."

After swearing them to secrecy, I finally brought the Pena Twins up to speed on my current predicament in hopes that they might help me see through the fog.

I shrug. "Maybe I don't want to be a rock star," I say, stealing a glance at Clive Brewer's lunch table. Since the Neptune hand-holding gaffe, looking at Clive's lunch table has turned into a full-blown obsession of mine. Enough time has passed that I should be able to relax by now, but I can't seem to let it go. I keep waiting for the moment when the truth comes screaming out and it all falls apart.

"Says the girl who smashes her guitar and dives into the freaking crowd," Rachel says.

"*Like* a rock star," Clara finishes.

"That was a one-time thing. And, if you recall, the

reason I came to this school in the first place was to try to get away from music and all that."

"You're not doing a very good job," Rachel says.

"Yeah, you're kind of shitty at that," Clara says.

"Not helpful," I sing-say.

"We can't change who we are, Rainey, not in here," Rachel says in her best after-school special voice, patting her heart.

I roll my eyes. Now that the season is over, I don't have to hear about soccer much, but the Pena twins have moved on to their second favorite topic: planning out my life for me.

"Look around," Rachel says, waving a limp fry to all corners of the cafeteria. "I'll wait."

I look around, then back at Rachel. I'm just glad Evan isn't here today or he would find this even more ridiculous than I'm finding it.

"You see all these people? Every single one of them is going to end up living a boring ass life."

"Bor-ring," Clara says.

"They just don't know it yet."

"No clue."

"But not you," Rachel says.

"Not you girl."

"You're different. You have a chance to be famous, chica."

"Famous!" Clara says.

"And rich and shit."

"But Shore wants me to totally change my sound," I

say. "And my look. I'm afraid if I sign with them, I won't even be able to recognize myself after a while."

"Yeah, because you'll look like somebody famous," Rachel says.

"And rich," Clara adds.

"It's not as guaranteed as it sounds," I say. "My parents have been professional musicians for thirty years and they're broke. My mom works in a law office."

"Your mom works in a law office?" Rachel asks.

"Which one?"

"I don't even remember." I wish I hadn't mentioned my parents. "I'm just trying to keep my options open. Besides, even if I do go to college, music isn't going anywhere."

"That's not the point," Rachel says. "Any of these chuckleheads can go to college, but none of them can do what you do."

She sounds just like Cassie.

"You gotta strike while the iron is hot," Rachel adds. "That's all I'm saying."

Clara licks the tip of her finger, then presses it against Rachel's now outstretched hand. On cue, they both make a loud sizzle sound.

I love these girls, but they're really not helping.

Mercifully, the bell rings, rescuing me from the Pena Twins. I drop off my tray, then turn the corner to head to class and nearly walk right into a wall, which turns out not to be a wall at all, but the massive, muscled torso of Clive Brewer.

"Sorry, shit, sorry, it's my first time walking," I say,

briefly looking up and making eye contact with Clive, then skirting quickly around him and practically running away.

"Wait, um, Rainey?" he calls out. I turn. "You got a second?"

His voice is higher than I remember. But he's as undeniably handsome as a daytime drama love interest, with a square chin, big eyes, and bullet proof hair. And the way his biceps bulge against the fabric of his sweater draws my eyes in a way I seem to have no control over.

"Sure? Okay," I say, swallowing as he closes the distance between us.

Oh my God, oh my God, oh my God!

"I should have done this the other day," he says. "When I saw you at the Neptune."

My heart jackhammers in my chest so hard I expect to see my shirt rising and falling.

"Done what?" I ask, certain this is the moment he's going to say it. *I know what you're hiding.*

But instead, he unzips his backpack and reaches inside. "Can you maybe sign this?" He pulls out and hands me the CD sleeve from *The Treehouse Tapes*, my first album.

In a daze, I accept it, looking at the picture of me up in my treehouse, looking straight down at the camera, my red hair vibrant against the snowy background.

"My sister thinks you're awesome," he says, finding a pen in his backpack and handing me that too. "But she's too chicken to ask you for an autograph. She's in ninth grade. It's her birthday pretty soon. And I thought this would be a cool present."

"Oh, okay," I say. "Yeah, sure. Who should I make it out to?"

As I stand there signing my autograph for Clive Brewer's little sister, whose name is Sarah, by the way, I realize that I have officially stepped through the looking glass.

Track Ten
Can I Change to Dare?

"Dare," I say.

Mia takes off one of her black Chucks and hands it to me. With a candle between us on the coffee table, an oversize shadow of her does the same thing across the treehouse wall.

"Lick the bottom of my shoe," she says, trying to keep a straight face.

"No way!"

She shrugs and reaches out to take her shoe back. "Then I guess I win."

I shake my head, then, after examining her shoe bottom to find the least disgusting looking corner, close my eyes and quickly lick it with the very tippy-tip of my tongue. I taste grass and rubber, but not some of the other horrible tastes I was imagining. I swish a huge swig of Coke around in my mouth, then toss her shoe back to her.

"Impressive," she says.

"Your turn."

"Dare," she says.

"You're brave."

"I trust you."

"That was your first mistake," I say, but don't know what to make her do. We've already both made each other run around in the freezing late November rain. She made me smell her armpit and I made her put Coke up her nose with a straw. Neither of us has chosen Truth yet, and the longer we avoid it, the more I can feel the stakes of the game slowly increasing. Suddenly, I have an idea and I feel underneath the loveseat until I find an ancient wad of gum that either Walden or I stuck under here when we were little kids.

"What are you doing?"

I pick at the wad until it gives with a snap, then hold it out to Mia. "Chew this."

"You're sick," she says.

"Says Little Miss Lick My Sandal."

"For how long?"

"Ten seconds."

She accepts the gum from me, deep uncertainty in her eyes. This is the girl who always needs fresh cream because she's so afraid of other people's spit, and for a second, I think she's not going to go through with it. Then, with a cock of the head and a heavy swallow, she pops the gum into her mouth and chews it while counting off ten seconds on her fingers. Then spits the gum into her palm before balling it up in a tissue.

"Wow," I say. "That was impressive."

"Still minty," she says and we crack up.

It's the Sunday after Thanksgiving, and Mia and I have been together all afternoon and now well into the evening.

We hit the Neptune, then snuck into Sullivan Street Jeans using Mia's key and continued to dream of all the ways Mia could re-arrange the store if she's able to buy it even though her mom still won't budge. Eventually, Mia took me home, then, at my mom's invitation, stayed to have dinner since Mom was making her famous chili with sausage and peppers. She also made a tray of cornbread and picked up some ice cream for dessert.

After helping do the dishes, we went out to the treehouse to listen to music, confounding my parents when we grabbed chips and sodas on our way out, both of them saying, "We just had dinner!" We were halfway through Nick Drake's *Pink Moon* when Mia looked at me and said, "Truth or Dare?"

"Okay, your turn," Mia says.

I pause before saying it, hoping I'm ready for whatever comes next.

"Truth."

"What was her name?" Mia asks, as if she's been waiting for the chance. "Your first girl?" Mia crunches some Doritos and swigs her Coke.

It seems amazing we haven't talked about this yet, and suddenly, it strikes me there might be a good reason we've talked so little about our romantic pasts.

"Juliet," I say, picturing Juliet's dark hair and pale skin. Her confident, gorgeous grin. How I felt like I was floating six inches off the ground the first time our lips touched on a dark beach with Lake Michigan purring out in the distance. Juliet wasn't just my first kiss with a girl. She was my first kiss period. Everything about it—about her—is still so vivid in my memory. Even the sound of Juliet's name evokes the smell of Freesia-scented body lotion. Makes me crave Nutter Butters and grape soda. Makes my heart ache a little bit for the memory of how she made me feel.

"Were you her Romeo?" Mia asks, a sweet hint of jealousy in her voice.

"Hardly," I say. "She and her sisters were all named after Shakespeare heroines."

"What does she look like?"

"Dark hair. Skinny. Shorter than me."

"Do you have a picture of her?"

I shake my head, wondering if I would want to show Mia even if I had one. "Just this," I say and dig a Polaroid out of an envelope. The picture has faded in the two years since it was taken, but still shows what it always has. Two traced handprints on a bedroom wall with the words *Juliet and Rainey Were Here* written beside them.

Mia takes in the photo and I wonder what she's thinking. "What happened?" Mia asks.

"Nothing," I say. "Everything. First love. Heartbreak. We don't even talk anymore. She lives in Michigan."

I can tell Mia wants to ask me more, but instead she hands me back the Polaroid and says, "Truth."

"Have you ever done stuff with a boy?"

I know it's kind of stupid, but I really want to know.

"Stuff?"

"You know what I mean."

I expect Mia to say no, but instead she nods in the affirmative.

"You *have*?"

"Twice," she says. "And that was enough. I consider it my own little beta testing."

"Tell."

"When I was thirteen, this boy named Derek kissed me at camp. That one doesn't really count, though, because it was just a peck. But the summer after my freshman year, I made out with Andy Stevens in the woods behind his house. He had a pool and a bunch of us went over. We were playing hide and seek and it was really dark. Somehow, we both ended up hiding behind the same tree. He said he thought I was cute and then we kissed. I didn't even like him, and I already knew I was into girls, but it was just one of those moments."

"Was kissing all you did?"

"No, we had sex."

"You *did?*"

"No!" she shouts. "Of course not. I was thirteen! But it was dark and everyone else was hiding. I let him feel my boob for five seconds and he totally got...you know. I saw it when he stood up."

"What?"

"A stiffy," she whispers, on the verge of cracking up.

My hands fly over my mouth. I can't help it.

"And that was the end of *that*," she says, dusting her hands off. "Wait, have you? Done stuff with a boy ever?"

"I've kissed a couple. And one touched my boobs, but there were no stiffies involved."

"How do you know? It's involuntary. And they get them all the time. I'll bet you just didn't know it."

"Gross," I say.

Pink Moon ends and I exchange it for the Avocado Tape that Mia made me last week. The cosmic, dreamy opening of Radiohead's "Subterranean Homesick Alien" comes on and Mia grins. Even though it's only been out for a few months, Mia recently proclaimed *OK Computer* one of the top five albums of the 90s, and I might agree with her.

"Good taste," she says.

"Okay," I say. "Your turn."

"Truth."

This time, I know exactly what I want to ask her.

"What did you mean that time when you said you were easily manipulated?"

"What?"

"At the Neptune, a month ago maybe, you said take it from someone who's easily manipulated. It was that day Cassie and I bumped into you in the street."

Her face sinks as she re-discovers the memory, and the weight of what it would mean to share it. Now I have to know.

"I change my mind, dare," she says.

"No way!" I say, knowing I might have finally found the key to hearing the secret side of how Mia ended up back home. I feel desperate to know, and a little scared.

At this point, I'm fairly well versed in the broad strokes of Mia's failed and deeply unsatisfying experience at RIT. The way she tells it, when she first got to college, the whole thing just felt off. Like she'd been mis-cast in a movie, given a part that should have been played by somebody else. Her whole life, she'd been a good girl. Done all the things she was supposed to. Gone to school, taken honors classes, gotten excellent grades, stayed out of trouble. But at college, she found herself distracted by this nagging suspicion that she wasn't supposed to be there. That it was all a game she didn't want to play anymore. She said she was torn between two sets of polarizing emotions, one side telling her she wasn't good enough and was going to fail, the other side telling her nothing she was doing really mattered. She started skipping classes and her grades started going down, putting her scholarship at risk.

The part I've heard far less about is the part that has to do with Leslie, the junior TA from her finite math class. I know they had a short fling that didn't last, but I've never been able to unearth the "stalker" part of the story that Walden heard about from Bethany, who heard about it from her friend. The closest Mia has come is when she admitted that she "sort of lost it." I've wanted so badly to hear the full story, but until now, it never felt fair to ask.

"I don't even know where to start. It's so stupid."

"I doubt that," I say.

"It's kind of a sad story. So, it may ruin our game."

I shrug.

"Okay," Mia says. "I'll tell you. Last fall I was in this finite math class."

I nod. I've heard this part before.

"The TA was this girl named Leslie, who was a couple of years older than me, and we started hanging out. Dating, I guess."

"Wait. How did you know that she was even available?"

"I could just tell," she says. "Can't you tell?"

I shrug. "I don't know. How do you know?"

"You just know. It's a feeling."

"Can you tell that I am? Is it obvious?"

"Honestly, not really," Mia says. "Although, it's hard to say because I already knew."

I wave my hands. "Sorry, I totally hijacked your story."

"It's okay. Anyway, we hung out for a couple months. She wanted to be really careful, so we always went to her apartment off campus. It was fun. And easy. We always watched movies and ordered Chinese food and stuff. I thought we really liked each other. At least I knew that I really liked her. More than that, even. I loved her, I guess. I'd never felt that way before. I had no control over my emotions. Have you ever felt like that?"

I nod.

"And then one day she totally changed. I'd go up to her after class and she'd be cold to me. Or I'd call her and she'd be weird, acting like she was too busy. I didn't understand. It made no sense. One day, I got mad at her on the phone. I don't remember exactly what I said, but I know I called her a bitch and she told me to leave her alone. I've told you how I was already struggling at school."

I nod again.

"I think this put me over the edge." She pauses, as if to gather her courage or arrange her memories in the right order. "After class one day, I followed her. I know it sounds super creepy, but I just wanted to talk to her. I wanted her to tell me why. I figured she was going to her apartment, but instead, she went to this condo on the other side of town. I waited outside for a while, wondering what to do. I should have gone home. Clearly it was over, whatever it was, but I couldn't let it go. I was just so gone. In her. I couldn't think about anything else. I was in a trance and I couldn't come out of it. Finally, I went up to the house and rang the bell, but instead of her, this man opened the door. It took me a second, but then I recognized him as one of the professors in the math department. I don't think he recognized me, but before either of us could say anything, Leslie walked up behind him. She looked at me, then said, *can we help you?* As if she'd never seen me before. The man asked if I was okay. I think he could tell that I wasn't. I walked away without a word. Why would someone do that to another person?"

"I don't know," I say.

"I went back to my dorm. I was so full of rage. And shame. I drank a whole bottle of wine in five minutes. I wanted everything to go away." Mia swallows. Her eyes grow moist with tears. "I had these pills," she says, her voice quavering, threatening to crack, "to help me sleep. I started taking them in high school because I used to have insomnia. There were only five or six left in the bottle, but I took them all at once. Then I immediately ran to the bathroom and stuck my finger down my throat and threw them all up, along with all the wine. I wasn't trying to kill myself. It might sound hard to believe, but I really wasn't. I've never had a suicidal thought in my life. It was just a stupid impulse. And nobody would have known. I would have gone to bed and had a horrible hangover the next morning. But my roommate came home while I was in the bathroom and found the empty pill bottle and the wine and she freaked out. She told our RA, who made me go to the hospital and then she called my parents."

Mia finishes her Coke.

"My mom came and got me, and the next day I was back here in Fairview with my tail between my legs."

"I'm sorry," I say, knowing those words don't even come close to capturing the hurt I feel knowing the pain and confusion she must have felt. "I'm sorry all that happened to you. I knew college hadn't been what you wanted it to be, and your grades and stuff, but I didn't know that—"

"I shouldn't have told you," Mia says, shifting uncomfortably. She looks like a wilted flower. "You probably think I'm so weird now. Some diseased creature. I'm sorry. Why do I always ruin everything?"

Her voice shakes with a sorrowful anger.

"Stop it," I say. "Don't say that. I don't think that." The truth is that I do feel a little rattled by Mia's story, but I don't want her to see that. And I know that I've just been trusted with something really important. "I really don't. That's how I felt when Juliet broke up with me. Out of control. I thought I would never get over it. It was horrible."

"River doesn't know, okay," Mia says. "About the pills or anything. Please don't tell him."

"I won't. I promise." I reach out my hand and Mia takes it. I tug gently and she gets up and comes over and sits down next to me. Her body seems totally limp, like a silk shirt on a hanger. I wrap my arms around her and she puts her head on my shoulder and cries.

"It's okay," I say, drawing circles on her back with my

palm. Over and over again. Just these slow little circles. "You're okay. I'm right here."

Track Eleven
This Time

My name floats through the darkness, gradually pulling me from sleep. The first thing I see is the orange numbers on my bedside clock (3:25), followed by my mom's face, softly back lit and rimmed by a halo of hallway light. She has her glasses on and her hair in a pony tail.

"I'm taking Dad," she says.

Only this time I don't ask where she's taking him. And this time they don't come home.

Every day, Walden picks me up from school and we drive to the hospital in Burlington, then take the elevator up to the 4th floor and sit in hard plastic chairs in Dad's room.

Sedated on heavy pain killers, Dad sleeps most of the time, and when he is awake, he's utterly miserable. Every time he comes to, it's as if he's awoken to find an elephant standing on his chest. Gripping the bed sheets with nervous fists, his eyes look big and afraid. A mossy layer of angry gray stubble encircles his chin. I cradle his clammy hands and tell him that he's okay, that it's going to be okay. But I don't believe it anymore.

My mom practically lives at the hospital, often bringing stacks of work files along. She makes me go to school during the day. I drink tea with Mr. Larson, who knows what's happening, but doesn't make me talk about it. He tells me my teachers will understand if I need my work excused under the circumstances, but I force myself to go to class, to do my homework. I know it's what my dad would want me to do. In AP English, we're reading *The Adventures of Huckleberry Finn*, which is basically about a kid trying to make the right choices in a world that's sending him mixed signals. Is it that art imitates life, or the other way around?

In the evenings, Mia comes over and we watch stupid action movies and mindless comedies. Sometimes, when Walden is gone, either out with Bethany or helping do sound at Club 182, Mia and I make out in my bedroom, kissing by the glow of a vanilla scented candle that makes the room smell like freshly-baked sugar cookies. With my dad fighting for his life, it feels impossibly selfish doing anything that makes me feel good, but it's also the only time I get a break from my fear and sadness. The only feeling strong enough to make me forget for a little while.

It's weird how life doesn't stop, even when your dad is dying. The world doesn't seem to notice at all. The sun sets. The sun rises. You still have to brush your teeth and put on clean underwear and eat breakfast. Django needs dog food in his bowl and his arthritis medicine stuffed into a hunk of hot dog to relieve the pain in his ancient joints. The carpet needs to be vacuumed; the toilet needs to be scrubbed. Kids go to class and teachers teach and it all keeps going while you sit there feeling like you're the only real person in the world.

One night, in the vanilla darkness, Mia and I take off our shirts and lay skin to skin, our bodies puzzle pieces nestled together. Her skin is impossibly warm and soft against mine, fragrant of rosewater, and I never thought it would be possible to love someone else's skin this way. Its softness and shape. Tracing its contours with my searching fingertips. Even the simple fact of its existence feels like a miracle. A gift I could never fully repay.

Mia's mom still won't budge on the loan and Mia isn't sure what she's going to do.

"We had a phone call with an admissions lady at RIT," Mia says, "and apparently, I still have my scholarship if I want it for next school year. They have a second chances policy."

"Oh," I say. "That's nice."

Mia shrugs. "I don't really want to go back to school. But maybe I should just do it, get my stupid mom off my back, and then reassess my life in a couple of years."

The thought of her leaving makes my heart ache. And I'm surprised to hear her even considering going back to school or abandoning her dream of buying Sullivan Street Jeans, but I also know how exhausting it is to live every day battling a tide of uncertainty.

"My mom says that I'm hiding from life," Mia says, absently winding a lock of my hair around her index finger. "That I need to face my demons, whatever that means."

"Do you think you are? Hiding?"

"I don't know," she says. "Maybe. Probably. But aren't we all hiding from something?"

One day, my dad's oncologist, Dr. Rudy, invites us into a separate "family" room and, after asking us to sit down on a strangely firm cornflower blue couch, tells us we should say goodbye to my dad. That we should start accepting the fact that he's probably going to die soon and we need to take whatever steps we can to prepare ourselves. He says the word *die* like it's any other verb. Eat. Play. Sleep. Die. Just things that people do.

"He's been so resilient, and he may respond to this latest round of immune boosting medicines," Dr. Rudy says. "But his symptoms, especially the dyspnea, which is that very labored breathing, are very concerning."

So, we say goodbye. The words feel impossible but they come out anyway.

Mom meets with the hospital's hospice coordinator, who urges both Walden and me to stay in the room because medical information is hard to process when you're stressed, and it's better if more than one person hears it. The hospice lady talks to my mom about portable bed options. About how to arrange for visiting nurses to come to the house to help. About how their job is to help my dad "be as comfortable as possible at the end."

My mom's new insurance policy will pay for Dad's hospice care, but not his days in the hospital. One day, I overhear Mom talking to Murph about selling more memorabilia to private collectors.

"I'm incapable of feeling sentimental," my mom says at one point. "I just need the money, Murph."

I bring my dad's white '57 Telecaster to the hospital. It's his number one, the guitar he bought for two hundred bucks when he was twenty-two and has spent over half his life playing like an extension of his body. I hold the case up to Dad, but he shakes his head.

"You play," he says.

"Any requests?" I ask, trying not to cry as I unlatch the Tele's battered case, which is scuffed and peeling at the corners, worn from a million road miles.

Dad shakes his head. On the windowsill sits a tiny fake Christmas tree Walden and I bought at the pharmacy yesterday. When you press a little button, the tree lights up.

I play "White Christmas" and "Jingle Bell Rock" and "The Christmas Song." I play "I'll Be Home for Christmas" and "River" by Joni Mitchell. We all sing them together, all four Cobbs singing in easy harmony the way we do, and before long, a collection of doctors and nurses has wandered into the room or crowded into the doorway to sing with us. The melodies are bittersweet in this place, but there are more smiles than tears. Music, as always, is magic. A light in the darkness.

Track Twelve
You Never Came Down

Christmas morning dawns clear and bright with a fresh dusting of snow on the trees and more coming down like big white confetti. I wander out to the living room where Mom is sitting on the couch drinking coffee alone. In the far corner sits the Christmas tree Walden and I bought from a guy at the gas station a few days ago and decorated by ourselves, trying and failing to feel festive as we strung the colorful lights and hung the usual ornaments. Under the circumstances, it felt about as meaningful as doing the dishes. On the floor, a small sprinkling of presents, far fewer than usual, rings the tree like a shirt collar.

"Merry Christmas, honey," Mom says.

"Merry Christmas. Wow, the snow is so pretty."

"Yeah, it sure is," she says wistfully.

I pour myself some coffee, then join her on the couch where we watch the snow through the bay window that looks out on the front yard. The snowflakes are dense and fat, so big you can almost see their intricate shapes and delicate designs as they fall.

"How long have you been up?" I ask, having my first sip of coffee.

"Just a little while," she says, but her tired eyes tell a different story. She has her hair down, though, and it looks especially red in the stark morning light, as if it's captured some of the snow's shimmery radiance.

"How was the night?" I ask.

"Not bad. Better than the night before. He was only up a couple times. We did okay."

I sip my coffee, trying to remember the last time I woke up and felt the magic of Christmas the way I used to when I was younger. That bubbly sense of excitement so big it could make your fingertips tingle and keep you awake half the night. Maybe it was because we were always on the road, or because we were homeschooled and didn't have other friends our age, or because my parents were weirdo hippies, but my family was one of those families that skipped Santa entirely. I remember watching Christmas movies as a kid and being confused by all the fuss everyone made about a big jolly guy in a red suit.

From the start, Walden and I knew that all the presents under the tree were bought with hard-earned money and that whatever presents we received were the result of some sort of sacrifice and effort. I know that doesn't sound very magical, but it was. My parents would often buy our Christmas presents throughout the year, picking up trinkets and interesting items at antique stores and unusual shops as we drove across the country and back again. Part of our Christmas morning ritual was in hearing the stories behind our ragtag assemblage of gifts. I still have the 50's-era antique piggy bank my parents bought from a flea market in San Antonio and gave me for Christmas a long time ago.

Our presents were rarely shiny and new, but always interesting, always meaningful.

"The stockings aren't up," Mom says.

"That's weird." I survey the exposed nails beside the fire place. "I guess Walden and I forgot them."

I hustle down to the basement and find the stockings stuffed into an old paper grocery bag. The stockings, green and red and white with images of snowflakes and snowmen and presents stitched into their slender bodies, were handknit by my grandmother when I was little, and I hang them as they always hang, from right to left by age. Rainey. Walden. Tracy. Luce.

As I hang my dad's stocking and read his name, it's impossible not to think about the fact that it's probably his last Christmas. Our last Christmas as a whole family. Will we still hang his stocking after he dies? What do you do with a person's stocking after they die? For that matter, what about their sweaters and their socks? With their guitars and their records? With all of it? By the time I sit back down, there are tears in my eyes.

"Come here," Mom says, patting the sofa. She puts her arm around me and I lay my head on her shoulder. I don't think we've lain this way for years, snuggled up like a single organism, but I don't ever want her to let me go. We sit there quietly for a long time before, eventually, Walden wanders out and then my dad calls from the bedroom for my mom's help.

An hour later, we're opening presents.

Django gets a rawhide bone as big as his head that he immediately wrestles to the ground and starts chewing. As always, he's oblivious to all the subtext around him, happy just to be here, among his people, in beautiful bliss.

Using saved-up gig money, I bought my mom a leather wallet and my dad a pair of L.L. Bean slippers that are fuzzy on the inside. I also got Walden a new Sony Discman because his recently broke. Sliding his hand over the Discman's smooth surface and slipping the provided headphones over his ears, Walden looks unusually touched.

"That's really cool, thanks Rainey," he says.

Dad puts on his new slippers and smiles.

"I'm never taking these off," he says. He's been home from the hospital for four days, his condition only slightly improved. He often wears his oxygen mask and fights through haggard coughing fits, but being home has eased something inside of him.

"This is for you, too," I tell my dad, giving him a final present I've kept hidden in my room. I'm nervous watching him open it, hoping he doesn't take it the wrong way, but I really wanted him to have it today.

When he first holds up and examines the hospital bracelet belt, which I was finally able to finish a few days ago when I snagged a final bracelet from his bedside table, he seems unsure of what he's looking at. Then his eyes catch sight of something familiar, and he realizes that each of the plastic bracelets has his name on it. I've strung them together with fishing line, and finished the belt off with a simple spring clasp.

"These are all my hospital bracelets," he says. "You saved them?"

"It's a belt. I thought maybe it could bring you good luck."

"Wow," he says, wrinkling his mouth and biting his lip. "I don't know what to say. It's amazing. Thank you." He buckles the belt around his sweatpants, joking "Who needs belt loops?"

When it's my and Walden's turn, my mom gets teary watching us open our gifts.

"I haven't had any time to shop," she says, shaking her head. "Sorry guys."

We each get a new book, the unabridged *Les Misérables* for me and *The Count of Monte Cristo* for Walden, plus a new pair of cozy flannel PJ pants. We hug her and Dad and tell them they didn't have to get us anything. That we understand.

"Hang on, I think we missed one," Walden says, giving me a coy look as I clean up the few scraps of wrapping paper dotting the floor.

"Pretty sure that's everything," I say.

But then he reaches into the corner behind the Christmas tree and pulls out a black guitar gig bag with a small red bow on it, which he hands to me.

"For me?" I ask, looking at the space behind the tree, unable to believe I hadn't seen the guitar hiding there in plain sight. He must have tucked it back there late last night.

"Your name is on it," he says, and I look at the tag, which says: *To Rainey, From Santa.*

With excited butterflies in my stomach, I slide open the zipper and pull out an ice blue Fender Jazzmaster with a brown tortoiseshell pick guard and attitude to spare. A Jazzmaster has a curvy, double cutaway body that's sexy and rugged at the same time. Elvis Costello plays one, and Tom Verlaine from Television. But I've only recently started wanting one ever since I found out that J. Mascis from Dinosaur Jr. plays a Jazzmaster. And J. Mascis rules.

"How?" I say, looking at Walden.

"How should I know?" Walden says. "Talk to Santa."

"C'mon."

"I've been helping my friend Rob with some recording projects. He asked if he could pay me in trade."

"Are you serious? This is really for me?"

"Just try not to break this one," he says, making my dad chuckle.

"Wow," I say, sliding the Jazzmaster's cut-away groove over my right leg and plucking out a few notes. I strum a G chord. The guitar is polished and gleaming, the neck smooth and fat and easy beneath my hand, perfectly worn from years of playing. Used guitars actually feel better than new ones, like slipping into a perfectly broken-in pair of jeans. I feel an instant connection. It just feels right. I'm in love.

"Thank you," I say.

"Merry Christmas," Walden says.

Moving slowly, but adamantly re-assuring us that he's up to it, Dad makes biscuits and sausage gravy for breakfast. We gluttonously devour two helpings each, sitting by the fire and listening to Christmas records on the turntable. Nat King Cole. Sinatra. Stevie Wonder. We stay in our sweatpants all morning. My Aunt Becky, my mom's younger, and only sister, comes over with a stack of gifts and a plate piled high with her famous homemade buckeyes. So does Murph, who comes bearing whiskey and wine. We all pile into the living room and watch *White Christmas.* We eat too many buckeyes and nosh on a spiral cut ham drizzled with maple glaze and Murph's famous Spam macaroni salad on the side. Don't knock it till you've tried it.

Between movies, I plug my new Jazzmaster into an amplifier and we all take turns playing it, agreeing it sounds and plays absolutely amazing.

"There's some magic in that guitar," Dad says and passes it back to me. "You're going to write some classics on that thing, I can feel it."

In the late afternoon, Mia comes over. After she says hi to my family and I show her my new guitar, we build a snowman in the fresh snow, powdery but just wet enough to hold its shape.

"How come nobody ever builds a snowwoman?" Mia asks, after we've secured a carrot for a nose and two rocks for eyes. We tie a purple scarf around our snowwoman's neck, then snap a frilly red tutu around her waist that I find in a box of costumes in the basement. We give her some pine boughs roughly arranged for a punk rock hairdo, a couple of oranges for boobs, then for the finishing touch, stuff one of my dad's cigarettes into her mouth.

"Her name is Marge," Mia says.

We can't stop laughing.

I give Mia a book of Emily Dickinson poems. She gives me a hand-knitted pair of mittens.

"You knit?"

"I'm learning. My mom is really good and she's trying to teach me. I think they're actually two different sizes, so don't get your hopes up. Merry Christmas, babe."

"Babe?"

"Yeah," she says, grinning, meeting and holding my gaze. "Babe."

I nod, liking the sound of it. "Babe," I say. "Okay."

After Mia leaves, we play Monopoly and eat more ham and a big bowl of buttered popcorn. My mom and Murph drink too much whiskey, and Aunt Becky tells embarrassing stories about when she and my mom were young. Eventually, we all end up crowded around the piano singing songs with my mom and I taking turns on the keys.

My tears from early this morning are the only ones shed, and it's the best day I can remember in a long time.

A few days after Christmas, my dad wakes up with a fever that won't break. He hobbles around the house like a drunken sailor. He's weak and irritable. A visiting nurse comes over in the afternoon to bathe him and help him change his clothes while my mom is at work at the law office. I watch the nurse confidently helping my grouchy dad, changing his shirt and pulling socks over his feet, sponging down his pale torso and combing his hair. I feel utterly powerless and afraid, amazed by her confidence and comfort with his ravaged body.

Cooped up together for too long, Walden and I start to snap at each other in a familiar pattern. It always used to happen on tour. We'd start strong, playing cards and chess all the time, trafficking in well-worn loops of inside jokes and sarcasm. Then, right around the middle of the third week, when his cologne and the smell of his farts had permeated every article of my clothing and every last strand of my hair, and he complained that I was taking up too much space, we started to get short with each other.

It doesn't help that a terrible winter storm blankets the entire state of Vermont, nearly two feet of snow falling in a single night, followed by temperatures plummeting into the single digits. It's so cold we can barely leave the house. We let the taps drip-drip-drip overnight to keep them from freezing. It also doesn't help that every time Walden catches me pondering the contents of my two naked envelopes, he gets agitated. He's been more supportive than I could have asked, but even still, I overhear him tell my mom that I'm dragging the whole thing out to get attention. That everybody already knows what I'm going to do. *Except me*, I think.

On New Year's Eve, something snaps in me. I can't take it anymore. Watching my dad practically disintegrate. Watching my mom try to stay strong. Watching my brother seethe in silence. Trapped in our tiny house with its chronic lack of privacy, I feel the intense need to be alone. To be free from everything around me. Just before midnight, I grab my letters and my Walkman and step out into the frigid, sub-zero December air, then plod through the thick snow and up into the treehouse for the first time since Mia and I played Truth or Dare after Thanksgiving.

Sitting down on the love seat, I click on the camp lantern, hoping the batteries still work. They do. *Let there be light.*

I slip my headphones over my ears, which are shielded from the cold beneath my thick wool beanie, then press play on Elliott Smith's *Either/Or* for the millionth time, which starts up in the middle of "Between the Bars." *Let there be sound.*

I pull the two white envelopes out of the inside pocket of my winter coat and toss them down on the coffee table, one beside the other, identical in the soft yellow light. Bright white and blandly official, they stare right back, utterly indistinguishable from one another.

Let there be decision.

Eeny, meeny, miny—

Thump. The treehouse trembles with sudden sound. I yank my headphones off and click the stop button, thrust suddenly into a deafening silence. Is it midnight already? But even after a minute, there's no sister sound to follow the first, which means it can't be the fireworks. Not yet, anyway.

So, what in the hell was that? For a second, I wonder if I imagined it. But I know what I heard, what I felt.

"Hello?" I ask stupidly, trying to make sense of the noise, which I'm nearly sure came from outside somewhere.

Curiosity has me first down the rope ladder, then back into the heavy snow and the winter wind. That's when I see it. A small raven, still and silent atop a crystal white blanket, looking entirely out of place there on the ground. Holding up the lantern and bending down to get a better look, I can see that one of its wings is broken, twisted unnaturally down and off to the side in a way that turns my stomach. The bird's neck is similarly off its axis. Snapped like a twig.

I look up at the side of the treehouse, then back down at the smashed raven, wondering how a creature with such finely tuned senses didn't see something so large. For a second, I wonder if the raven did it on purpose just to be free of this miserable weather. I watch the bird, waiting for I don't even know what, until my ribs rattle painfully with the cold, but the raven's chest reveals no movement. Not even a final tremble.

Now feeling really good and freaked out, I go back up to the treehouse and wait for my heart to slow down. The envelopes are still sitting on the coffee table where I left them, staring at me, interrogating me, daring me. I feel immobilized, utterly stuck and unsure of what I should do. Which future I should step into, wondering if it even matters, hating that my dad won't be there to see it no matter what I decide.

"I don't know what I want, okay," I say, fighting tears. "You tell me."

There's another sound outside, echoing and far away. Which means that, just like that, it's officially 1998.

I lay back and listen to the fireworks, which make the whole world tremble. The treehouse pulses and it's like I'm stuck in a snow globe and someone is knocking on the glass.

"Happy fucking New Year," I say to nobody.

When my dad steps into the treehouse, for a second I'm sure

it's a dream. But he's really there, bundled up in his winter coat, heavy gloves, and rabbit fur hat, shaking with cold, and winded from the climb—yet wearing an unexpectedly mischievous grin.

"I came to make sure you hadn't gone into cryo-freeze," he says, trying to catch his breath. "What are you doing out here, Rain Man? It's freezing."

"I don't know," I say, my eyes darting to the two envelopes. "I guess I just—"

"Wanted to be alone?"

"Kind of."

"I'll go," he says. "Just wanted to make sure you were okay. Don't stay out here much longer, okay. It could be dangerous."

"Don't go. Please. Stay."

Dad nods, then rubs his hands together and slowly eases himself down into the chair across from me. I hate how I've gotten so used to the sight of him in pain, straining through even the simplest physical task. But he hates it when we try to over-help or baby him.

"I was kind of hoping you'd say that," he says. "That rope ladder is impossible. Who designed that system?"

"Pretty sure you did."

"Not a chance," he says.

He looks down at the envelopes, then back up at me.

"Have the envelopes spoken?" he asks.

"Not yet."

Dad nods. For obvious reasons, we haven't talked much about college or the record contract the past couple weeks. I know he worries about me, and knows I'm managing a lot, but his sickness is all consuming, sucking the air out of everything.

"I passed a dead raven in the snow on my way out here," he says.

"I saw it," I say. "Talk about a bad omen."

Dad shakes his head. "Not necessarily. In a lot of cultures, ravens are symbols of transformation and rebirth."

"Even dead ones?"

"Well," he says chuckling, "I guess it's all how you look at it, but sure, why not?"

His eyes wander up to the ceiling and the mural he and my mom painted. As his eyes roam around, I see them stop on the Polaroid of me about to jump in the puddle. Slowly, he gets up and un-pins the picture, studying the image of his young daughter.

"I love this picture," he says, his thumb gliding over the image of me.

"I found it in all the stuff you had in the studio. I thought it was kind of cool."

"Your mom took this," he says. "We were having a picnic in Phoenix, I think it was, and there was a big rain storm that chased us all inside this huge church. We were playing downtown somewhere and the venue had arranged for an outdoor barbecue lunch for all the bands. I remember Kenny Loggins was there. And Bill Withers. Maybe it was a festival. Anyway, just as we sat down to eat, the sky opened up and we all ran inside this church with our plates of chicken and whatever. When we came back out after the storm, the sky was that incredible baby blue that it sometimes is after it rains, and there was a huge rainbow.

The biggest one I ever saw. It filled up the whole sky. But you didn't care, you just couldn't wait to jump in all the puddles. Your mom grabbed the camera and caught you on the first one."

He hands the photo back to me and I re-pin it to the wall.

"That's how I always think of you, Rain Man," he says. "Up in the air somewhere, floating, hovering above it all."

"I'll bet I made a hell of a mess, though."

"Impossible," Dad says, shaking his head. "You still haven't come down."

He reaches out and I put my hand in his and he squeezes it. I squeeze back.

"It's freezing out here," he says, and we both start cracking up at how cold we are, our mingled breath like smoke from a fire. "Should we go back inside and thaw out?"

"Yeah," I say, then, seeing the cover of Mia's mix on the table, I make a spontaneous decision. "Wait. Dad, I want to tell you something."

"Okay."

Looking into his eyes, which are sunken and tired but still so full of the love and kindness that has protected me my entire life, I don't feel afraid anymore. I just need him to know. I need him to know before it's too late.

"You know my friend Mia," I say.

"Yes," he says, saying the word slow, sounding confused.

My heart is pounding and my hands start to tremble.

"We're, uh, kind of, more than just friends. She's

actually my...girlfriend. I guess. Yeah, so, I wanted to tell you that."

"So, you?"

"Like girls. Instead of guys. For dating and stuff." I steel myself to say the two stupid little words that I don't want to hide from anymore. That I need to prove to myself I can say. "I'm gay."

"Okay."

"Okay?" I'm not sure what I thought my dad's face would do when I finally told him all this. But he looks far calmer than I expected. As if he knew it was coming. "It's really okay?"

"It's really okay," he says. He rubs his chin and goes inside himself for a moment. "Rainey, I love you more than life itself. And there is nothing you could ever do or say that would make me love you any less than that. I just want you to be happy. That's all I've ever wanted. But thank you for telling me."

"Mom doesn't know yet," I say. "Or Walden."

He puts his finger up to his lips. I smile.

"Happy New Year, Dad."

"Happy New Year, honey."

"I love you."

"I love you too."

Track Thirteen
How Can the World Still Exist?

My dad, Lucien James Cobb, dies in a portable hospital bed in our living room on January 9th, 1998 at ten in the morning. We're all there when he takes his last breath. His eyes are already closed.

When he dies, something dies in me too, slips out of me like steam from a cup of tea. I feel reduced. Diminished. Less than.

We make arrangements. We have a funeral, but not a burial because my dad wanted to be cremated, followed by a huge bash at the house full of friends, family, and dozens of musicians, some of whom my mom has known for close to thirty years, and some of whom are famous and have songs playing on the radio somewhere right this second. There are stories and lots of singing. There are guitars and banjos and gorgeous voices in soaring harmony. There is too much wine and whiskey, and enough tears to fill an ocean.

Somehow, my mom holds it together. Turns herself into a sponge that soaks up the grief and memories that pour out in a flood. I don't know how she does it, but she does. Witnessing first her strength and stoicism, and then the inevitable release after the mourners have said their goodbyes and she wrings herself out, is almost more than I can stand.

She sacrificed everything. Her passion. Her happiness. Not to mention the momentum she was building in her solo career. She gave all of it up to take care of my dad, but has nothing to show for it but a dead husband and a mountain of bills to pay.

When I look around the dinner table and see we're no longer a quartet, but a trio, that's when it starts to feel real. Meet the Cobbs. Tracy, Walden, and Rainey. Luce doesn't live here anymore.

I force myself to say the words. Hoping that if I can get more comfortable with them, it won't hurt so much. *He's dead. My dad is dead. My dad is dead. My dad is—*

But words are only words.

The three of us endure long silences and re-heated meals where we barely exchange a syllable. My dad's chair glares at us. A cruel joke. Empty as a dried-up lake. My mom tells me I need to eat, but I pick at my food like a baby bird. Walden practically lives at Bethany's apartment, a one-bedroom on Locust Street. I barely leave the house. I live in my sweatpants. I read books. Watch movies. Drink endless cups of coffee until my nerves are frayed and humming. My mom and I briefly revert back to a state of physical intimacy that we haven't shared since I was a little girl. Powerful magnets drawn together, we spend hours wrapped in each other's arms, tangled up like the wooden planks of a house after a tornado has blown it apart. I cry so much I don't even know where the tears are coming from anymore.

My mom just lets me cry. And she doesn't tell me it's going to be okay. I love her so much for that.

Desperate to help, to relieve some of the pressure, I beg her to re-consider Shore's offer to pay for the hospital bills. I'd sign for five albums if it could make the pain go away.

She shakes her head, then wipes away my tears with the sleeve of her sweatshirt. "It's taken care of," she says. "You don't need to worry about it."

"Taken care of? How?"

It turns out that even though my dad didn't have health insurance, he did have life insurance. A one hundred-and fifty-thousand-dollar policy he'd been quietly, but persistently maintaining over the past twenty years.

"I never even knew," Mom says. "Sneaky bastard."

The payout will cover my family's extensive debt to a hospital that couldn't save my dad but will gladly accept half of his life insurance. I don't blame the doctors and nurses who did their best, yet the logic feels cruel. But the relief in knowing my mom won't be saddled with my dad's hospital bills for the rest of her life is immeasurable. Maybe then someday she can fly again.

Mom says that she's going to work at the law office for a little while longer, then reassess. Walden and I urge her back to music.

"We'll see," she says.

I tuck my matching white envelopes into my dresser. Cassie sends flowers and calls me three times, but I don't feel like talking to her.

"I miss him so much," I tell my brother. "It hurts so bad I don't know what to do. I can't take it."

"I know. I miss him too."

I tease out chord progressions on my Jazzmaster and scribble scraps of bruised, broken lyrics. They're not full songs, at least not yet. Right now, everything feels too unresolved, so I compose incomplete melodies and unfinished choruses.

Mia and I go on endless drives. Sometimes we talk, sometimes we kiss and do other things, but mostly we listen to music. We listen to The Sundays and Indigo Girls and Dinosaur Jr. We listen to Ida and Fleetwood Mac and Cocteau Twins.

I curate and co-host a classic blues night for Mia's radio show, then a Motown night. I'm surprised how much I enjoy talking into the microphone, introducing the songs and then saying little things about them. Sharing the music that I grew up hearing and playing; the music that inspired my parents to make their own. When I play Ma Rainey, I find myself opening up about her, this early blues singer I'm named after. How her real name was Gertrude Pridgett. The Rainey came from the man she married. How she was born in 1886 and died in 1923. How her gravelly singing style lives on through Louis Armstrong and Janis Joplin. How she wrote a lot of her own songs, which was pretty uncommon for blues singers in those days.

After the show is over and the microphones are off, I tell Mia the rest.

"Ma Rainey was bi-sexual."

"No way, really?"

"She was married to a man, but she wrote lyrics about female lovers. And legend has it she had a fling with Bessie Smith."

"I love her even more now."

Almost every night, Mia and I wind up at the Neptune Diner where we sit in the same corner booth and Pat brings us the usual.

Every time I see a family eating together across the restaurant, or someone out for pie and coffee with their dad, I feel a rush of anger, not understanding why they get to have their dad but I don't. I'd give anything for one more day. One more hour. One more minute.

"I wish I knew how to make you feel better," Mia says, re-arranging the salt and pepper shakers and rotating the pitcher of fresh cream so that its handle is out.

"Just being around you helps. It's the only thing that helps."

"Then I'm here," she says. "As much as you need me."

I start wearing the hospital bracelet belt I made for my dad. The fishing line snaps one day, so I shore up the bracelet with some heavy duty paracord.

I go to school. When the bell rings, I go to my next class. I write down my homework in my notebook. The Pena Twins tell me dirty jokes at lunch and dip their fries in salty ketchup. River offers to get me high (I decline). Mr. Larson makes me chamomile tea with honey.

"I feel numb," I tell him. "I was so sad at first, and now I just feel numb."

"That's how I felt when my dad died," he says. "I

thought there was something wrong with me, like I was doing it wrong."

"Your dad died?" I ask, surprised.

He nods. "Skin cancer. When I was in fifth grade."

"I'm sorry," I say.

"It's okay."

"How long did it take until you felt better?"

"Honestly, I don't even know," he says. "I just know that I did. Eventually. And so will you, Rainey. I promise."

That's when I lose it.

How do you do this? Please tell me. How do you lose the most important person in the world and then keep living your life? How do you wake up tomorrow and the day after that? How do you move on?

I don't know. But somehow, that's what I do. What we do. Seconds become minutes become hours become days become weeks.

The hole in our lives doesn't go away or get filled up. It never gets any easier, but somehow, we learn to live with the pain. To carry it around with us.

We learn to keep living anyway.

Track Fourteen
Puddle Jumping

Like love and heartbreak, death has a funny way of pulling songs out of me. Two summers ago, when I was fifteen and I'd just gotten home from spending a week with Juliet at her family's resort on Lake Michigan, songs began pouring out of me. I'd sit up in the treehouse and practically take dictation, caught in a trance as melodies and words flooded my brain. Some were love songs about Juliet. Okay, a lot of them were love songs about Juliet. But some, like the "Anger" songs, were about my mom, and how I felt about things in general. How I felt stuck in my life as a homeschooled kid who played full-time in the family band and had logged a million road miles before I hit puberty. How I just wanted to be normal for a change. An ordinary girl. All the emotions I poured into those songs broke free from their melodic vessels and spilled out into my life. They led to me quitting the family band and going to public school for the first time.

All I wanted to do was blend in and disappear. To get out of the spotlight. I felt so strongly that was the right thing. But like nearly everyone in my life has pointed out,

I've done a pretty lousy job at blending in and disappearing. Almost two years after a Nirvana-obsessed girl who wore purple lipstick made me the greatest mixtape of all time and inspired me to change my life, I'm left wondering, for the first time, if I did the right thing. And what does it mean for future decisions if my own internal compass doesn't even point me in the right direction?

In the weeks after my dad dies, I slowly, at first, and then very-very quickly, transform the scraps of melodies and broken lyrics in my notebook into nine brand new songs, most of them in the Elliott Smith-inspired vein of "The Magicians" and "Two Doors Down." I disappear into the same type of creative trance as I did two summers ago.

When I first wrote "Jesus Wears a Blonde Wig," a new musical direction opened up. A tablespoon of Ramones, a dash of The Breeders, a sprinkle of The Clash. But I can see now that "Jesus" was only a rage-fueled detour, not a new homebase for my songs. Rage can eat you up inside, and I don't want to live that way.

I listen to Elliott Smith even more carefully, trying to figure out how he does it. I listen to the Beatles, too, spinning *Rubber Soul* and *Revolver*, those mid-60s albums when they were on the bridge between Beatle-mania and psychedelia, thinking about something my dad said. About how the Beatles started their songs quickly, but finished them slowly.

I sit on my bed with my legs crossed and my head down, playing the songs on my Jazzmaster over and over again, looking in the corners and turning over the stones. Bringing the butterflies safely into my net.

I experiment with layered vocals and lush harmonies, sometimes not doubling but tripling my voice, then soaking it in reverb until it sounds like a choir beneath an inch of water. I write the most vulnerable lyrics I've ever written. My emotions feel raw and naked. I couldn't hide them if I tried, so I don't try. I don't worry about whether or not they're radio ready. I just stay open, and let them come. The muse is never wrong.

Walden and I basically move into Paradise Avenue over February break. We live on Cokes and hot dogs and boxes of Little Debbie snacks. For days on end, we don't consume a vegetable or even leave our property. But we record a whole album in a single week.

At night, Walden does quick mixes of what we recorded that day. River comes over and lays down lead parts. I let him get more experimental, and encourage a long solo over the extended, droning outro of a song called "Coin Toss." Walden swells the mix behind River's solo, the music getting louder and louder until you almost can't take it anymore. When the music finally cuts out, the sudden silence is even louder than the preceding riot. It has to be the album closer.

Evan comes over, but only once. He likes the new music, but it's when he says, "I'm really happy for you, Rainey," that I can feel the way he's beginning to write himself out of this particular story. He has a girlfriend now, this short, smiley, studious girl named Samantha who's new to our school this year. They sit together at lunch and hold hands in the hallway and bond over math proofs and prog rock and spend all their time together, perfecting their homework and analyzing Tool and Yes albums like Bible study.

And, River informs me, recently losing their virginity to one another with the help of a condom River gave him.

"You mean, Evan..."

"Did the deed," River finishes. "Our little boy is all grown up."

I try not to be hurt that Evan didn't tell me himself. Truthfully, it's nice to get a breather from the full weight of Evan's affection, but I also feel sad not to have him around as much. And yes, a little jealous that he found a girl he likes more than me. Petty, I know, but it's the truth.

As River would say: *emotions are a fickle thing, Rainey.*

Walden spends the first two weeks of March mixing and mastering the album's ten tracks, which add up to a run time of thirty-six minutes and fifty-eight seconds. It's the exact same run time, down to the last second, as *Either/Or*, a subtle tribute to Elliott Smith we achieve by drawing out "Coin Toss" to be almost seven minutes. Walden barely knows who Elliott Smith is, but he's willing to humor my obsession.

We sit in the studio and listen to the songs over and over and over until we can't think of ways to improve them. I can still smell Dad: cigarettes, Budweiser, Old Spice, and the rich, musty tang of old paperbacks. His memorabilia, much of which has been sold, is still piled against the wall. His white '57 Telecaster sits on a stand in the corner collecting dust.

"I can't even tell if it's good anymore," I say about a

song called "The Day Before Tomorrow" after we've listened to it five times in a row.

"That means it's done," Walden says.

The songs hold up a mirror to my life over the past six months. Every one of them is about Mia or my dad, at least in one way or another. There's a sister song to "Jesus Wears a Blonde Wig," a sweet and sour ballad called "The Thing Around My Neck." A poppy number called "Snowwoman" that's got jangle piano and bells that could have been an outtake from *Pet Sounds*. For the album cover, I choose the mid-air picture of me as a little kid, the one my dad says he loved so much and remembered so well.

I call the album *Puddle Jumping*.

When the first box of CDs arrives in April, I smile and trace my finger over Walden's hand drawn logo on the back, tucked down there in the bottom right. Treehouse Records.

I read the track names. Then the credits.

Music and lyrics by Rainey Cobb.

Recorded, produced, and mixed by Walden Cobb.

"Our second album," Walden says. "Too cool."

For the sleeve notes to *The Treehouse Tapes*, I wrote my lyrics into a schematic of a brain, divided up into nine sections, one for each song. I do the same thing for *Puddle Jumping*, except the schematic is the shape of a heart.

"It feels a little Valentine-y," Walden says, when I first show him the sketch.

I change the heart's shape to be less greeting card perfect and more biology textbook raw. And then make it black with the lyrics in white. At the very bottom, in print almost too tiny to read, I write: *For my dad.*

"Are you going to send Cassie a copy?" Walden asks.

"She'd probably hate it."

"That's how you know it's good," he says. But I don't share his bitterness. I don't blame my confusing roller coaster ride with Shore records on Cassie. And I don't blame her for being cold to me when I finally call and tell her I'm not going to sign with Shore because I want to see how far my own songs can take me—at least for now. I blame myself for being too naïve to see what was right in front of me. I should have known it the second I sat down in that make-up chair in New York City and let them take off my jewelry.

To celebrate, Mom takes us to Ponderosa and we all eat huge steaks and steamy baked potatoes smothered in butter and sour cream. Walden and I get hot fudge sundaes for dessert delivered in tiny baseball helmets. Walden gets the Brewers. I get the Houston Astros.

"Your dad would have loved this so much," my mom says, wiping away tears.

When we get home, we play Yahtzee and listen to records and really laugh together for the first time since Dad died.

As we're putting the score sheets and dice back into the box, I look up at my family.

"I have something I want to tell you guys."

So, I do. I say those two words again.

"Oh my God, I have goosebumps," Mia says. "What did they say?"

It's the next night and we're at the Neptune, tucked into our usual booth.

"My brother reacted like my dad did," I say. "He was classic Walden. Supportive. And cool. But kind of muted."

"Your brother's so mysterious."

I shrug. "I guess so."

"And kind of cute. If I wasn't gay..." she says and I hold up my hands.

"Okay, stop! Stop right there. That's so gross."

"What about your mom?" Mia asks, giggling. "Did she freak?"

"A little bit, at first," I say, remembering the way Mom's eyes widened when I said *I'm gay*, and she nervously folded and re-folded a cloth napkin. "She asked me if I was sure."

"They all do that," Mia says. "They hope it's just a phase."

"She said she needed a few minutes to let it soak in. But then later on, she said she loved me and she was glad I told her."

"Rainey, that's amazing," Mia says. "My dad lost his shit and wanted me to go to therapy so they could talk me into being straight. You should be more excited."

"She did say this one thing that kind of made me mad, though. She said the world is a cruel place and that she didn't want me to get hurt. She said that life is hard enough."

Mia shrugs. "The world is a cruel place. And this does make it harder. You'll see."

"I guess." Every once in a while, Mia says something

that reminds me that, even though we're so close and have so much in common, we're at slightly different places in our lives.

"Hey," Mia says energetically, perhaps sensing my shifting energy, "you didn't get disowned and that calls for a toast." She holds up her water glass, which I clink with my own.

"To not getting disowned," she says.

I laugh. "To not getting disowned."

Pat comes by and pours us coffee, and as usual, asks if we want the usual.

"Actually, I'd like a slice of apple pie," Mia says. "With some vanilla ice cream. But can you put the ice cream in a dish, please, instead of right on the plate?"

"Really?" Pat asks, looking shocked. "No Swiss fries or gravy or nothing?"

"No, thank you."

"What about you?" Pat asks me, as if we're playing a practical joke on her.

"I'll have apple pie and some ice cream too. But you can put the ice cream on the same plate."

"The pie will get soggy," Mia says.

"I like it like that."

Mia shakes her head, aghast at the thought of ice cream touching her pie crust, then turns to Pat. "And can I please have some—"

"Fresh cream, I know," Pat finishes. "Be right back."

I reach into my bag and pull out a copy of *Puddle Jumping* that I've wrapped in Christmas gift wrap, which was all I had. After Mia rips off the paper, she holds the CD to her chest, then cradles it, gazing down at the picture of me. Using her fork, she pries the shrink wrap loose, then opens the CD case and looks through the booklet, at the heart schematic, which she'd already seen in concept, but not yet the finished version.

"I can't believe you just made an album and now I'm holding it in my hands," she says. "Hardly anybody ever does things, really does things, but you do."

I shrug, trying to seem casual, but glowing from her excitement and praise, feeling that happy weight in my chest that Mia makes me feel.

"When's the album release show?" she asks.

"Next Friday. At 182."

Pat brings out our pie, and I'm about to take a big bite when Mia waves me off. After reaching into her purse, she stuffs a birthday candle into the center of my pie.

"My birthday's not until May," I say.

"Yeah, but we're celebrating. We have to do it right." She lights the candle, then looks deeply into my eyes. "Make a wish, Rainey."

The album release show for *Puddle Jumping* is the band's first show in almost six months. It's hard to believe it's been half a year since I was on a stage. Since I smashed my Telecaster. And impossible to fathom that my dad has been dead for almost four months. Four months is 121 days. It's 2,904 hours. It's 174,240 minutes. And he's been gone for every single one of them.

Some days I make it all the way to dinner and the sight

of his empty chair before I remember he's gone and I have trouble breathing for a few seconds. Some days it's worse, and when I wake up, I've swallowed a bucket of lead and I can't stop crying.

Poser gives me a huge hug and tells me how much he loves the new album.

"Even if it only sells ten copies?" I ask.

"Don't sell yourself short," he says. "I'm sure it will sell at least twenty."

I punch him in the arm. He hugs me.

"Do you think I made a mistake?" I ask.

He shakes his head. "Are you kidding? You told a major record label to eat shit. Do you know how long I've wished I could do that. You're my hero. And you're still going to conquer the world, Rainey. It just might take five minutes longer now."

The show is sold out, but bittersweet. Since Evan isn't my manager anymore, and he's AWOL in Samantha-ville, he doesn't come backstage. During the opening act, I catch sight of him cuddled up with Samantha on the couches, lost in their own little world of two. I miss his nervous jokes, the protective look in his eyes before I go on stage. The way he steadied and calmed me just by being there and believing in me.

There's also the fact that River recently broke the news that he's going to Syracuse next year, and that this is probably his last show with us. He was accepted to a summer fellowship program and is leaving a few days after graduation for New York, and then the rest of his life. In six weeks, he'll be gone and who knows when we'll see each other again.

"The good news is that since I mostly just take up space in this band, you guys will have no problem replacing me," he says.

"I don't want to replace you," I say.

Walden is more circumspect and says he'll miss River, but that he also knows two or three guitar players he thinks will be able to handle River's parts. But with no River, and no Evan, will it even feel the same? Will it even be fun?

Now that I've officially decided I'm not signing with Shore or going to BU, Walden has started booking a summer tour to promote *Puddle Jumping*. Philly. D.C. Baltimore. Raleigh. He talks about loading up our gear and piling into Howard the Duck like he's fantasizing about a trip to the moon. But imagining all those long hours back on America's endless gray highways sounds exhausting. Sleeping in Walmart parking lots. Standing by the side of the road after Howard busts a tire or drains his battery. Scarfing McDonald's from paper bags. If I'd signed with Shore, Walden and I might be piling into a shiny new tour bus this summer instead of a thirty-year-old rusty RV. We might be booked into theaters and music halls instead of basement bars and tiny clubs. We might be opening for mid-sized bands on their way up. Walden says that once *Puddle Jumping* starts getting reviewed and catches fire, it's only a matter of time.

He may be right. I hope he is. But in the meantime, it's hard not to think about how River said I do things the hard way.

As we take the stage and I tease out the opening chords to "Ordinary Girl" on my keyboard, having decided to open with a familiar song to loosen up the crowd before filling their ears with new music, I scan the audience one more time to be sure.

Cassie Plimpton isn't there.

But Mia is, perched behind the merch table, wearing a T-shirt with my face on it and looking up at me with those green eyes.

After the show, Mia and I get pepperoni slices at Mr. Matt's and eat them off paper plates as we walk the darkened, tree-lined streets of Burlington. It's a cool night, and I'm glad I grabbed my cardigan before we left the club.

"The new songs sounded so good," Mia says, nudging up the sleeves of her jean jacket between bites. "And people were buying the new CD like crazy." A light breeze tickles and lifts the tips of her blond hair, somehow shiny even in the darkness. It's funny, and kind of wonderful, the way her compliments still send butterflies through my stomach.

I love you, I think. The words bubble up like carbonation in a can of soda. Rising, rising.

"Thanks," I say.

We walk all the way up Main Street to the broad palatial green that fronts the University of Vermont along University Terrace, my heart beating fast from the incline. A fat three-quarters moon perches low in the sky like a partially eaten wheel of cheese. Mia pulls me down onto the lawn, claiming her feet hurt and we lay side by side looking up at the stars—bottomless, endless, perfect—our fingers just barely touching through the tall grass.

"I want to tell you something," she says without looking over.

"Okay."

She's quiet for a moment and I turn and look at her. She looks back.

"What is it?" I ask.

"Nothing," she says, giggling. "I forgot."

"You're so weird."

"You're weirder."

I wiggle through the grass and kiss her. She climbs on top of me and kisses me back, cradling my neck in her hand and gently massaging me as we kiss. I put my hands on her hips and love the feel of her, the weight of her, the sureness of her. Nervously, I look around between kisses, but the green around us is empty, and so are the sidewalks.

We kiss some more and then, as her face hovers above mine and I feel electrically connected to her, as if our bodies are tethered by invisible strands of buzzing thread, the words rise up and slip out. I'm not sure I could stop them even if I wanted to.

"I love you," I say, my voice barely a whisper. My heart is hammering and I look past her as I say the words.

"You do?"

I look back. Our eyes meet.

"Yes," I say.

"I love you too."

And then we melt and melt and melt into each other.

Track Fifteen
Most of Us Can't Just

"Well, what's this for?" Grandma Rose asks as Mia secures the paper Burger King crown atop her head, carefully arranging it so it doesn't mess up her freshly done hair, which we've coiffed and styled.

"You're queen for the day, and every queen needs her crown," Mia says and Grandma Rose smiles proudly. I'm still burping up the Burger King kids' meal we ate on the way over to secure said crown.

Surprisingly, spa day was my idea. Mia said that her grandma was having a tough time lately, and remembering something my mom told me once, about how they used to paint her mom's nails when she was sick, sparked the idea in my mind. So, we grabbed some nail polish and makeup, cruised through the BK drive thru, and went to visit Grandma Rose.

We paint Grandma Rose's fingernails, and then her toes, both bright red, each of us working on one side of her. I've never painted someone else's nails, and I'm a little embarrassed at how clumsy I am. Several times I smear paint past her nail and onto the surrounding skin, having to wipe it off quickly with a Kleenex so it doesn't stain. But Grandma Rose doesn't notice at all. She's in heaven. Mia brought along a boom box and plays a Sinatra CD while we work. Grandma Rose sings "Fly Me to the Moon" under her breath, looking at us in wonder as she gobbles another truffle.

"Who are you again?" she asks me.

"Rainey. I'm Mia's friend."

"You've met a bunch of times, remember Grandma?" Mia asks.

"We have? If you say so. Don't ever get old girls, I tell ya. These golden years aren't all they're cracked up to be."

After the nails, we do Grandma Rose's makeup. Eye shadow. Mascara. It's while Mia is applying blush that Grandma Rose says, "I'm so proud of you, sweetie."

"Really? For what?" Mia asks.

"Your mother told me."

"She did? Told you what?"

"That you're going back to college."

Mia's eyes widen. She looks over at me, then back at her grandma.

"Aren't you?" Grandma Rose asks.

"Oh, no. Yes. I am. I just didn't know she told you."

"She tells me everything," Grandma Rose says, patting the back of Mia's hand. "She's so proud of you. So am I. It's time you made something of your life, honey."

Mia looks like she's about to cry.

"I can't believe she remembered that," Mia says as we're

driving away. "She can't even remember what she had for breakfast."

"You're going back?" I ask. "You decided?"

She nods. I remember when we were laying in the grass after my show.

"Is that what you were going to tell me? The other night?"

She nods.

"You said you forgot."

"Sorry. I didn't know how to tell you."

"But what about the store? What about your plans?" I don't add what I really want to say, which is, *what about me?* "How can you just give up so easily?"

"I'm not giving up. My mom wouldn't budge." I can hear her trying to stay calm.

"If you say so."

"What was I supposed to do?" Mia asks.

I can feel my sadness and shock sliding into anger. I try to stop it, but I can't.

"I don't know, try harder."

"Well, we can't all be perfect," she says. "Not everybody's dreams work out as neatly as yours."

I can see that she wishes she could take it back. That her words and her meaning haven't aligned.

"What are you talking about? My dream was for my dad to get better, and now he's dead."

"I didn't mean it like that," she says, gliding her finger down the driver's side window. "I'm sorry. I wasn't talking about your dad."

"Then what did you mean?"

"I don't know. Let's just forget it."

"What, you think that I think I'm perfect or something?" My palms feel sweaty. The car feels too tight.

"I sometimes think you don't realize how easy things are for you."

"Are you actually being serious? Literally nothing is easy for me. I feel like I have weights tied to my feet."

"Oh my God, open your eyes!" Mia says, raising her voice in a way I've never heard before. "School is easy for you. Music is easy for you. You think your life is so tough all the time, and I know losing your dad has been horrible, but most of us can't just turn down record deals and scholarships because making a decision feels inconvenient."

"Wow," I say. My heart hammers in my chest, a wounded animal fleeing for its life. Seconds pass. A minute. She reaches out for me, but I yank my hand away. "Don't touch me."

I'm angry about the hurtful things she said, but what cuts deepest is that I can't imagine my life without her, but clearly, she can imagine her life without me.

"I'm sorry, okay?" she says. "I'm really really sorry. But can't we have a little honestly once in a while without it being the end of the world? This is what it means to be in a relationship. Sometimes you blow up at each other. Tell me something terrible about me that's been on your mind. I can take it. That'll make us even."

Across the yard, Django watches us through the living room window with his nose pressed to the glass. My adrenaline is racing and I feel a cruel urge within me. I hate the way we're talking to each other, but I don't know how to stop.

"You're a phony," I say.

Mia huffs sarcastically. "Says the girl who's always pretending not to want the things she spends all her time trying to get."

"Fuck you," I say, then get out of the car and slam the door on my name as it leaves her lips.

Track Sixteen
I'm Starting to Question Your Commitment

"Okay, next question," Rachel Pena reads from a folded over copy of *Seventeen*, stuffing a fry into her mouth. "A girl you've never met in your life says 'what's up,' sits down at your lunch table and starts unpacking her Hello Kitty lunch box—"

"Oh, Hello Kitty no!" Clara says, cracking herself up, then upending the salt shaker onto a puddle of ketchup before dredging her fry and popping it into her open gullet.

Every day the Pena Twins dip their fries in too much ketchup, and every day it makes me think of Mia dipping her fries in too much gravy. It's weird how when your heart hurts and you're missing somebody, the world serves up constant reminders of that person. I never thought I'd feel nostalgic for the way somebody eats fries.

It's been a week since my fight with Mia, since her harsh reality check, since my *fuck you*. I still can't believe all the words we said to each other. How did things get out of control so quickly? One part of me never wants to see her again. Another part misses her so much it hurts. And yet another part is still rattled from the truth inside her words.

Just for the record, I don't think I'm perfect. And I'm doing the best I can. But I can understand how someone could look at me and, dead Dad aside, wonder what the hell I could ever have to complain about. And yet, also for the record, that doesn't make things easier.

I keep thinking that if only one of us would apologize, the fever would break, and we could go back to normal. Back to being us. The people who said *I love you* that night beneath the stars. But she hasn't even called. And every day it feels more impossible to pick up the phone and make the first move to make things right.

"Do you, A, offer up some Oreos," Rachel reads. "B, politely introduce yourself and your friends, but then roll your eyes when she's not looking. Or C, say, 'Excuse me, but do you have a reservation?'"

"Oh my God, C all the way," Clara says, laughing with her mouth open so that I can see a pale glob of half-chewed fry on her tongue. For near-adults who are headed to top tier colleges in the fall, Rachel to NYU and Clara to Vassar, the Pena Twins still have some seriously questionable eating habits.

"All the way," Rachel says.

"Reservation, that's too good," Clara says. "I'm totally using that."

"For all the girls that suddenly sit down with us?"

"You never know."

"That's true, you never know. There are some *weird*

bitches out there. Rainey, what do you think?" Rachel asks. "C all the way, right?"

"I really don't know," I say and take a small nibble of the tuna sandwich I made for myself this morning. It's a sad sandwich. Not enough mayo. Stale bread. I wash it down with a swig of chocolate milk, which only makes it worse.

"Girl, don't take this the wrong way," Rachel says, setting the magazine down and looking at me seriously, "but I'm starting to question your commitment to passing this quiz."

Clara snorts, then eats another fry.

"Those quizzes are kind of stupid," I say. In the past two weeks, we've taken quizzes on *Do You Have a Big Mouth, Which Hot Celeb You Should Be Dating, Does He Like You,* and *Are They Really Your Friends?*

"But how else are you going to know if you have too much attitude?"

"Do I look like I have too much attitude?" I ask.

The Pena Twins exchange a worried glance, the kind that I've been inspiring a lot of the past few months. Don't get me wrong, the Twins have been amazing. Listening to me. Trying to cheer me up. But just like after I got dumped by Juliet two years ago, I can't talk to anyone about my break up with Mia. River says he doesn't want to get involved, and even though Walden says he's there for me, he doesn't really know what to say.

Straight kids can broadcast their break-ups on the evening news and it's fine, even expected, but I'm forced to sit here and pretend nothing's wrong. Not to mention, if I told the Pena Twins that I'm on the verge of tears at lunch again because I'm heartbroken over a girl with eyes the color of mushy peas whose skin I love more than oxygen, I'm not sure if they would want to be my friends anymore. That's fucked up.

Across the lunch room, Clive Brewer sits stone faced beside a motormouthed Mandy Thompkins, who seems to be in the middle of a riveting story that she's telling with her whole body. At the next table over, Evan and his girlfriend Samantha are sitting alone, their bodies so close together they look like a four-armed sea monster. For two years, Evan sat in the seat right next to me. That one right there. Until he didn't. Until one day he told me he and Samantha were going to sit *over there* and I pretended I didn't care. It's been hard losing Evan, and the hardest part has been admitting to myself the way I took his friendship for granted. It all seems so clear in hindsight. The way I assumed he'd always be there to listen to me and care about what I had to say. To make me feel good about myself. I think this is part of what Mia was talking about. My selective blindness. How I get so caught up looking inward that I completely stop looking out at the world and the people around me. Evan thought I was so special that even I had started to believe him. Turns out what Evan really wanted was someone to love him back. It's been right in front of me for two years, and it's only now starting to make sense.

Note to self: Sometimes the heaviest truths are the ones hiding in plain sight.

The bell rings.

"Hey, I can ditch math," Rachel says, taking my hand.

I shake my head.

"I'm good."

"Girl, you do not seem good. You seem like you need to eat a whole bunch of ice cream and let it all out and I'm here if you need me."

"I'm okay."

"Are you sure?"

"Yeah, thanks you guys."

I'm dropping my half-eaten sandwich into the garbage bin when a voice calls out "Ask her!" Looking up, I find Evan and Samantha standing right in front of me, holding hands, lit up like a pair of glow worms.

"Ask me what?" I ask.

"What color tux do you think I should wear to prom?" Evan asks.

"What?"

"Tux. What color tux do you think I should wear? I think classic black is the way to go, but Samantha thinks I should wear—"

"A white jacket," Samantha cuts in. "I think he'd look so cute, don't you? With black pants and a bow tie. Like James Bond or something. Very chic." Samantha is short, barely five feet tall, with high cheeks and jet-black hair. She smiles a lot, and when she does, it takes over her whole face. Even her dark eyes and bright white teeth seem to be smiling. She's a nice girl who has done absolutely nothing wrong except fall in love with my best friend, which is why, on principle, I can't stand her.

"I really don't know," I say. "Just whatever will look good in the pictures."

"I'm telling you, nobody else will be wearing white," she says.

"*That's* what I'm worried about," Evan says. "The kids around here think I'm weird enough already."

Samantha nudges him playfully. "Are you going?" Samantha asks me. "To prom?"

"I doubt it," I say, making eye contact with Evan. He and I have spent the last two years joking that we would go to prom together since neither of us was ever with anyone. "Isn't prom still over a month away?"

"Yeah, but it's never too early to plan the perfect outfit," Samantha says. "I already have my dress. It's yellow, with lacy sleeves. It's so pretty. And Evan made us a reservation at Starry Night Café. He's such a romantic."

"Sounds life-changing," I say, trying to connect Evan with the word *romantic*, then skirting awkwardly around them. I hear Samantha say something, but I can't make out what it is. I'm halfway down the hallway when Evan catches up with me and pulls me into a little alcove.

"Why are you being so weird?"

"I'm not being weird."

"I just mean, are you okay?"

"I'm fine," I say. "You should get back to your dream girl before she sends out a search party." I hate the hurtful spite in my words.

"That's not fair."

I shrug.

"Don't be mad because I found someone who actually likes me back," he says.

"I'm not mad."

"You are. I know when you're mad. But you don't have any right to be."

"You knew the situation," I say. "I never asked you to like me that way."

"I didn't know the situation when I *started* liking you. Remember that part? How you let me like you for an entire school year before you finally told me? And it really messed me up, okay?"

"I didn't know how hard it was for you," I say.

"That's because you only care about how you feel."

"That's not true. I care how you feel. You're my best friend."

"Then please start acting like it."

We look at each other for a long moment, then he walks back down the hallway, links arms with Samantha, and disappears into the crowd.

In Chemistry, I start writing Evan an apology letter, but it doesn't sound right, so I tear it up and make a list about Mia instead.

Things I Miss About Mia
1. Her bizarre obsession with melted Swiss cheese. Who even likes Swiss cheese?
2. The way she really listens to me when I talk
3. Her incredible mix tapes
4. How she always wants fresh cream
5. The way she drives even slower than me
6. The way she twirls my hair around her finger without thinking about it
7. Her breath in my ear

8.   Her absolute belief that ghosts are real, even if nobody else can see them
9.   Her lips. Kissing her.
10.   Her mushy pea green eyes

In homeroom, I squirt some honey into my tea and stir it so long I lose myself in the spoon's metronomic circles until I can feel Mr. Larson looking at me.

"Sorry," I say, setting the spoon down.

"It's okay." He twists his wedding ring in a circle. Mr. Larson and Matthew aren't officially married because they're not allowed to be, but last summer, they exchanged vows and commitment rings. "I take it you two still haven't talked?"

As always, when we're talking about anything gay-related, I look around the room to be sure no one is listening to us.

"No. She hasn't called."

"And you haven't called her?"

"She started it," I say, not believing how childish I sound. "She's the one who jumped on my case first. She should call."

Mr. Larson opens his mouth to say something, but instead slides his fingers over his new mustache, an ill-advised facial hair choice that makes him look like a used car salesman.

"Do you think that I think I'm perfect?" I ask.

"What? Why would you say that? Did someone say that?"

"Mia said that I don't appreciate how easy things are

for me. Music, and school, and stuff. And that I've been too casual about my opportunities. Or something." I replay Mia's words in my mind for the thousandth time. "She said most people can't afford to turn down record deals and scholarships because they can't make up their mind. What do you think?"

"I don't agree with the first part," he says.

"And the second?"

Mr. Larson shrugs.

"I guess it does sound kind of insane when you say it out loud," I admit.

"Kind of?"

"Hey!"

"Well, c'mon Rainey. You must know what she means. At least a little bit."

And I do. Mia's words still sting, but I think I finally understand why they came out. Watching me let my dream sail by because it didn't feel right when she couldn't make hers come true must have felt especially cruel.

"I don't think I'm a very good friend," I say. "I keep letting everyone down."

"That's not true. You're doing your best under extraordinary pressure. But remember that honesty is a sign of strength in a relationship. Doesn't mean it won't hurt sometimes, but being willing to take a good look in the mirror once in a while never hurt anybody. Take it from someone who needs to do it a little more often. Or so I'm told."

Mr. Larson checks his watch, sips his tea.

"How do you guys get over it?" I ask. "When you have a bad fight?"

"We ignore each other, sometimes for days," he says, "until Matthew gives in and either apologizes or tells me I'm being ridiculous."

"That's very mature."

"I think you're going to find that every couple has their own system. And that most adults are no more mature than kids are. They're just better at faking it."

I sip my tea and wave away a wasp that's hovering. Every year, as the weather warms toward summer, wasps find their way into Mr. Larson's room. Maintenance has been up on ladders and examined all the nearby trees looking for the hive, but nobody can figure out where they come in. There's a girl in homeroom who's allergic so Mr. Larson has to keep an epi-pen on hand at all times.

"I'm cursed to lose the people I care about," I say.

"That's not true, Rainey."

"It feels like it's true."

"Look. You probably shouldn't be taking relationship advice from someone who hasn't dated in over fifteen years."

"*But*," I say.

"But, I think you're both a little too much like me. Maybe one of you needs to be more like Matthew if you're going to make things work."

"You said every couple has their own system."

"Yes, but the system takes some time to form itself. There's an adjustment period."

"She's leaving anyway," I say, thinking about how Mia is going back to Rochester in August.

A wasp lands on the desk and goes to work on a honey smear.

"At the end of the summer. That's three months away," Mr. Larson says, then drops a textbook on the wasp's head. "Last time I checked, life is happening right now."

Track Seventeen
Rochester Isn't on the Moon

It takes an hour before either of us gets a bite, but finally, Mia's line slips suddenly into the water, and she sits up as if she's been goosed, jostling the small rowboat so hard I have to steady myself.

"What do I do?" she asks, sounding panicked.

"Reel it in. But not too fast, and not too hard. You don't want to rip the hook out or break the line."

With gritted teeth, Mia slowly cranks away as her pole bends under the hooked fish's weight and effort not to be caught. She's concentrating hard and looks deeply uncomfortable, affirming her assertion, which I had found hard to believe, that she's never been fishing before.

"Oh my God, there it is!" she squeals as the fish breaks the surface and starts flopping about, desperate to be freed. "It's so strong."

In spite of Mia's reaction, the perch is a small one, no more than six or seven inches long, and probably only about a pound. But she's fighting it like she's got a giant marlin on the end of her line.

"Keep reeling," I say. "A little higher. A little higher. Now try to hold him still."

I wrap my hand around the fish and take hold of its wet, slimy body. Being calm, but firm, I tilt the fish's body away from me, then slip the hook free from its mooring. The fish's eyes are black as a starless night and frozen with fear.

"Do you want to touch him?" I ask.

"Are you kidding? No way."

Stroking the fish's green-gold body, tears well up in my eyes.

"Goodbye, fish," I say, then look up at Mia. "Now you say it."

"Really?"

"Yeah. You have to say it. It's what we always say."

"Goodbye fish," Mia says.

I lower the golden perch into the water, let go, and watch as it paddles down, down, down until it's swallowed by the darkness.

"Well, that was totally terrifying," Mia says. "Let's never do that again."

I giggle.

"But it is nice out here," she says, looking around the pond, which sparkles with afternoon sunlight. Water bugs dart across the surface like restless fairies, and even though it's only late afternoon, some of the peepers are already singing. Mia waves at the air. "Kind of smelly, though. You used to come out here with your dad?"

I nod. "All the time. Fishing was our thing."

Mia leans forward and I kiss her, then rub my fishy hands on her bare legs.

"You're so dead," she says, frantically washing her legs with palmfuls of pond water, then splashing me until my T-shirt is completely soaked and I can see my bra through the fabric. I can't stop laughing.

After Mr. Larson's pep talk the other day, I went straight to Sullivan Street Jeans after school. I took Mia's hand and led her into the back room and looked right into those big green eyes.

"I'm sorry," I said. "You were right. I'm the worst."

"No, you're not. And I wasn't right!" she said. "I hurt your feelings. I never want to hurt you again. I was such a jerk. I've almost called you a million times. I was afraid you wouldn't ever want to talk to me again. I thought I screwed it all up."

"I needed to hear it," I said. "I've just been so overwhelmed by everything. I didn't know how to handle it all. I'm glad you said it."

"I'm sorry too," she said.

We hugged desperately and I buried my face into her neck and inhaled her rosewater scent, feeling like I'd come home. Feeling desperate not to leave.

Since then, we've been nearly inseparable, even acting more like a couple, at least when we're around my brother and mom. Occasionally, I catch my mom studying us as Mia and I share a blanket on the couch or hold hands across the table.

The fact of Mia's leaving still hangs over us like distant, threatening rain clouds, and we've agreed that life has shitty timing when it comes to love. But we've also agreed that we might as well focus on the positive, which is that we still have the whole summer together. At least, minus the days that I'll be on tour.

And as Mia keeps reminding me: Rochester isn't on the moon.

"You can come visit me anytime," she says.

As I find myself falling deeper and deeper in love, which feels a bit like drifting further and further out to sea, I try to pretend it won't make it hurt even more when she leaves.

That night, after Mia leaves, I make Evan a mixtape. I take my time, filling it with songs by bands I know he loves (Yes, Tool, King Crimson, Rush) and some I hope he'll love when he hears them (Pavement, Ida, My Bloody Valentine). I play with the sequence, trying out songs until the transitions are perfectly optimized. Sometimes smooth and seamless, songs slipping easily one into the next like a series of breaths, other times deliberately chaotic and surprising, as if throwing on the lights in a dark room. Evan's preferred listening pose is prone on his carpeted bedroom floor staring up at the ceiling, and once he's settled, he hates getting up to skip ahead or fast forward through crappy songs. So, I lean on sure things, songs that I hope will make him think of me and how much he means to me. I sneak in an Elliott Smith song, and feeling majorly sappy, like a mother crying over a photo album of her children long after they've grown up and moved away, I end side 2 with Queen's "You're My Best Friend."

For the cover, I cut up pictures of Evan and me, making our faces into circles, and arrange them across pictures of tree branches, so that our faces are fruit on the tree. It's silly, but I know it will make him laugh.

An hour later, he looks surprised to find me standing on his front porch. He's in sweatpants, holding a can of Sprite, his index finger bookmarking a doorstop of a Tom Clancy book. The mix tape is in my back pocket, messily wrapped in newspaper because I didn't have any wrapping paper.

"Can we talk?" I ask.

"Okay."

We go up to his room, and when he shuts the door, I hand him the tape.

"I made you a mix," I say.

"You did?" He peels back the newspaper, smiling when he sees our stupid faces hanging like apples from the tree branches. I watch as he reads the track list, nodding to himself in a stew of satisfaction and curiosity.

"I'm sorry that I haven't been a very good friend. These last two years would have been impossible without you, and I just don't want you to hate me."

"Rainey, I could never hate you. You act like our friendship is over because we had one argument."

"I just—" I say, but I can feel myself staring to cry.

Evan spares me an ugly display of blubbering by hugging me. "We're still best friends, okay."

"Promise?" I ask.

"I promise."

Then we lay on his floor, our faces side by side, our legs sprawled in opposite directions, and listen to music the way we've done a hundred times before. It feels so good, and I'm proud of my mix as the songs sail by.

"King Crimson, nice," Evan says approvingly when "21st Century Schizoid Man" comes on.

I smile. I knew he'd like that one.

As the calendar inches past my eighteenth birthday in late May, Walden plows ahead with tour planning, adding midwestern dates in Cleveland, Indianapolis, and Chicago. We leave for tour on June twenty-fourth, three days after I graduate from high school, and will play fourteen shows in fifteen days before returning home on July ninth. Murph has been helping us out, crafting a decent press release for the new album, nudging us toward "Snowwoman" as the first single because of its upbeat tempo and sing-along melody, and making the most of her deep rolodex by sending *Puddle Jumping* out to a far wider swath of radio stations, newspapers, and magazines than Walden and I ever would have been able to on our own.

In spite of my mom's warning never to read reviews, I devour every press clipping Murph gives me. Seriously, how are you supposed to resist gobbling up every little thing people say about you? The *Boston Phoenix* gives it 3.5/4 stars and says that my new album "sounds like the love child of Stevie Nicks and Kurt Cobain fell in love with the love child of Elliott Smith and Alanis Morrissette." The Village Voice calls the album "a hypnotic blend of layered vocals, deep hooks, and gut-punch lyrics that lay bare the soul of a girl mourning the recent loss of her father, the late-great Luce Cobb, who died of lung cancer this past January." *Arts and More* isn't in love, though, calling *Puddle Jumping* "more a step sideways than forward from her first album, and frankly, a little boring at times. We expected more from such a promising young artist."

"That's why you don't read reviews," my mom says.

I have a strange nightmare where I'm walking down the street and perfect strangers keep stopping me to tell me I'm boring.

The first week of June, we begin rehearsing with a new guitar player named Pete Brewster who's a friend of a friend of Walden's. Pete is thirty-two, but looks twenty-two with his wiry frame, huge blue eyes, and arms completely covered in tattoos. Pete always brings along his two-year-old daughter, Violet, to rehearsals because his wife, Sandy, works afternoons as a dental hygienist. Wearing massive ear phones to protect her tender ears, Violet colors way outside the lines and constantly pets Django, who she calls "Tango," while we rehearse out in the studio.

As Walden promised, Pete, who has played in a lot of bands, but mostly works as a session player, is a talented guitarist who shows up to our first rehearsal with all the songs from both my albums, plus "Jesus Wear a Blonde Wig," already memorized. When I ask him how long it took to learn them, he says "a couple days."

"You're not the only one with a freakish memory, hot shot," Walden tells me.

Pete is a sweet, soft-spoken guy who listens well and asks thoughtful questions. Musically, it was hard for me to imagine we could ever replace River, but Pete is a seasoned pro whose playing is polished to a shine and inventive as hell, and I can almost immediately feel our sound leveling up in his experienced hands. Pete never strays too far from the established blueprints of my songs, but finds clever ways to add new depth and shade and texture.

On rehearsal breaks, Pete changes Violet's diaper and gives her sloppy zerberts that make her cackle. He seems like he'd be an easy guy to spend the summer driving around with. But still, Pete is almost twice my age, and it doesn't feel the same as playing with one of my best friends. With River, it was always hanging out more than practicing, but the second rehearsal ends, Pete packs up Violet and they're gone, like he's just another guy heading home from work. Which, of course, he is. Coordinating the tour dates with his availability is akin to planning a land war in a distant country, and we have to re-schedule some of the shows to work around his schedule. Pete says he likes playing with us, and loves my music, but it's a gut punch when he can only commit through the end of this calendar year because he's already booked some studio dates and a tour with another band in early 1999.

"If we have to, we'll find somebody else," Walden says to the worried look on my face. "I told you. There are a million guitar players out there who can handle this material."

"But we're only a trio," I say. "Isn't it kind of weird if

one of us is always a different person? I think people are going to notice."

"It doesn't matter."

"Yes, it does."

"No, it doesn't, and you want know why?"

"No, but I'm sure you're going to tell me."

"I will. Because you're the *only* one people actually care about."

"That's not true! People care about you. And they cared about River too. And they'll care about Pete. People want to feel connected to a band, like they know them."

Walden shrugs. "Yes. True. Sometimes. But we're not that kind of band. Nobody knows who Alanis Morrisette's guitar player is. Do you?"

I chew on my cheek while I try to conjure up a name I don't know.

"He shoots, he scores," Walden says. "The crowd goes wild."

Track Eighteen
Aw Shucks

"This thing is seriously messing up my hair," River whispers, adjusting his graduation cap so that it lays jauntily to the side, before we have to separate and line up in alphabetical order. With my black gown swooshing as I walk, I take my position in line, right behind Amanda Christopher and right in front of Seth Daniels. In my pocket, there's a tiny slip of paper with my name on it, written phonetically so that the director of guidance announces it correctly. *Ray-knee Cobb.*

As we march into the humid gym, a thousand people rise from bleacher seats to cheer us. I've always felt a little cynical about the idea of graduation, wondering if the ritual is really necessary, but flocks of butterflies take flight in my stomach as their voices roar. I look around, desperately searching for my family, and glimpse them just before I sit down, way off and up to my right, five rows from the top. Three across: my brother, my mom, and my aunt Becky. When they see me looking, my mom waves frantically, and I half wave back.

The valedictorian speaks. Then a local business owner.

Followed by the chosen faculty speaker, an English teacher named Mr. Willis, who talks about living a life of service, of planting trees you never get to sit under, but will provide shade for future generations to rest beneath.

I feel mushy and moved by the whole thing in a way I didn't see coming, one of those moments where you realize you're in the middle of something important and you wish you could slow time down.

A huge brass, or maybe it's iron, bell hangs in front of our high school, and according to tradition, every graduate must walk out and ring the bell to formally complete their passage into what's next. After I take my turn, I look around at my classmates, their futures as varied as their features. Kids I barely know come up and wish me good luck with everything. I hug and take pictures with Ms. Ofalko and Mr. Larson. I high five the Pena Twins, whose family I meet for the first time. Evan and I exchange huge hugs and pose with our families. Evan's graduation gown is bedecked in honors cords of various colors, twice as many as I have.

My mom takes pictures of everything and everyone with her new camera.

"I'm just really proud of you, okay," she says, hugging me for the tenth time. "You did it. You really did it. God, I wish your dad was here to see this."

"Mom," I remind her.

"I know, I know, I'm sorry. Last time."

We had promised not to talk about my dad so that we could both get through the day without totally losing it.

Walden takes it all in without saying much, ambling awkwardly with his hands stuffed in the pockets of his wrinkled khakis, perhaps wondering how it would have been to go through all this instead of getting his GED in the mail.

Mia is there to celebrate River, along with their mom and younger sister. I'm also introduced to a tall, handsome man with wavy blonde hair and a deep California tan, who looks like an older version of River. It's his father, a man I've never met before. River's father is energetic and gregarious, counter to the portrait of the absentee jerk I've heard so much about over the past two years. Mr. McRae chats up River's teachers and shakes a lot of hands, looking proud and acting lordly, but I can see how hard it is for River to have him here.

"He's so full of shit," River says. "Pretending he cares about my life or has had anything to do with it. I wish he hadn't come."

"Forget about him. This is your day."

"Yours too," he says.

"Damn right."

River laughs. We plop down on a small hill and let the sun warm our backs. Down below us, our fellow graduates are still hugging and posing. I pull up my gown to let my legs breathe.

"What now?" I ask.

"The future is a fickle thing, Rainey," he says, and I elbow him in the ribs.

"Don't start."

He puts his arms around me and I lean into him, this wonderful boy I care about so much who's about to leave for college.

"I'm going to miss you," I say.
"Aw shucks."

Track Nineteen
I Feel Everything

I blink and I'm on stage in Philly singing my new songs to strangers. Blink again and I'm in Cleveland. I'm in Chicago. The crowd is large. The crowd is small. The crowd is singing along. The crowd is bored. I feel loved. I feel hated.

I feel everything.

I'm in the McDonald's drive thru. I'm stuck in traffic. I'm riding shotgun with my feet splayed on the dash, scribbling in my journal and making lists to pass the time. Signing autographs for strangers and selling T-shirts with my picture on them for twenty bucks a pop. I'm sweating and dusty by the side of the road with my thumb in the air after Howard the Duck's battery dies in the middle of the night. I'm playing rummy with Pete. Trying to ignore my brother's relentless snoring. Bombing the RV with Glade air freshener to minimize the overwhelming boy stink. Chewing my eraser and trying to conjure up a five-letter word that means "stockpile."

I'm scarfing a gas station hot dog and slurping another value-sized fountain Coke. Searching for a decent radio station on a barren stretch of highway. Arguing with

Walden over whether to wait out this traffic jam or get off at the next exit. Sending a post card to Mia every chance I get. I'm reading *Les Misérables* for the third time in six months, baffled all over again by its epic greatness. I'm low on deodorant. I'm in desperate need of a shower. I'm waking up from another vivid dream where my dad is still alive, then silently sobbing into my pillow when the truth punches me in the head all over again.

I'm having the time of my life.

I can't wait to go home.

My mom meets us for the last show of the tour at the Middle East in Cambridge, Massachusetts. She's there for the show, but she's there for another reason, too.

"Where are they?" I ask her. "Do you have them with you?"

"What, in my purse?" she asks. "They're in a box in the car."

"Have you looked at them?"

She nods.

"What do they look like?"

"Like ashes, I guess," she says.

"Yeah. I guess that figures."

"It's going to be good." She puts her arms on my shoulders.

"Is it legal?"

"I have no idea," she says. "Probably not. Maybe we'll all get locked up. That would be a plot twist Dad didn't see coming."

Remarkably, as we're warming up in the dressing room before we go out, I look at the Middle East's show calendar taped to the white concrete wall and find that just last night, Elliott Smith played here. Tracing my finger down the paper, I can hardly believe his name is actually there, right above mine.

July 7th: Elliott Smith

July 8th: Rainey Cobb

Of course, it's probably not as amazing as it seems. Certainly not a cosmic coincidence sent here to tell me something or change the course of my life. Touring musicians are constantly intersecting, winding toward and around and away from each other, in and out through the same cities, the same clubs. The same invisible footprints.

But still.

He was here. Last night. He was right here. I close my eyes and imagine the sound of his heavenly voice and intricate finger picking echoing off the walls like a memory sequence in a movie. It's a comforting thought that energizes me and helps me fight through the end-of-tour tiredness that's worked itself into my bones. But it's when I step on stage and see Elliott Smith standing toward the back of the modest crowd that I fully leave my body and start to levitate. He's wearing a black T-shirt and a baseball cap pulled low over his eyes, but I recognize him instantly. Elliott's face is handsome and kind, but also rugged and worn, as if he's on his third lifetime in the same body.

"Holy shit, Elliott Smith is here," I whisper to Walden, who's arranging his drum chair and organizing his sticks.

"Yeah," Walden says. "His manager asked me if he could come back and say hi after the show."

"What? He did? When? Why didn't you tell me?"

It's now been at least a minute since the house lights went down and we walked out on stage. Walden glances over at Pete, who, as usual, looks calm, unconcerned about whatever it is we're talking about, or the fact that we're making several hundred restless people wait.

"You were in the bathroom I think," Walden says. "What's the big deal? People come back all the time."

"There's no big deal," I say. "It's just—"

"Rainey, chill. Okay. He's not the pope."

"Right."

Luckily, performing is the one place in my life where I almost never feel nervous, and I manage to get through our set without blanking on any lyrics too bad or falling off the stage. Instead, I tap into some new found energy drawn from Elliott's presence and we play our best show of the tour. It helps that we've been playing my new songs every night for two weeks now, road testing their peaks and valleys, finding the right way to bring them over.

Elliott watches the whole show rooted to the same spot, nodding his head, sipping his beer.

"Great show," Elliott says, then holds out his hand, which I shake. "I'm Elliott." His greasy black hair juts wildly from beneath the brim of his hat. His eyes are a deep and sleepy blue-grey.

"Hi," I say. *Be normal. Be normal. Be normal.* "I'm Rainey."

When I ask, Elliott explains that today was a day off for him and his band, and that when they saw I was playing at the Middle East, they decided to hang out in Boston for the day and come to my show.

"Your new album is really cool," he says. "I think I like it even more than the first."

"Thanks," I say, trying to process the idea that all this time that I've been listening to Elliott Smith's music, Elliott Smith has been out there listening to my music. The world really is a strange and incredible place.

"But I hate it when people compare albums so forget I even said that," Elliott adds, laughing nervously.

I'd heard that Elliott Smith battled depression and could be socially awkward. Cassie Plimpton said he was the shyest person she'd ever met. As an introvert, I've always felt it takes one to know one, and Elliott is obviously shy, but I find him to be more gentle and reserved than just plain shy. There's also something painfully open about him, like a wound that needs to be sewn up.

Walden comes over to meet Elliott. So does Pete, whose wife and daughter came down from Vermont for the show. Pete has little Violet propped up on his hip, and she keeps yawning and rubbing her sleepy toddler eyes. She keeps asking about Tango the dog, not understanding why he isn't here when he's been everywhere else she's ever seen me.

"I'm really sorry about your dad," Elliott says to me, when it's just the two of us again, his voice soft and intimate enough that I have to lean forward to hear him. "He was awesome." Elliott looks across the room where my mom is talking to the club manager. He turns back to me. "I had all those Luce and Tracy records when I was a kid. I still listen to them sometimes. They were so great. Anyway, sorry."

I have the urge to say to Elliott all the gushing and overwhelming things I feel. I want to tell him that *Either/Or* is maybe my favorite album ever at this point. That it's been my constant soundtrack over the past year. A blanket. A balm. A best friend. A Rosetta Stone. That it's worked its way into the nervous system of my creativity and had an incredible influence on my most recent songs, including the new album he claims to like so much.

Instead, I ask where he's playing the next couple nights and how his tour is going. Elliott holds up a pack of Camels and motions toward the door. I nod, then follow him outside. He lights up and I tell him thanks but no thanks when he offers me one, the lone abstainer in this impromptu smoking lounge. A heavy kiss of fryer grease and old garbage mix with the smell of cigarettes.

"You just graduated from high school, right?"

I nod. "Like five minutes ago."

Elliott shakes his head in wonder, presumably at how young I am. "Are you doing music full time now?"

"I'm not really sure yet. Maybe, I guess. We head home tomorrow for a while, but my brother is already booking fall shows. There's some festival stuff out west. He mentioned Europe and Japan the other day. But. I don't know."

Elliott looks around, then back at me, through me.

"You can say the rest," he says.

I have no real reason to, but I trust Elliott. There's something sort of broken and honest about him. "My dad really wanted me to go to college," I say, "and I still might. And there was this label that was trying to sign me, but it wasn't the right fit because they wanted me to change pretty much everything about myself, so my brother and I are going it alone, at least for now."

"*Treehouse Records*," he says, puffing on his half-smoked cigarette. Yellow nicotine stains blanket the first two fingers of his right hand. Same as my dad. "I dig the logo. You'll have other offers. If you want them. The indie thing is pretty cool, too. But you seem like you might not be so sure."

"I love music so much. But it's all I've ever done, so there's also this small part of me that feels like I should be doing something else." I look down at the black X on my hand that signifies I'm under 21. "I grew up in clubs like this. Being underage in a bar is basically my default position." Elliott chuckles softly. "And I'd kind of forgotten how draining the road can be until we went back on tour and I ate McDonald's for two weeks straight. Sorry, this all probably sounds really stupid."

"No, it really doesn't," he says, "and don't worry, I say stupid things all the time." I can tell he understands at least part of what I'm talking about. At the same time, it's ridiculous and surreal to be standing here telling Elliott Smith about my problems. But he's easy to talk to, and it's been a while since someone seemed interested.

"Any advice?" I ask.

He laughs softly. "I am about the last person who

should be giving advice," he says in a hesitating way, as if there's something else he wants to say. Elliott drops his cigarette to the ground and stubs it out.

"You're a songwriter," he says. "It sucks, but what else is there? Anyway, when I'm stuck, I just listen to Elvis Costello. That usually helps."

"I'll try that," I say.

"Anyway, I gotta go, but it was really nice to meet you. Good luck, Rainey."

He's about five feet away when I call out his name and he turns back to me.

"I wanted to tell you—" I begin, then shake my head. "I really love your music. That's...I just wanted to tell you that, while I had the chance. Sorry. I'm not great at honesty. Clearly."

He smiles and nods ever so slightly, then holds up his hand (palm out, fingers together) in a way that could either be hello or goodbye. I hold up mine and for a frozen moment Elliott Smith and I are standing there—just like that.

Track Twenty
Do You Guys Want to Say Anything?

Walden Pond and the replica of Thoreau's cabin haven't changed much in the past eight months since I was here with my dad. I can't say the same for me.

The cabin is still shockingly modest. You can circle it in a dozen big strides. There's still nothing on the walls. The bed is still tiny. The desk comically small. I remember my dad tossing me the camera and hopping onto Thoreau's bed for a quick pose. The devilish smile in his eyes.

The pond's namesake takes it all in, predictably unimpressed by the spot where a quiet writer and philosopher chose to live, write, and garden almost a hundred and fifty years ago.

"This is why I never wanted to come here," Walden says, knocking his fist against the cabin, and looking around. "I knew it would be underwhelming."

"It was the book more than this spot," my mom explains.

"Be honest. Was it your idea or Dad's? Naming me?"

"It was fifty-fifty," she says, but Walden isn't buying it. "Dad's," she finally confesses. "He loved that stupid book."

"I fucking knew it," he says.

"Walden!"

"Sorry. But I did."

We walk down to the rocky beach. A low stone wall curves around the embankment and merges with the shallow hillside. Tall trees growing on the slope tilt toward the water, leaning out for their portion of the sun. It's strange to see people sunbathing and splashing, to hear "Don't Stop Believin'" spilling from a distant boombox in this place mythologized for silent tranquility and poetic reflection.

"Should we do it right here?" Walden asks. "Did he say where?"

My mom shakes her head. "Not here, it's too busy. He only said *near* the pond. He wasn't that specific."

We walk back up the path into the sun-speckled shade and amble along quietly. Squinting, as if she's seen something, my mom peers through the trees, then motions for us to follow her as she steps between the pines and maples, which swallow her like one of the baseball players in *Field of Dreams*. We follow her until we step into a shallow outcropping that overlooks the pond but is concealed enough that we won't get busted. I hope.

"Let's do it here," my mom says, opening her purse and taking out a small, plain cardboard box.

"They're in *there*?" I ask, shocked at how un-ceremonial the box is. It might as well be full of nails or old Legos.

"No," she says, opening the box and removing a small plastic bag knotted at the top and stuffed with dusty gray ash. "In here." The ashes look heavy and substantial, as if they've been mixed with sand and tiny rocks.

For a few seconds, we all stand there looking at my dad's ashes. I feel overcome with emotion, and yet, there's something comically surreal about the whole thing. About the cartoonish discrepancy between this bag of tiny rocks and my dad the human being. I almost start laughing. My thumb briefly traces across Dad's hospital bracelet belt, which I still wear every day.

"I thought they would be in an urn or something," Walden says.

"Your dad didn't want that."

"Why?" I ask.

"He said Thoreau wouldn't have wanted one," she says. "And it's not like we're going to keep them on the mantle above the fireplace. Do you guys want to say anything?"

I look at Walden, who shrugs and looks back at me. I want to say something, but I don't know what. The moment seems to want silence. Nodding, my mom opens the bag and sprinkles a third of the ashes onto the ground, right in among the leaves and grass and broken twigs, then passes the bag to Walden, who sprinkles out another third, then hands the bag to me. It's lighter now, almost empty.

I love you, Dad, I think, then sprinkle out the rest.

Track Twenty-One
I Worry Anyway

By the end of July, "Snowwoman" has become a heavily requested staple on indie and college radio stations all over New England and *Puddle Jumping* has sold over ten thousand copies.

"I can't believe this," I tell Walden.

"I can," he says, his voice soaring with triumphant enthusiasm. "I told you we didn't need those assholes."

"I know, I know."

We get a small write up in *Rolling Stone*. Another in *Spin*. The irony is not lost on either of us. It's not exactly the cover of *Spin*, but one thing at a time. At Murph's urging, we re-release "Jesus Wears a Blonde Wig" as a single and add it to *Puddle Jumping* as a bonus track, which I am philosophically opposed to because it messes with the whole *Either/Or* run time synergy thing, but give in to pretty easily once Murph goes to work on me.

"It's got hit single written all over it," she says. "And the video makes you look like Xena the Warrior Princess."

"Isn't it, I don't know, too controversial?" I ask.

"That's what's so great about it," Murph says. "People will buy the album just to see what all the fuss is about."

"I thought you said doing all this ourselves was a bad idea."

"I said there were no guarantees," she corrects. "And there still aren't. You've caught a good wave. Don't jinx it by trying to make sense of it."

The video gets a handful of plays on MTV 2. The album keeps selling. Twenty thousand. Twenty-five. My mom tells me to ignore the numbers and focus on the music, but they make my head swirl anyway. I imagine twenty-five thousand copies of my CD in a massive, tilting pile like something out of Dr. Seuss.

Occasionally, I still think about college, about my deferred admission status at BU, about wonderful Nina and the Cherry Garcia. But I also feel compelled forward as if drawn by an oversize magnet out there in the distance somewhere.

Keeping up with the demand for *Puddle Jumping* on our own proves impossible, so with Murph's help, Walden and I sign a contract with an indie label called Flower Moon that will help us with ordering, shipping, and distribution in exchange for a small cut. All we have to do is put their logo next to ours on the back of the CD. I retain full rights to all my songs.

With the earnings from tour and album sales, I open my very first bank account. Mom also takes me to a dealership and helps me buy my first car, a 1994 teal Hyundai Scoupe, for which I write my first check and to which I quickly develop an irrational attachment.

I work occasional shifts at Cuppa Josephine. My mom works her last days at the law office, then starts rehearsing for a solo tour that starts in September. She seems happier, but sometimes I hear her crying late at night behind her closed door.

River calls me from his summer program at Syracuse and makes me laugh. Evan and I get together once in a while and I kick his ass in Mario Kart for old time's sake.

Every other waking minute, I spend with Mia.

We drive along the winding backroads and endless small towns of northern Vermont. We gawk at cows and jump into swimming holes. We eat maple Creemees and drink our iced coffee from Ball jars. We pick blueberries and eat handfuls of the sun-warmed fruit right off the bushes. At an antique store called the Wood Bull, I buy Mia a silver-plated jewelry box with an elaborate filagree pattern carved into the top. We keep a blanket in the trunk of my car and lay it out in grassy fields so we can look up at the sky and decipher pictures in the clouds. We never see the same things.

The fact of her leaving is a physical presence, an itchy wool coat against my collar. Mia convinces me we shouldn't talk about what will happen to us after she leaves.

"We're happy right now," she says. "We're together right now. Why do we have to worry so much about tomorrow?"

"Because tomorrow isn't that far away."

Mia takes my hand.

"I love you, and you love me, and I don't think that's changing anytime soon, do you?"

"No," I say.

"So, why worry?"

I worry anyway. I worry that Mia will stop loving me. That she'll fall in love with her next TA and forget the name Rainey Cobb ever existed. That the solid ground beneath my feet will turn to dust.

One day in the middle of August, Mia gets into a car with her mom and leaves for Rochester, which is 309 miles away, but who's counting? She calls me when she gets there. At first it makes me feel better to hear her voice, to hear her say she loves me, but after she hangs up, I feel empty and alone.

I ask Walden if he wants to go to the movies, but he and Bethany are going out to celebrate their anniversary. Mom is just leaving for dinner with Aunt Becky and invites me along, but I realize I don't really feel like talking, so I just decide to stay home.

After everyone is gone, I go up to the treehouse and dig one of River's old joints out of the drawer in the coffee table and hold in the smoke for as long as I can. It's the first time I've smoked pot since my promise to Mr. Larson, and it goes right to my head. All I can hear are the crickets singing in the tall grass and I might be the only person left in the world.

It's a warm night and before long a thin layer of sweat has glossed my brow. The crickets become musical, secret rhythms revealing themselves to my overly-attuned senses.

My Jazzmaster is propped on the couch, and I pick it up and start lazily strumming, my fingers falling into well-worn shapes, meandering across chords. I pluck out a scrap of Bonnie Raitt, then a scrap of Elliott Smith. I picture Elliott's kind and weathered face. The way a smile seemed to cost him something. I remember how he seemed to want to protect me somehow. The advice he couldn't help but share. I mumble sing a melody that ambles by, repeating it on a loop until its randomness forms first into syllables and then into words. As I keep playing the chord progression, I open up my journal and scrawl down the words that come, as they so often do, on the dancing dust of memory.

Just the grass and the moon.
Just the sun and the rain.
She's a pebble of glass that's still eating my brain.
Alone, well okay.
I'll just try not to care.
I'm me and I'm me, and that's all.
So there.
A black bird, broken winged, that still thinks she can fly.
A mute voice, trapped inside, that forgot how to cry.
I'm floating in space. I fell out of my chair.
I'm me and I'm me and I'm me.
So there.
I'm me and I'm me, and that's all.
So there.

As usual, music is magic. Only an hour ago I felt so lonesome I could cry, but now I wear an unexpected smile. My loneliness isn't gone, merely re-channeled, re-born.

I stare at my words and feel that familiar twang of

satisfaction that comes after I've written something new, as if I've been whisked around the room unexpectedly on a gush of summer air, then set down gently where I used to be. Only changed into something new. Something more. Something beautiful and strange.

This is what I do. I turn blank pages into songs.

Maybe when you find something that makes you feel a little more like yourself, you should just keep doing that thing.

I'm a songwriter.

What else is there?

Hidden Track
A Girl Can Dream

The waitress sets down Mia's cheese fries and my chicken Caesar salad, then, after refilling both our coffees, turns to leave.

"Excuse me?" Mia says. "I asked for some fresh cream."

"Is something wrong with that one?" the waitress asks. "I filled it up an hour ago."

"Oh," Mia says, looking shy. "Well..."

"It smelled kind of funky," I interject.

The waitress smells the cream, then shrugs, and walks away with it.

"Thanks," Mia says. "They don't know me very well here yet."

We're in a diner called the Oasis, which is about a ten-minute walk from the off-campus apartment Mia shares in downtown Rochester, NY, with a senior psych major named Frances, who I saw only once the entire weekend, and then only briefly when she stopped by to grab a couple of books, some hair ties, and a jug of Diet Coke from the fridge.

"Hi, bye," Frances shouted as she breezed through the

room with her arms full. "At Justin's if you need me. Toodles."

Mia adjusts her plate so that it's square to her body. She tidies the salt and pepper shakers. "Can you believe you can't get a side of gravy here?"

"A crime."

"Oh my God," Mia says, grinning, "I almost forgot to tell you. There's this girl in my women in literature class that's *obsessed* with you. The other day she was all Rainey Cobb this and Rainey Cobb that to her friends. If only she knew the girl sitting right behind her had seen Rainey Cobb naked."

I shake my head and try not to blush, but I can practically feel the blood rushing to my cheeks, which seems to please Mia. I mix the dressing into the lettuce, then have a bite.

"Caesar salad?" she asks.

"I ate a lot of fast food on tour," I say, thinking about the endless barrage of Quarter Pounders and Whopper Juniors I consumed during September and the first half of October as Walden, Pete, and I crisscrossed the Midwest, South, and Northeast to crowds that seemed to be a little bigger and know the words a little better every night.

Out the window, at the junction of two busy roads, stands a broad maple tree whose leaves have turned a deep golden yellow and dance in the fall breeze. Mia reaches into her bag and pulls out a folded piece of paper that she slides over.

"The nuclear launch codes?" I ask.

"Directions back to the highway. It's pretty easy."

"Thanks."

"I feel like you just got here," Mia says. "When do you leave for California?"

"Wednesday."

"It's so far. Do you think Howard will even make it?"

"I forgot to tell you. We finally got a new RV."

"What? Howard's gone?"

"Howard's gone," I say, thinking of the strange, but celebratory, day last month when Walden and I used some of the profits from *Puddle Jumping* to buy a lightly used Winnebago with less than twenty thousand miles on it. Working microwave and coffee maker. Bunks that don't squeak and have heavy duty privacy curtains. They gave us fifteen hundred bucks for Howard against the Winnebago. Then a mechanic with greasy hands and the name Tim sewn onto his shirt front took the keys from Walden and drove Howard out of sight. Walden claims they probably sold Howard for scrap and then flattened him into a pancake with a hydraulic press, but I prefer to think of him enjoying an overdue retirement with an older couple somewhere who fire him up for an annual camping trip and otherwise just let him be.

"But we're flying to California," I say. "The festival bought us plane tickets."

"Wow, VIP."

"It's not that big a deal. Do you want me to quiz you some more? Before I go?"

Mia has a big finite math exam tomorrow morning. She knows the material cold, but is still convinced she's going to fail.

"You don't have to keep pretending you care about my classes. I know all this must seem pretty boring."

"It doesn't seem boring," I say. "And I'm not pretending."

Mia shakes her head, visibly annoyed at herself. "Sorry," she says. "I know I promised not to do that anymore. I'm working on it." She eats a fry, then pulls out a stack of multi-colored index cards being strangled by an aggressively wrapped rubber band. "Maybe just one more time. I have to send my grades to the scholarship people at the end of every semester and I don't want them to regret giving me a second chance."

She hands me the stack of cards and I start undoing the rubber band.

"Who else is playing at the festival?" she asks.

"Just some bands. Nobody you've heard of."

Mia rolls her eyes. "C'mon, who?"

"Pearl Jam," I say. "Sarah Mclaughlin. No Doubt. Green Day. Sheryl Crow. Lots of people. But we're fortieth on the bill. You can barely read my name on the poster, and we're only playing for twenty minutes."

"You don't sound very excited."

"No, I am," I say, gnawing a bright green piece of romaine to mush, wishing I actually liked the taste of salad. "It's just that it's my first big festival gig. And I'm not crazy about flying."

"You're going to do great," she says.

Our eyes meet across the table.

"So are you," I say.

When our plates are empty and we've been through

Mia's note cards five times, we sit in silence, both of us knowing what comes next. The part where I drive Mia home, then hop on the highway and drive back to my life, which bears absolutely no resemblance to my girlfriend's. And then back to our nightly phone calls where we say we love each other and pretend the distance doesn't hurt as bad as it does. That it won't take a toll on us. That we'll be okay.

I reach across the table and take one of Mia's hands in mine. She looks down at our nestled fingers, then up at me. When the waitress starts coming our way, Mia moves to pull her hand back, but I tighten my grip just enough not to let her go.

As the waitress asks us if we want anything else, her eyes quickly steal a glance at our held hands, then she drops the check on the table.

"Pay at the counter," she says flatly.

After she's gone, we crack up.

"Did you see her face?" I ask.

"I think the whole state of New York saw her face," she says. "What's gotten into you?"

"I was just thinking about how nice it would be if two girls could sit in a stupid diner in some stupid town and hold hands and nobody would care. I want to live in *that* world."

"I'm not sure that world exists," Mia says.

I squeeze her hand a little tighter. She squeezes back. We don't let go.

"A girl can dream," I say.

The End

About Benjamin Roesch

Benjamin Roesch's debut novel, *Blowin' My Mind Like a Summer Breeze*, won the 2023 Next Generation Indie Book Award for Young Adult Fiction. He has an MFA from Lesley University and is a writer, musician, teacher, podcaster, and award-winning essayist. For twelve glorious, exhausting years, he was a high school English teacher, and is now a full-time writer based in Burlington, VT, where he lives with his family. Oh, and his name is pronounced "Rush," like the band from Canada.

www.benjaminroesch.com
@benjaminroeschwrites (IG & Tik Tok)
@bbroesh (Twitter)

Rainey's story starts in
Blowin' My Mind Like a Summer Breeze,
winner of the 2023 Next Generation
Indie Book Award

Available now in ebook and paperback!

Also from Deep Hearts YA

Stone Feather Fang
A.G. Rodriguez

The gods—the cemi—have left the world of Ke', and their lush and verdant Andolin Islands are now inhabited by impious followers.

Teenage priestess Hildy Rios is tasked with saving her religion. In a special ritual called the Telling, she must somehow reawaken her people's love of the gods. Her effort is the last hope of her people: after this Telling, there will be no more chances, as the cemi will vanish into the past, their power forever lost to the world of Ke'.

The weight of her world on her shoulders, Hildy rewrites the Telling's story—and her own. She weaves a tale of her distant ancestor, a boy named Jenaro, blessed with the ability to see and speak to the cemi; a boy who, though long past, becomes as much a part of the present by way of the Telling's power.

For three days, Hildy brings to life the tale of Jenaro and his yearning for adventure, how he is haunted by the cemi of death, and who—like her—is fighting against the shackles of his family and society. For three days, Jenaro becomes real, and the power of the cemi to reach across time should be enough to convince Ke's people, but their impiety runs so deep…

Hildy and Jenaro. Two people joined by cursed blood, but separated by centuries of time. Only the cemi know how their tales will end.

Available now in ebook and paperback

Also from Deep Hearts YA

Cage of Nightingales
Elizabeth Hopkinson

Two boys. One meek, one rebellious. Both discover a power that will set them free…or sever them.

In a highly structured eighteenth-century society, the city-state of Angelio is known for two things: its music and its guardian, the Archangel Michael.

At Angelio's music school—nicknamed the Cage of Night-ingales—castrato singer Carlo is destined for fame at the opera… at the price of his freedom. Charity pupil Tammo hates the school and the restrictive future it offers, dreaming instead of escaping to live in the woods to charm birds with his flute.

When Tammo meets Carlo, their lives change forever. With the Archangel's help, they are granted the power to fulfil each other's deepest desires—but every gift demands a price.

As music opens doors to a glittering world beyond the Cage, the bond between them is tested by ambition, longing, and the fragile promises they have made. And their choices will shape not just their futures, but that of Celestina—a young aristocrat who will become entwined in their lives in ways neither of them can foresee.

Cage of Nightingales is a story of found family, and queer identity—featuring a tender portrayal of an asexual, nonbinary eunuch at its heart.

Available now in ebook and paperback